CW00819963

Other historical novels by Maggie Freeman

The Girl in the Great House
Daughter of the Sea
The Clock-Mender

Maggie Freeman

THE WIVES
OF
KING
CANUTE

First published in Great Britain in 2024 by
Speckled Mountain Books

ISBN 978-0-9933044-4-6

Cover design Natasha le Coultre

www.speckledmountainbooks.com

With many thanks for their help
to
Steve, Jan and Malcolm

Prologue

You look back and you think, what has made me as I am?

You have to fight what is happening to you, you think, yet you know you have no choice but to accept it, there is nothing you can do. Nothing any more.

Your slave, your Cornish slave with her dark hair plaited in a braid that hangs well below her waist, has brought fresh lavender, you smell it bunched beside you, sharp and aromatic as it often is after rain, and you think, where has she found it, in this dark time of the year? You think, perhaps the darkness is the product of my eyes, my eyes are failing me, maybe I am going blind.

You take hold of her thin hand and you feel the gold ring that you gave her loose on her finger. You twist it round. Don't lose it, you say, with it you can buy a passage to Greenland if you wish, or the lands beyond.

That's what I dream of, she says. That freedom of the sea you love. She begins to sing then, quietly, a song about the Whale Road to the rim of the Earth. The breath of the wind tugging at your hair, the great whales surfacing beside you. On the horizon the green trees of the New Found Land will swell up like waves before you. Life will begin again, she says.

You hear Emma then, she has come in the room and she is talking to the bishop beside her, you recognise him from the shuffle of his feet and the smell of incense on his vestments, and she puts a silver cup of sweet wine to your lips, and feeds you sugared plums, and how is it that each time they leave you, you fall into a deeper sleep? The wine will make you better, she says. But you don't know. You've always trusted Emma but now you wonder... You wish your sight was clear.

And the other one, Elfgifu, you've written to her many times commanding her attendance and she hasn't come, even though your royal seal was affixed to the letters which is a surety that they will have been delivered to her in Norway - why does she not come when you yearn for her so? Why do your sons not come? Why now does no-one come whom you love and have always trusted?

You were always an outsider, an invader. Not belonging. This was never your country. Where you felt at home was always Denmark. Those two women taught you to love this land, the one showing you its traditions of hospitality and generosity; the other, a foreigner like you, understanding the politics of state and church, she manipulated the church which was richer than the state... There's been peace here all the time you've ruled. Peace they both wanted, peace and prosperity. Yet how they hated each other.

Think on this slave girl who cares for you unremittingly. I will care for you until you die, she says.

I cannot die a sickbed death like this.
I've asked for my sword. Bring me my sword, I've said.
I long to feel the weight of my blade in my hand.

1. Elfgifu, London, 17th November 1001

Elfie's mother took her by the hand and pulled her through the dark rooms of the palace to the entrance to the queen mother's chamber. 'This is the place,' she said.

The great door stood open. Heavy curtains, the saints embroidered on them a blur in the November dusk, hung in folds about the huge bed. Oaken angels knelt atop each bedpost. Candles burned at the head of the bed, their flames the only warmth in that chill room.

Elfie hung back. 'No,' she said. 'No, Mama, I don't want to see her. I don't want to go in.' How afraid she had been of the tiny old woman, who had dominated the court and laid down the law to her son King Ethelred, her voice sharp, her fingers jabbing and crabbed, her head balding.

'You've no reason to fear the dead.' That was Wulfrune talking. 'Look.' She lifted up her ten-year-old daughter and Elfie saw the waxen face of the queen mother; her closed eyes, a stillness about her that rendered her barely recognisable, for she had always been the active power in the court. Aelfryth, the king's mother, autocratic and dominating, compelling everyone to do her will. Reduced to this. Powerless, a husk; she couldn't move, she couldn't speak.

'Her spirit has left her. We all come to it in the end.'
Wulfrune knelt on the boards by the bed, dragging Elfie
down next to her, her arm around her to give her courage,
and together they recited the Lord's Prayer,
companionship and comfort in the familiar words. Then
Wulfrune prayed for the kingdom: 'Our Lady, I fear what
may come to pass with the queen mother's strong
guidance gone. Let no harm befall any of us in the
emptiness that will follow Aelfryth's death. Grant good
sense to our king in all he does. Though that may be too
much to ask,' she added, standing and pulling Elfie up
beside her. 'Lord knows what he'll do now his mother isn't
here to make him toe the line.'

Nobody could have guessed what was to happen: that in
early December Ethelred's meek wife, Queen Elfgifu,
would simply disappear. Go missing. There was no trace of
her anywhere. No message left behind for anyone;
nothing. Her sable-lined cloak lay flat in the iron-bound
chest in her chamber, the mare she loved to ride was
restive in the stable.

The queen was missing and rain fell. Day after day the
rain fell, grey, heavy, cold, as if the whole world were
grieving. The river was full to bursting its banks from the
unceasing rain, the days were overcast and dark.

Prince Athelstan led a search party of palace children in
rain-sodden cloaks along beside the river. 'What can have
befallen her,' he cried, 'so soon after our grandmother's
death?' Grey rain fell, the falling drops making circles in
the swollen river.

'That's not her, is it?' cried Elfie, pointing to something
on the far side.

'Can't you see it's just a log?' That was Prince Edmund,
the youngest of the royal brothers.

'What's the point in looking for the queen here?' said Wulfstan, Elfie's younger brother. Wulfgeat, the older one, was attending a council meeting with the king which Athelstan should have been attending too. 'It's a waste of time. What would she be doing here, on a day like today?'

'This is the place she loves most in the whole world,' insisted Athelstan.

'Nobody would want to walk here today,' said Elfie, and shivered. Last night she had overheard her mother saying to her father, 'So you think the king has killed her?'

'I wouldn't put it past him,' her father had replied.

Meanwhile Ethelred, the powerful and noble king of England, had dismissed his councillors and was striding into the great hall of his palace, his scarlet cloak flowing from his shoulders, his mighty sword in its scabbard at his side, his arms weighted down with gold rings, the heavy gold buckle of his belt resting on his belly; the jewelled knife that he used to cut his meat snug in its sheath. His pale blue eyes were liquid-bright, his straight hair straggled to his shoulders. He demanded wine, lashed out with his foot at his favourite bitch that slunk up to nuzzle at his hand. He yelled at a slave to take away the wooden throne on which the queen had been accustomed to sit beside him. 'Get rid of that damned thing,' he cried. 'She can't be arsed to come to the great hall, so burn it! Burn her bloody throne. Toss it on the fire. Let it burn, let it burn! If she won't fulfil her duties, she has no need of it any more.' He dug his knife into the roast boar on the platter brought before him, he called for his minstrel to sing of the glories of his great, rich kingdom.

In the hearth flames licked round the wooden dragons that had been the arms of the queen's chair, smoke issued from their gaping mouths, their tails crumpled into ash.

5

Dogs pissed on her silk cushions that had been tossed down among the rushes and the old meat bones.

Halfway down the table Elfie sat stiff beside her mother, hands clenched in her lap. She was thinking: the lost queen and I share the same name. Elfgifu. Elfie was only her nickname, a baby-name, a shortening. We are like sisters, the queen and I, Elfie thought, like twin lambs or like peas in a pod, because we share the same name. The pale queen had stood godmother to her at her baptism and had always been generous to her. She had insisted that Elfie be allowed to join in the princes' lessons with her brothers when she wanted to. That girl likes her letters, the queen had said to Elfie's mother, she's clumsy at her weaving and embroidery, you must allow her to be like a boy, to learn with the princes as she wishes. As if the queen had wanted for Elfie chances that she had not had for herself. With the queen's sudden and unexplained disappearance, Elfie felt part of herself had been stripped from her, a layer of her being lost. It was her first close acquaintance with tragedy, would not be her last. It was as well she did not know what was to come, how her whole world would change. She searched for her gentle namesake everywhere, in every room of the palace, in every corner of woodland and meadow, in every barn or enclosure.

'Why should you be able to find her when no one else can?' asked her mother, drying her hair when she came in from the rain.

'I have to find her,' said Elfie. But she never could.

At Epiphany, the end of the twelve days of Christmas, the weather changed. The wind turned to the north-east. It hurtled from Russia, from Viking lands, whipping at bare faces, translating the river's edge to ice. A bitter invader, killing more of the poor in their flimsy hovels than the Viking longship raids along the south coast, which were so feared, ever did. Snow fell on the frozen land, snow overnight and in the daytime too. Transforming the land; whiteness over everything. The palace children donned bearskin cloaks, they ran out in waxed boots into the thickly falling snow. They threw snowballs that wouldn't compact, they shouted, they turned their faces up to the sky, opened their mouths and stuck out their tongues to catch snowflakes, they caught snow-feathers in their lashes and shook their heads and giggled and ran indoors to the warmth of the huge fire in the great hall, with the vast bowl of the iron cauldron bubbling above it, the scent of stew rising toward the rafters. The shutters of the hall were closed against the cold, the room was dim as a vast cave. The minstrel stood at the far end, where the queen's throne had been. He folded himself over his lute and began to play, his arms were round it as if it were a woman. 'Not this song,' interrupted Elfie's mother suddenly. 'Don't sing about the terrible killings in Southampton. It'll give the children nightmares. Elfie, off you go to bed, my little one.'

In the moonlight that came through cracks in the clouds Elfie crossed under the still-falling snow to her family chambers. How white the snow lay, how bright, a feather quilt concealing the land. She stretched out her arms. Maybe this is the only shroud that Queen Elfgifu will ever know, she thought, this quilt of fine snow-feathers, and she imagined the gentle, icy queen fallen lying dead beneath the snow, reaching up her arms out of the snow to pull her down to be her companion underground, and she shivered, and ran fast to shelter.

For all Elfie's ten years England had been beset by attacks from the Vikings. Oh yes, there had been pools of safety, times of calm, happiness in the rich yield of farmland and of forests, in the evenings listening to the old songs, played on lute and harp, and the reciting of legends at feasts in the great halls. The companionship of family and of friends, the heroic court with all its splendour: all bathed in a sea of bliss against the dark threat and ever-present danger of attack from marauding Vikings who would steer their longships with their striped sails out of the emptiness of the ocean, anchor them to step ashore and wallow in an orgy of theft and rape and killing, in torching houses and robbing barns heaped high with grain and hay against the coming winter: making people homeless, penniless, leaving them starving.

King Ethelred and his sons were even now marching with the army to the Kent coast to ward off invaders. How furious the king had been at the support the Vikings were getting from Duke Richard of Normandy, across the Channel: 'Richard's so damn greedy for their trade, the slaves and gold and silver those villains have stolen,' he'd complained. 'There must be some way to stop him. Got to get my head around the problem. Maybe forge some kind of an alliance with that damned duke. If the bloody Vikings didn't have a safe haven with him, we'd stand more of a chance of defeating them.' He buckled on his jewelled sword, fitted an iron head to the silver-trimmed shaft of his spear, balanced it in his right hand.

2. Emma, Normandy, February 1002

Emma, the fourteen-year-old daughter of Duke Richard I of Normandy and his Danish concubine Gunnor, was clutching her skirt, climbing the rickety ladder to the top of

8

the lookout tower out on the headland. She balanced on the platform, grasping the rail, her cloak jetting out from her shoulders, her blonde hair escaping the confines of her shawl and flapping like a pennant in the sea breeze. *Welcome*, it might have been signalling. *Welcome to all Vikings. I want you to come.* She stared out over the grey restless sea to the pallid line of the pale horizon, her eyes watering in the sharp wind as she strained to make out the silhouette of a Viking ship dipping in and out of the waves. Hurry up and come, she was thinking, Hakon is late, he's ten days late, what does he think he's doing, not arriving when I'm here waiting for him? All Northmen were welcome but especially Hakon, kinsman to her mother and to herself an honorary uncle who once or twice a year would anchor in the bay and offload bolts of fine silks in rich colours from China that she knew when she unrolled them and wrapped them round her shoulders, staring at her reflection in the silver plate on the wall, would suit her well. There'll be no silk this time, she was thinking, Hakon will be on his way back from Ireland, and he'll be carrying a cargo of slaves. 'A musician I'll capture for you, a gifted musician, little one,' he'd promised, ruffling his friend Richard II's sister's soft hair, 'I'll bring you the greatest of musicians, the Irish have a gift for music. I'll find someone who will sing of your beauty in all the great halls of the western world. You'll be world-famous. They'll write books about you.' Emma had felt her lips curve in a cat-like grin, she'd straightened and thrust out her new breasts and he had laughed. She had wondered for a second if perhaps he didn't find her as beautiful as he professed; but that thought flitted from her brain in her longing for him to bring her treasure – brooches carved with crosses, or amber beads polished to a fine sheen, perhaps looted from a monastery. Beads she'd attach to gold pins on her dress. Something that would make her status obvious to all, that's what she wanted. She liked people to know of her riches and her rank. She pushed an imaginary thick gold ring up her arm (fine white skin she had; the minstrel Theodor sang of it).

But at that moment the only ship in sight was a simple fishing boat coming into harbour. When it dipped in the trough of a wave all the treasure she could see was the glitter of silver herring and cod in the hull. She sighed and climbed down the tower to where her slave Eseld, a Cornish girl perhaps five years older and a foot taller than herself, waited, ready to pull her cloak straight around her shoulders and adjust the pins, then step back to walk three paces behind her mistress, a long presence as she picked her way past the windbreak of pine and birch, back along the stony road, through the bare-branched orchards toward the buildings of her brother's court.

At the small rectangular chapel Emma paused to enter and kneel and pray in the shelter of the stone walls for her godfather Hakon's safety - *Keep him safe, Lord, let not such a magnificent man be swallowed up by the waves.* She whispered in Norman French at first and then slowly translated her words into Latin to make sure that God would understand. Important words, words that really mattered, she believed, should always be in Latin, which was why she had had her mother appoint a priest to teach it to her. Emma liked her life to be ordered; she found security in the routines of the church. A rightness and discipline that she knew must reflect the truth of life. A repetitiveness at one with the rising of the sun each day, the rhythm of the cycle of the moon. Far distant from the random battles her brother fought, his changing friendships. Look at him now in the great hall as she passed by the door. Oh, he was charming, yes he was,

gurning away like a ferret. Entertaining a messenger from
the English King Ethelred; giving him to understand that
he'd break off all dealings with the Vikings, no doubt. Lying
through his teeth. Everyone knew her brother depended
on the Vikings for trade goods, the luxuries of life, walrus
bone combs and whalebone gaming pieces, glass beads
and silver shoulder brooches, dirhams, silver coins traded
from Azerbaijan and made into jewellery, which jingled as
one walked. *Jingle jingle in and out of doors. In and out the
fire's warmth.* All things necessary for a civilised life, the
Vikings brought. They were often cousins of her mother's,
whom she was always pleased to see. Oh, so and so, she'd
exclaim, throwing her arms around them, how are you?
How's unt Maud and the little ones? What, Sigrid's fifteen
already, she got married last winter, did she? Twin boys –
imagine that, she was always such a skinny one, I can't
believe it ... Gunnor believed her cousins had every right to
obtain their riches looting the south coast of England. They
were brave pirates, great adventurers, skilful sailors, she'd
say, of course they should behave as they do. The foolish
English were at fault for having so little concept of honour
that they would pay tribute rather than fight. Last year
Hakon when he came to Normandy had had his men
heave ashore a lead chest full to the brim with silver coins,
all newly minted and glittering in the sunlight when he
opened up the lid, the treasure he had been given when
he approached a monastery. 'They pay us to go away,'
he'd said scornfully. 'I'll leave it another year and then go
back and attack them again, see what else they have to
offer. Those monks and farmers – their only concern is
their crops and their beasts and their gardens, they don't
understand the glory of fighting, the triumph, how good
success makes you feel. The power of a sword dripping

with blood. Living in peace – pah! What's the point of that?'

Gunnor had slipped her arm around his shoulders, hugged him fondly.' Take care of yourself, my dear cousin,' she'd said. 'We love you dearly.'

A year ago Hakon had stolen a little gospel from a monastery close to the coast, that he gave to Emma. 'Here's a pretty toy for you,' he'd said. Its vellum binding was embossed with jewels, the initial letter of each chapter illuminated in gold leaf, the paint vivid scarlet and blue. The black ink of the script sat neatly on the small pages. 'A gaudy thing,' he'd said, tossing it to her. 'What it's for I don't know.' He couldn't read.

'The gospel of St John,' Emma had said reverently, turning it over in her hands, opening it, studying it with great care. She loved that gospel, kept it in the chest beside her bed, would take it out from time to time and slowly unpick the meaning from the words. She would polish the jewels on the cover. It gave her great pleasure.

She wondered sometimes, if the English could make something so beautiful, if they might have knowledge that was of greater value than her mother's kinsmen's fighting skills. Blood dripping scarlet from a drawn sword blade might well give a man a passing rush of ecstasy; but this gospel kept its beauty. Rich and lasting. Several of her friends had brothers who had been slain in battle. How transitory life could be. You needed to keep as firm a hold on it as you could.

'Emma.' It was her brother's voice behind her.

She stopped and turned. 'Richard?'

'King Ethelred's taken me by surprise this time,' he said. He was looking anxious, biting his lip. 'I'm not sure it's a good idea. There's that question mark over what happened to his first wife. I've talked it over with your mother, though, and she thinks that's just foul gossip, and it's a proposal truly worthy of your consideration.'

'What do you mean?'

He put his arm through his sister's, led her back through the gate and out into the countryside. He was an outdoors man, could always think more clearly when he was among trees – though the orchards they were walking through were miserable enough at this time of year, all bare dark branches made jagged by the pruning saw. And the cold was bitter, a thin snow was falling. She pulled her hood up around her neck, thought longingly of the great log fire that would be blazing back in the parlour.

'It's got to be your decision,' he said at last.

'What on earth are you talking about, Richard?'

'Your mother's all in favour of it,' he said.

'In favour of what?'

'Him. You know. King Ethelred of England. Damn silly Anglo-Saxon name.' He stopped, looked down at her and sighed.

'What are you talking about, Richard? You're not making sense.'

'The messenger in the hall came from him.' He sounded glum. 'It's not what I'd have wished for a sister of mine. He's forty if he's a day. What would you want to tie yourself up with someone so ancient for? And people say - well, people always talk, don't they? I dare say it was just an accident. You know how people make up stories. Maybe she ran away. They never found her body. His last wife, that is.' He sighed deeply. 'You're fourteen, you know. Your mother keeps reminding me. High time you were married, Emmy. And this – this King Ethelred. He'd do you fine. High status. Rich. A mature man, not some hare-brained firebrand. Being a queen would suit you very well, Emmy. You've always had a high opinion of yourself. A sense of your own dignity.'

'A queen?' Emma was not sure what he meant.

'Yes. King Ethelred's asked for your hand in marriage. You should consider it seriously if you truly want to marry a king, as Ma says you do. There's a general shortage of kings in need of a wife at the moment. King Sweyn of Denmark is still shacked up with that Bratislavan princess. Old Ethelred is desperate to form an alliance with me. He takes it for granted that if you two marry I'll help him against the Vikings.'

'You wouldn't support the English king against Ma's cousins, would you, Richard?'

'Of course not. Damn profitable trade, the Vikings bring here. And most of them are family of some sort, and I'm not fighting family. What would people think of me if I did? Anyway, have a think about it, about marrying old Ethelred, sister. His proposal is worth considering. In lots of ways this seems too good an opportunity for you to miss.'

'I've never thought of being a queen.' And yet hadn't every girl who had listened to the old songs dreamed of just that? The riches, the respect, the power that she would have... Also how satisfying it would be, she suddenly thought, in a ray of bright radiance, to outrank her brother. You're so squat and plain, no one will ever want to marry you, he'd teased her back in November, when she had that terrible cold and might not have been looking her best. His words had stung. If she were a queen she would sweep past him with head held high and rustling skirts. A headdress of silver lace, if not a crown of gold. Her brother would have to bow before her.

'Ethelred is as rich as Croesus,' said Duke Richard. 'Worth bearing that in mind. Your tastes are too expensive for me to support, sister mine. Commissioning that Book of Hours, well, that was a bit... you shouldn't have done it, Emma. It cost me much more than was reasonable.'

Oh, but it was such a beautiful book, Emma thought, complete with its gilt illustrations and jewelled cover. A book to match your beauty, the head of the scriptorium had murmured. How could she have resisted buying it? Images of the seasons, he'd promised her. Sun gold, hay gold, buttercup gold. Hounds hunting with jewelled collars. Peasants with gold pitchforks. Maybe she should have mentioned it to her brother before she commissioned it, maybe she should have considered that if she ordered it in his name it would have brought dishonour on him not to pay for it. But she had wanted the book, had been certain it was her right, as sister of the Duke of Normandy, to own it. How could her brother not see that?

Marriage would free her of any need for family approval, Emma thought. As Queen of England, she'd be her own mistress. Independent, tra la. Silk skirts trailing, bunched in her right fist, fingers glittering with gold rings. All hoity-toity in a gold crown. Married to Ethelred, one of the richest kings in Europe, she'd be free to do as she wished. Visions of fine fabrics and rich gold jewellery floated through her head. She'd have on her throne a silken cushion filled with soft goosedown and embroidered with symbols of the spring: apple blossom, and twining leaves. She'd employ women to do the embroidery and to make the gold and silver fringing. No need to prick her finger doing the work herself. She'd live in the lap of luxury. So comfortable she'd be, so much admired. People would give her gifts to gain her favour. She imagined them kneeling before her, palms outstretched.

She turned back to her brother. 'The messenger, Ethelred's messenger, I saw him with you in the great hall, is that what he came to say? That the king of England is proposing marriage between us.'

'I told him it's up to you. You must decide. You have a strong mind of your own.'

'Very well.'

'You mean...?'

She didn't hesitate. 'Yes,' she said. 'Yes, I'll marry him.'

3. Elfgifu, Winchester, early March 1002

A vast orange fire blazed in the half-dark at the heart of the great hall in Winchester, a hall with walls built of vertical oak trunks, the scent of the wood still new. A venison stew bubbled in a cauldron and unleavened bread baked on iron griddles. Courtiers, men and women, lazed on benches, gossiping, now and again bursting into song.

King Ethelred seized the drinking horn. 'To our alliance with Normandy,' he shouted. 'To my new young, pretty young wife.'

'To the alliance.' Elfie's father took up the toast when the king passed the horn to him and drank deeply from it. Elfie glanced doubtfully at him, grabbed some bread from a griddle, dropped it because it was so hot, pulled her sleeve down over her hand and held it with that, the warmth seeping through the fabric as she walked out into the yard, turning to Prince Edmund as he followed her: 'How can your father marry someone who's only a little bit older than me? She's years younger than you. The whole idea is ridiculous.'

Edmund shrugged. 'You know what my father's like.'

Elfie tore off a fragment of the bread. 'You want a piece?'

'Thanks.'

'I... your mother, Edmund, she was lovely, she was my godmother too, I loved her, she was always kind to me, she always took time to speak with me, she was so gentle and generous, has your father forgotten her already?'

'He... you have to face reality. He's king, he has a job to do, he needs Richard of Normandy on his side against the Vikings... creating family ties through marriage, that's the easiest way to do it.'

'The king's in his forties, he's an old man. My father says nothing but trouble can come of this marriage.'

'Nonsense! It will bring peace. That's the whole point of it.'

'Oh,' Elfie snapped. 'Of course it won't. Don't be ridiculous. Don't argue with me.' She rubbed her eyes with the back of her hand, tossed the last of her bread to a dog that had followed her out of the hall, and broke into a run. 'Race you to the forest!'

But Edmund outstripped her, reached the tall pine at the edge first, turned his back to it and held out his arms, and she tumbled into them, then wriggled out of his grasp. 'Nothing will be the same any more,' she complained. 'Everything will change. Believe me, it will. Emma will be your stepmother, she'll have children, what will happen to you and Edward and Athelstan then? She'll favour her own children.'

'We are the king's firstborn sons. Nothing can change that. Our father is the king, he will always honour us, not allow some half-Norman to take our place. Forget your fears. Everything will go well, I swear it on my life.'

4. Emma, England, spring 1002

The new queen came with the spring. In a slight south-westerly breeze she took ship from Normandy across the Channel. She sat amidships, hooded in a leather cloak that protected her from the spray. She was certain that she was doing what was right; that she was about to fulfil the role that God had ordained for her. Queen Emma; queen of England. She was the chosen one. She drew herself up tall and stiffened her neck, imagining the weight of the crown on her head.

The gentle breeze propelled the *Star* across the blue surface of the sea. Behind her sailed the three boats carrying the iron-bound trunks of Emma's belongings and the baggage mules with their scarlet harness, their jingling buckles that would carry her, her servants and her goods along the long road to Canterbury. A soft sun shone; fleecy clouds swept along and dappled the slight waves with intermittent shadow. A calm journey; a little slow. Emma ordered the captain to set the oarsmen to row, but he ignored her. She thought: maybe it's for the best. I can take this time to make the transition from being subject to my family's wishes to being independent. In control. In charge. Her lips slipped into a smile in appreciation of the change.

'Enjoying the journey, missy?' asked the captain.

She ignored his insolence.

Slowly they drew closer to land and she could make out features: a sandy bay, and beyond the beach a cluster of fishermen's huts, a windmill, and ploughed fields glazed with green, and beyond that a great forest.

This was the shoreline of her new country, a thin slice of coast suspended between sea and sky, part obscured by mist; her new kingdom. Queendom. She would rule side by side with her husband, she was set on it. She imagined her hand overlapping his in their grasp on the throne.

Small boats rowed out to greet her, red pennants flying from their masts; in one a minstrel sang a song of welcome to her, and she tossed him a silver penny in appreciation, which he caught in his hat.

Then her four boats beached at Rye. Her men loaded the mules with the wooden trunks of her luggage – her books, her fine clothes, her bedlinen, her cushions; earthenware jars of honey, cinnamon and nutmeg, cheeses and quince paste and crystallised fruit. A girl had to take care of herself, for who knew what the uncivilised English might eat.

King Ethelred wasn't waiting for her on shore, which was what she had been anticipating. Instead his oldest son Prince Athelstan bade her welcome, showed her to a rose-gold tent. The setting sun shone through the fabric. She was glad the weather was good, that it wasn't raining. Lying on her bedtime couch among a festival of blankets (the spring nights were still cold), cushioning her head on her arm, she was thankful that she was here at last: desirous of taking the royal oaths to make all certain. She wasn't one to let the opportunity to become a queen slip away from her. Tomorrow she would meet her husband for the first time. It was good that he was old and wouldn't live long. She wondered about marrying Prince Athelstan afterwards. He stammered, though; not a good attribute in a king; and besides he was too thin and pale, she felt.

Emma. Daughter of Duke Richard I of Normandy. Sister of Duke Richard II. Destined to be Queen of England. A peace-maker. A pawn, a pledge of the truth of the treaty brokered between King Ethelred and Duke Richard, which stated that Ethelred would not attack Normandy; nor would Richard any longer provide a safe-haven for the Vikings, a launching place for their raids on the south of England: he would no longer furnish them with food nor buy their plundered goods and slaves. That was what he had declared; time would tell if he intended to keep his word.

Emma was satisfied to be becoming Queen of England. Granted, she'd have preferred to be Empress of the Holy Roman Empire, but that post wasn't presently vacant, and so England would have to do. She rode sidesaddle on her grey palfrey, the silver bells on the harness jingling to announce her passage through the Kent countryside, drowning out the singing of birds in trees, hedgerows and sky, the great concert of thrushes and tits, robins, larks and skylarks, finches, sparrows and nightingales that announced her arrival, tra-la along mud-ridged lanes, picking her way between fields weeded by stooped peasants who straightened their backs to stare open-mouthed at this grand parade of strangers under a banner they didn't recognise; ignorant peasants whom she would soon be the ruler of. She inclined her head now and then to them in acknowledgement of their awe at the sight of her and her retinue.

They passed into woodland, under the wide branches of chestnut and oaks whose leaves were just unfurling, and on into the rich scent of bluebells in bloom reflecting the colour of the afternoon sky; on out into orchards of apple trees the branches of which were cupped with pink flowers whose petals drifted in the slight breeze, drifted like snowflakes into the rich hum of bees. They landed in Emma's blonde circlet of plaits, dotted her silken sleeves, pooled in her lap.

It was evening when their escort ahead halted. Prince Athelstan had disappeared off somewhere and Aelfhelm, ealdorman of Northumbria, was now in charge. He rode back to Emma. 'Canterbury, ma'am,' he said, gesturing ahead.

A small town of timber houses. A market place. Cattle tethered by a well. The stone cathedral rose among monastery buildings blushed pink by the setting sun; early twilight softened the shabbiness of the streets, turning them rosy.

Emma pressed her lips together. She was weary from yesterday's boat trip, which had made her feel queasy; from her early rising and her long ride through the countryside. Her bum felt sore. Frankly, she had expected more than this. Where was the king, her husband-to-be? He should be here to greet me, she thought.

Then here he came, at last. King Ethelred. Of medium height, medium build, straggling shoulder-length dark hair grizzled at the temples. A green woollen tunic that exaggerated his round belly; laced leggings. Only a great gold torc around his neck indicated his wealth. I'll have to teach him how to dress, Emma thought. He exuded physical strength; he was obviously still active. A shame: when she had been told that he was a man of forty, she'd anticipated that he might die quite soon and that she would be left to rule all of England on her own, which would have suited her organising temperament very well. Never mind: she would take every opportunity time granted to learn to understand the rules of government, the world of men. She would learn how to bend him to her will; after all, she'd succeeded with her brother, who did pretty much as she wished. She stepped forward, smiled up at him.

Ethelred looked down at this gurning dumpling. Blonde hair bleached almost white an inheritance from her Danish mother, no doubt: he had fought off invading Danes all his life, so it was not a look he was enamoured of. That and the rosy Norman apple cheeks. Plus her hair was teased into a rigid crown of plaits which suggested she was self-contained, self-controlled; he preferred his woman abandoned. She was clever, he had been told, blessed with a gift for languages; she spoke three. She looked younger than he had anticipated, more suited to romping with the palace children than to taking her place seated on a throne beside him. She would have no experience of love-making; he supposed he'd have to teach her, and, frankly, he didn't know if he could be bothered. She really wasn't his type. His first instinct was to send her straight back to Normandy; but, Lord, if his treaty with Duke Richard were to hold, it would make so much difference to his life. No longer the problems raising tax to pay for the men and ships to defend the coast against the Vikings, no longer his perpetually having to summon up his courage and ride out at the head of a troop to fight them. He sometimes half-thought he might be getting old: he dreamed of a peaceable life. Of taking his ease, hawking and hunting, enjoying the country ways. Listening to the chanting of songs in the great hall in the evening. Tales would be made of his life, he knew. There would be epic poems about the battles the great Ethelred had fought and won. He coughed to clear his throat. 'Welcome, most gracious lady, to the city of Canterbury,' he said.

She stared up at him blankly. He found that offensive but tried again. 'Welcome indeed. Your apartments are prepared for you, mistress. My lord Aelfhelm will conduct you to them.' She still didn't answer and he snapped, 'In this country one answers when the king speaks to one.'

Aelfhelm had to explain that the lady Emma couldn't speak English. Only Danish and Latin and her native Norman French, in all of which she was fluent.

'Then for God's sake make sure she's taught English before our damned wedding,' snapped Ethelred. 'If she can't speak English by July I'm not marrying her. I don't want to see her again till then. Tell the archbishop I'm postponing the coronation. You come from bloody Northumberland, Aelfhelm – you must speak Danish. That wildcat daughter of yours, Elfgifu – Elfie, is that what you call her? – does she speak Danish? Well, the two of them will have a language in common. Get your daughter to teach English to Emma. We can't have a queen of England who has no idea of the language of her subjects.'

A small window too high to see out of was cut into the southern wall of the chamber where the two girls sat side by side to study. In the latter half of May the circling sun cast a rectangle of yellow light on the earth floor, that slid slowly from south to north. Come June the sun was higher in the sky and that rectangle disappeared around midday because of the thatched overhang of the roof. Every day Elfie held her breath, longing for its reappearance which would mean that her laborious task of teaching Emma to speak English was nearly finished for the day.

Emma was painstaking in her study. She wrote down every word, each with its translation into Danish and Latin. 'I've got to get this right,' she insisted. She demanded to know the everyday words of the court, such as a queen would need to command meals to be cooked, linen to be washed and mended, rooms to be cleaned and prepared for guests, and for the bestowal of gifts. She needed words that would express her learning: words about the use of pen and parchment, the technique of illuminated manuscripts, about the Church and its hierarchy of bishops and priests, friars and abbesses and monks and nuns, about the lives of the saints she venerated. She needed as well to know the language and customs of government, of the *witan*, the council-meeting of nobles, of charters and land bills. She took her role as future queen very seriously.

Many of these things Elfie had learnt from the lessons she had shared with the princes and their tutors, but sometimes she had to check facts with her father, and then Emma grew impatient and hurled pens or cushions at her, and shouted at her for being an ignorant slut.

Elfie spent her eleventh birthday still shut up in that close chamber, longing to be outside at this time of year that she loved most of all, when everything was new, the grass springing up, the flowers opening wide; this time when one could stretch one's body that was at last freed from its winter confinement by running for miles through woodland and meadows, leaping like a lamb in the fields, hair loose to the wind, heart thumping, filled with the exhilaration, the pure joy of the sun and the southerly breeze.

Every previous summer of her life she had spent on her father's estates in Northumberland.

But this year Emma was unrelenting. Pedantic. 'I have to learn,' she said. 'Teach me.' So this year Elfie knotted her legs under the table and tempered herself to the Norman girl's diligent study. She was no longer a person but a book or a well in which Emma must dip the pen of her thirst for knowledge.

Elfie got constant headaches, her back and legs ached. At night she sobbed herself to sleep. 'You're doing a grand job. It'll soon be over,' her mother consoled her, sitting beside her, rubbing the back of her neck.

24

At the beginning of July Emma was summoned before Ethelred to be examined on her command of English. He sat on his throne, his grizzled hair straggling beside his hawkish face. She stood before him, feet slightly apart, hands clasped in front of her. She had had her woman do her hair in the English fashion, and braided amber beads through it. Behind her stood Elfie, still as a pillar, in a plain apron fastened with silver shoulder brooches.

'The nobles won't consent to our marriage if you can't speak their language,' Ethelred warned again. He lounged back on his throne, knees spread wide, knuckles gripping the ends of the carved arms.

Emma licked her lips. She hated him, she thought. He was old, arrogant and uncouth. But he was the means for her to acquire riches and power. 'Turn the boar on the spit,' she began, flat-voiced. 'Spread the linen on the hedges to dry. I present you with this gold ring as a token of my appreciation of your service. Saint Cuthbert's ear is preserved in a reliquary at Barking Abbey. I bestow the field known as Stone Field on my steward.'

'Fine, fine, you'll do fine,' said Ethelred. He had fought several skirmishes with the Vikings along the south coast that spring and was anxious for his proposed treaty with Duke Richard of Normandy to be ratified by the marriage as soon as possible. 'You're not perfect, but you'll do.'

5. Elgifu, Canterbury,11th July 1002

The coronation went ahead on a day of heatwave, at noon when the air was still and bright. Banners hung limp, birds were silent, leaves wilted, even bees flagged as they sucked at pea-flowers. It was so hot it was an effort to walk. The whole court had decamped to Canterbury and waited there. And at last the horns on the hilltop blasted out to announce Emma's arrival. As she entered the main street of the town she was mounted on her grey palfrey whose mane was plaited with silver and scarlet ribbons, whose bridle trappings of gold and silver jingled as she stepped. Emma was robed in yellow silk, and a golden circlet held in place a lace veil that kept the worst of the road dust from her face. A great crowd of servants followed her, both men and women, leading horses laden with iron-bound chests: they walked two abreast and as they progressed they pressed the inhabitants of the city up against the walls of the houses; there were cries as a child was trampled.

Elfgifu and Prince Edmund had climbed up on the roof of a peasant's cottage and straddled the thatch as if it were a great horse, or a dragon. 'Heaven be thanked that she's getting married at last,' said Elfie. 'I really hated teaching her English. Being stuck indoors all spring with that humourless bully.'

'All over now,' said Edmund. 'Back to normal life.' He plucked a straw from the roof and leaned over to stick it in her hair like a feather.

Once the procession had passed the two slithered down and ran fast through the back streets to take up their state positions with their families to welcome the new queen. 'By our lady, Elfgifu, you look as if an imp has dragged you backwards through a hedge,' scolded Wulfrune. 'What have you been up to this time?' She smoothed her daughter's skirt, picked straws out of her hair and plaited it firmly, fitted on her headdress so her daughter would look meek and conventional. 'Stand straight. That's better. Now behave as befits a subject welcoming her new queen.'

But the new queen didn't look Elfie's way. Her eyes were all on Ethelred. He was standing at the doors of the cathedral in the heavy silk of his scarlet tunic, a purple cloak, ermine-trimmed, swinging from his shoulders. He wore a gold circlet on his greying hair. The events of the last few months had aged him; his beard was greying, his shoulders were stooped. At the sight of his bride his face turned pale and he stood still as a stone.

Someone – Prince Athelstan, his older son, together with Prince Edmund, took an arm each and led him forward to meet her. He didn't look at his bride again.

This is like watching a play, Elfie thought; a miracle play, a scene from the Bible perhaps. I have no part in it. But I must keep watching because it's significant. It will affect all our futures. Who knows what will happen.

The king stepped back. He glanced behind him but he was hemmed in by his sons, his councillors and his palace staff, the archbishop and a platoon of dark-robed monks and priests. A semi-circle of strong men preventing his escape; forcing him to carry out the pledge he had made.

Sweat circled under Emma's armpits, rendered Ethelred's hands sticky, dripped from the archbishop's nose: he was sweltering in his ornate robes.

Priests started to chant the wedding anthem and a monk swung the censer before him. The burning incense made the king cough uncontrollably. His spittle sizzled on the censer, his eyes began to weep. 'I must go,' he whimpered, but his followers had linked arms and would not let him pass.

The queen-to-be was a mere girl, not as tall as him. She was a little chubby, fed on good Norman cream and apples. One could glimpse her pale blond hair to the side of her veil. She stretched out a hand to the king: a small hand heavy with rings of twisted gold, a solid wrist weighted down with silver. Pale-skinned from her indoor life.

The princes Athelstan and Edmund were now both at their father's side. They walked him forward. Emma placed her hand on his arm; her knuckles clenched white as she gripped him so tight he couldn't escape her. 'This way,' insisted a priest, and the king had no choice but to walk beside her into the cathedral.

'*Gloria*,' sang the choir; '*Gloria, gloria, alleluia*,' gasped the congregation.

'A determined woman, so I've heard,' said Wulfrune over Elfie's head.

'Interesting times to come, I fear, my dear,' said Aelfhelm, moving with their sons Wulfheah and Wulfgeat to join the procession into the cathedral.

Wulfrune turned to her daughter. 'She comes as a peacemaker, Elfie,' she said. 'You have to be strong to make peace. Strong to maintain it too. It's a fighting world out there, my dear. Vicious. Never believe otherwise.'

The ceremony began with a baptism which was strange when Emma had been baptised as a baby: but her Norman name was no longer acceptable; she had to take an English name if she were to be Queen of England. 'No one has informed me of what her new name is to be,' complained the archbishop. Ethelred looked harassed, as if he were trying to dredge something up from his memory. 'Elfgifu,' he muttered in the end. 'I baptise thee Elfgifu,' pronounced the archbishop, dipping his finger in the holy water of the font and making the sign of the cross on Emma's forehead.

A shiver of shock spread through the congregation in the cathedral, a hiss of, '*No,*' it was so strange that the king should give his young bride the name of his former queen, whom rumour still whispered that he had had murdered. Earls and ladies glanced at each other, thinking the same thing could happen to this one. But for the moment she

28

looked plump and solid enough, and Ethelred was smiling (wolf's smile? people wondered) as he escorted her up the steps to her throne and seated himself beside her. She placed her hand on his arm; she was breathing shallowly, you could tell she was excited. The archbishop anointed her with oil and then the deed was done; she was Queen of England at last, glory be. '*Gloria,*' sang choir and congregation once again, '*Gloria, gloria, amen,*' their voices welling up in a great wave that filled the cathedral, and the bells in the tower began to ring, ding-a-ding, on and on, loud and monotonous. Queen Emma-Elfgifu clenched King Ethelred's arm as they processed down the nave, through the doors that stood wide, out into the open air, followed by the congregation.

'Are you coming?' Wulfrune said to her daughter, holding out her hand. They were nearly the last in the cathedral. A novice in a black habit was beginning to sweep the floor.

Elfie stayed crouched on the bench with her hands round her knees. 'Why does Emma have to take the dead queen's name?' she hissed. 'She has no right to it. It's my name too. I don't want her to have it. I feel as if she's taken everything she can from me.'

'Don't be bitter,' said Wulfrune. 'Forget it, that time is past. We are moving on to a new world. Come on, my dear, let's not miss the feast and the dancing.'

And the songs and drunken laughter and fights inside the hall, while outside in the deepening twilight the children chased each other through the courtyard, ghost-like in their pale clothes; the new moon swelling brighter, the stars a glitter, the earth breathing out the day's heat, making the leaves rustle. A barn owl was calling, was answered by its mate. Elfie stood still to listen. 'I wonder if their chicks are fledged,' she said out loud to no-one. How much I belong in this natural outdoor world., she thought.

'Hey, stop that!' shouted Prince Edmund, lazing on his back on the grass in the summer sunshine the next day. He grabbed the end of the stout stick with which Elfie was threatening him.

She heaved the stick back and thwacked him.

'For heaven's sake!' He jumped to his feet and seized the stick from her, hurled it away for the dogs to race after. 'What on earth's the matter? What's got into you?'

'Your father,' she sobbed, brushing the tears from her eyes with the back of her hand. 'I can't stand him. How could he?'

'What's he done this time?'

'He's only given that horrible wife of his my name.'

'I wondered how you'd feel about that.'

'My name. He's gone and had her baptised with my name. She's not to be called Emma any more, he said she's got to have a good Saxon name. My name! How dare he give my name to that arrogant Norman bitch?'

'Calm down, Elfie.' Edmund grasped her arms, he held her close. 'There, stop crying. There's nothing to cry over. You're making a fuss about nothing. It's a political decision. It makes political sense for the people to think she's a good English woman. Though I don't suppose anyone who meets her will believe she's English just because she's got a new name. Not when her Norman accent is so strong.'

'But it's not just my name, it's your mother's name! Your mother was such a lovely person, Edmund, this must make you angry too. Do you think your father is so stupid that only one name will do for all of his wives, his memory is so bad that he has to call all of his wives by the same name?'

'Elfie, calm down.' He stretched out a hand to comfort her. One of the dogs came back with the stick in his mouth, dropped it on the grass next to them and wagged its tail wildly. 'It really doesn't matter, Elfie,' Edmund said.

'It does, Edmund.' Her voice breaking with tears. 'Her having the same name as me – it makes me feel tied to her, in a strange way. As though we'll share the same future. As if we're an ugly kind of twins. As if our fates are bound together. As if we'll destroy each other.' The dog nosed at the stick and started to bark, wagging its long tail. 'I don't want anything to do with her.'

'You're imagining things, Elfie.'

She jumped up and hurled the stick for the dog, which went chasing after it. She brushed the dirt from her hands on her apron, looked up at him with blue eyes strained with seriousness. 'Edmund, you must resent her too, taking the place of your mother. Especially when she's younger than you.'

He swept his hair back from his forehead and sighed. 'My grandmother used to keep a tight rein on my father,' he said. 'Since she died he's been making the most of his freedom to act as he wishes. I'm only a younger son, there's nothing I can do about it.'

6. Emma, late summer 1002

Over the weeks that followed, the new royal couple were seen strolling together everywhere, Emma always with her hand tucked proprietorially into the crook of Ethelred's elbow, the top of her head coming almost to his shoulder. She had become slimmer, perhaps the natural result of entering her mid-teens. He was decked out in a purple linen tunic decorated with gold fringing, and silk trousers, while she wore a silk dress the creamy colour of the ivory whalebone casket carved with the story of David and Goliath that her brother had sent as a wedding gift. She kept such a tight hold on her husband that it was only rarely that he got to break away with his sons and go hunting and hawking, enjoying the outdoor freedom and energetic exercise that all his life he had loved. In the long church services she dragged him to his head nodded, his eyes closed until she pinched him to wake him up. His face grew pasty, he was slow and listless.

7. Elfgifu and family, London and Northumbria, autumn 1002

In the Witan, the council chamber, where Emma-Elfgifu was not permitted, Ethelred was wide-awake and angry. 'Like a bull goaded with a spear,' said Aelfhelm, coming back from a September meeting. 'I always thought before that he was ill-advised, but that damned new wife of his has made him so furious that he's a hundred times worse now.'

'What's the matter this time?' asked Wulfrune, looking up from her embroidery.

'He's decided to kill all the Danes in England.'

'What?' Wulfrune's needle stopped still in mid-air, her mouth an open O. 'That can't be true – you must be joking.'

'Every single Dane in England – he says he'll kill them all. For God's sake, what does he think he's playing at?'

'I don't believe you.'

'He's worked it out in detail. What's worse, there are men in the Witan who support him. Isolationists who believe in a perfect English race. As if there were such a thing. As if we weren't all descended from Gauls and

Romans and Celts, and the Danes who've been settling in our country for centuries, before the Romans even.'

'But the Danes... you and I...we are... our grandparents... Danes live in every town and village, they've settled, they farm the land, they've taken English wives, they are part of the fabric of the country... you must be mistaken, it's nonsense, it can't be true.' She laid down her embroidery and got to her feet, felt her husband's forehead to see if he had a fever, if it was some affliction that had addled his head.

'Oh God, Wulfrune, what can we do? The king can't be dissuaded.' He flopped down on a bench, he buried his head in his hands. 'I've tried so hard. There's nothing I can do. He won't listen to me.' He was shivering uncontrollably. 'The trouble is, there are fellows on the Witan who back him up, they're after political advancement, and riches... they think they'll be given the land of the Danes who are murdered.'

Wulfrune sat beside him, put her arm around his shoulder. 'Why, even his own wife, Emma, she's half Danish... Do you think that's it, Aelfhelm? That he hates her, and, and... no, no, he wouldn't. She's only a child. Do you think it's she who's driven him to this?'

'I don't know the reason. But I'm not prepared to be involved. I'm going to visit my estates in Northumberland, and check everything is in order. I've told the king. He's forbidden my going but...'

'If you stay, you'll be able to make him see reason, I know you will.'

'There's no hope of that. I've tried my hardest. Other councillors too...'

'You must be able to stop him.'

'It's too late. Ealdorman Pallig from Devon... You know what good friends he was with the king. Always by his side.'

'His wife's Danish. Gunnhild. A lovely woman. So generous, you can tell she's of royal blood.'

'He's left the court. He's taken his family and servants back to Devon.'

'He's someone whose judgement I trust utterly. He has a good head on his shoulders,' said Wulfrune. 'Aelfhelm, you must be right. Tell the boys to get ready. I'll tell Elfie. We'll leave in the morning.'

'I must be able to get him to see reason.'

'If Pallig's left the court...'

'You're right. I don't want to put all your lives at risk. We'll have to go.'

They led their horses from the stables into the pre-dawn light. They hung leather bags of their belongings behind their saddles, they wrapped the iron and silver rings on bridle and harness with cloth to silence them, they led their horses across soft grass to hush their hooves. Away from the palace; into the great forest north of London, where in a coppice of hornbeam hung with the gold leaves of autumn, the rising sun catching light to the topmost branches, doves cooing a merry backdrop to the desperate secrecy, the fear with which they travelled, they readied themselves and began their gallop northwards.

By quiet tracks the first day. Aelfhelm chose their route by the direction of the sun, the length of the shadows falling before them. At nightfall they camped towards the northern edge of the forest, where the lightness of open fields was visible through a curtain of branches hung with autumn leaves that rustled in the breeze. 'That song we all know so well,' murmured Elfie, slipping her hand in her brother Wulfheah's.

Tomorrow they would go on. But that night they lit no fire, they were wary of attracting attention to themselves; only stale unleavened bread and cheese and apples to eat. They wrapped themselves in blankets, lay close together for warmth. With dawn the next day they moved on, and the following day, not stopping with friends as they usually did, because who knew who would be supporting the king, where anyone's loyalties might lie, who might send him messages telling where they were. 'I'm in haste to get to my estates,' Aelfhelm said to all who questioned him. 'I've not been home in over a year. I suspect my steward of cheating me, I have to check.'

And here they were, home at last, coming into the cobbled courtyard surrounded by stone buildings, and Egbert had taken the weary horses, was leading them to the drinking trough, was rubbing them down, and Margaret had run out to greet them, still with her shuttle in her hand, trailing a long strand of brown wool, she was embracing the boys who hugged their old nurse back, she was throwing her arms round Elfie and clutching her to her bosom with such force that she lifted her off the ground: 'My little one, sweetheart, how you have grown, I wouldn't believe it, you'll be a young lady soon, I don't want you to grow up, I want you to be my charge for ever and ever...' and the housekeeper was bustling round, she was shouting instructions to the servants for beds to be readied with fresh linen, and for the cook to prepare food, for Michael to fill the ale cup. The dogs were bounding round them and leaping up too.

Elfie was down on her knees with her arms round Brindle's neck, Brindle who'd been hers since he was a puppy. The two of them, the girl and the dog, they were in a world of their own, they jumped up and ran off down the track through the stunted pines to the beach and the sea. Elfie threw fir cones and Brindle leapt up to catch them, she threw sticks and he chased them, ears flapping, tail waving like a flag, across the sand where she was slower, her feet sinking in. She kept on running right to the sea's edge. She kicked off her boots, she knotted up her skirt, she stepped tentatively into the rim of the sea, the cold North Sea waves that had rolled all the way from Norway to slide up the bones of her feet – so cold at first, and then, as she got used to them, the waves felt warmer, for though it was autumn the sea still held some residual summer heat, and she waded in up to her knees, the waves splashing thigh-high. Brindle was panting off up the beach chasing a gull, and she raised her eyes to the horizon and stared at that vast encircling line that limited her vision, and wondered as ever what lay beyond it. I'd like to explore all far off unknown places, Norway certainly, Russia and eastwards perhaps; and she laughed out loud, glad to be away from the court, glad of her freedom to be herself.

Every day of that beautiful autumn Elfgifu ran on the sands with Brindle at her side, loving the freedom, forgetting all the unpleasantness of down south earlier in the year. Her skirt was looped up and her feet splashed in the salt sea that was sun-warmed at the edges, so cold she flinched when she paddled far out; cold (she had her cloak with her) when she took boat with fishermen out to the Farne Islands and she laughed at the thousands of puffins popping out of their holes, and watched the grey seals, that strange aquatic cross between slugs and sleek dogs, basking and diving, swimming, humping their backs; and she slipped into the dark chill chapel of St Cuthbert that was like a cave, and joined in the prayers of the resident hermit, a lame old fellow whose name she never learned, who from the smell of him never washed. She and Brindle clambered over the rocks to fetch driftwood that had been washed up by the sea, for the hermit to burn to keep himself warm in the winter; the sea-washed wood was so silver and smooth that she stroked it.

She stood waiting for the fishermen to fetch her, staring back at the mainland with its great forests of oak and beech, its clearings with thatched houses and gardens, her father's great house strong as a castle, green meadows of cattle and sheep beside clear-running rivers; the pigs rooting for acorns at the forest edges as the autumn drew on.

One stormy day in early November, when out on the island the wind tore at Elfie's sleeves and skirt and whipped her long hair into rats' tails as she added yet more driftwood to the huge heap she'd made at the side of the chapel, the hermit came out to say, 'God bless you, my child.'

'My mother has forbidden me to come again until the weather is warmer,' said Elfie. 'So farewell for the time being.'

The hermit raised his hand in blessing. 'May the Good Lord keep you safe always, through all the troubles and changes that are to come in your lifetime.'

Elfie clambered into the boat, and as the men rowed her back to the mainland, toward her father's house, she slipped her hand under her cloak and rubbed her chest, cherishing the old man's blessing as if it were a jewel she could polish and carry with her for ever.

8. Elfgifu, Northumberland, late 1002

News came that King Ethelred planned his massacre of the Danes for St Brice's Day: November 13th. Aelfhelm, still in Northumberland with his family, made ready to ride back to London to try one last time to dissuade him, but Wulfrune rushed out and grabbed his stirrup. 'Don't. There's no point, my dearest, my sweet heart,' she gasped, hanging on though his horse was rearing, hooves flailing in the air. She was flinching, frightened. 'Think,' she begged. 'Just consider. The king has so little support that no one will do as he orders. It's not feasible. The Danes are so fully integrated, they're so much a part of every town and every village, that it's not possible to separate them out and kill them all. It can't be done. If you go, if you argue with Ethelred, you'll inflame the situation, the king will feel bound as a matter of honour to carry out his plans. But if you stay here, my dearest, where you're safe – ignore him and then he can change his plans without dishonour ...'

Aelfhelm calmed his horse, and sat there, biting his lip. 'What you say makes sense,' he conceded at last. He jumped down and tossed the reins to Egbert. 'Bring me my hawks,' he commanded.

At that moment a man galloped into the courtyard and reined in his frothing horse. Roger the bailiff – 'Wolves,' he was shouting, 'wolves, my lord, attacking the sheep. Two gone already...'

'Show me,' said Aelfhelm, swinging himself back up into his saddle, grabbing a spear from the stack by the stable door, checking its sharpness, and setting off at a fast gallop up toward the meadow where the sheep grazed alongside the forest.

In the chill of November, days of grey fogs, coughs raking the chests of the native Northumbrians, the walls of Aelfhelm's castle bleeding drops of moisture, news from the south arrived in dribs and drabs. The messengers were given warm mead to soothe their dry throats, they spoke in the hall. Everyone there was silent, awaiting the solemn news.

In Oxford an angry mob had pursued the Danes to the church of St Frideswide, the messengers said: there the mob had not respected the sanctuary laws, they had set fire to the building, the Danes inside couldn't escape, they had been burned to death. In the smouldering ashy aftermath the charred corpses of warriors defending the door with sword and axe were found, the bodies of mothers curled around their children to shield them from the flames, of lovers entwined in each other's arms. Fleshless bones fell together.

May the Lord have mercy on all their souls, wept Aelfhelm and his family and people.

In Devon the sailor Pallig was killed with his fair wife tall Gunnhild and their small child. 'My God, not them,' wept Aelfhelm. 'Not my dear friends. How can Ethelred be such a fool? He knows that Gunnhild is the sister of King Sweyn Forkbeard of Denmark. His vengeance will be swift and terrible.'

'Swift and terrible,' shouted Elfgifu into the east wind as she galloped her mare across the wide sands at Bamburgh, as the grey waves rolled in and shattered, her hair and the mare's mane threading the bitter wind. The mare's hooves splashed in the sea, they thundered on the sand.

'Gunnhild was indeed King Sweyn's sister,' said Wulfrune. 'I have known her so long. And her dear innocent daughter. Ethelred had no reason to kill them, how could he have been so cruel as to kill them?'

King Sweyn was a black cloud. A bogeyman, a great devil with a barbed pitchfork on the points of which were speared the wriggling bodies of the many foes he had slain; and yet there was still space for those he was to slay in the future. That villain who had fought and slain his very own father in order to gain the throne of Denmark. The man who at his own father's funeral rites, in front of the ferocious piratical Jomsburg Vikings who constituted his guard, had made an oath that he would become King of England. Oaths counted, even when everyone was drunk. Sweyn, king of Denmark, already ruled parts of Norway and Sweden too. He would certainly seek to avenge his sister's death. He would not renounce his determination to conquer England.

'Ethelred's a fool,' said Aelfhelm. 'No point in his marrying Emma of Normandy to form a political alliance against the Vikings, if he then does his utmost to make Sweyn mad. He can't be fool enough to believe Emma's brother will support him against Sweyn. Richard has much more sense than to attract the hostility of such a powerful man.'

'Who knows what will become of our land?' wept Wulfrune.

Elfie put her arms around Brindle's neck, cuddled the big dog close to her.

From Russia the bitter wind came, from Scandinavia, the icy homes of the Vikings, from Norway and Sweden and the more fecund plains of Denmark whose harvest was to be the spear-shafts and axe-handles, the bows of King Sweyn's formidable army.

The family stayed in Northumbria till after Yuletide. Its midwinter darkness was lit by the orange flicker of the flames of the huge birch fire lighting up the great hall, reddening the pale cold faces of the family and their retainers, and of those Danes who had fled North and sought safety with them.

'Let them all be fed,' Wulfrune had ordered, walking into the kitchens; and the cooks had scooped deep into the stores of wheat to make bread. Aelfhelm had gone hunting with Wulfheah and Wulfgeat and they had shot two stags, speared four wild boar, slit their bellies in situ and gutted and skinned them, leaving the entrails for hungry wolves and foxes to scavenge. Egbert heaved the carcasses onto the sled and led the carthorses over frost-rutted tracks back to the hall, with ropes hoisted the carcasses high into an oak tree to hang out of the reach of wolves. A boy stood guard with a catapult and a bag of stones against plundering ravens.

Elfie was used to the sight. She was just thankful that the family had the wherewithal to fulfil its obligations of hospitality to their friends and dependants. Starvation was always a near thing. 'Let me come hunting with you tomorrow,' she begged her father, but it was hawking they went, she with her young kestrel Speckle on her wrist. She caught five wild ducks. They hung from her saddle, bouncing against her mare's belly. When she got home, she handed them over to the thrall Padraig who hung them in the oak tree. A tree of dead things; a tree to give life to the household. The carcasses blew in the bitter wind from the east; by the morning they were stiff with ice and rattled against the branches.

In the great hall the refugees, the strangers with their wild hair and strange accents who had fled from the south, sang songs of the losses they had suffered; they plucked the lute and sang praises of Aelfhelm's generosity, his upholding of the traditions of the land. Wulfrune, in a green woollen dress with a circlet of gold at the neck, filled the warm mead-cup, carried it round and offered it to all, for them to taste its sweetness. People laughed, they told tales, they gossiped. Elfie pulled her warm cloak tighter round her shoulders, curled up on a cushion on the floor with Brindle's head warm in her lap. She lifted Brindle's ear and blew in it, and he shook his head. She was certain that this was the right way to live, the traditional way, with generosity, hospitality and loyalty, in companionship with others.

Someone began to sing the old, old tale of a dragon living in an underwater cave in a lake. The dragon in the story was a female, battling to protect its young from formidable enemies. How vivid the story-telling was; Elfie would have liked to believe it, but a dragon was a creature she had never encountered and whose existence she doubted. She stood up, and, calling Brindle to follow, went out of the hall. The moon was up now; a half-moon that shed its light into the courtyard and silvered the track through the pines to the sea. How bitter the wind was. She pulled up her hood and tugged her cloak tighter around herself. 'Come on, boy,' she called to her dog, and started to run, the thump of her feet pumping heat into her chest.

Beyond the pines, the sea stretched dark and secret in front of her. The moon cast its light like a road across the water, its reflection broken and rippled by the inward-rolling waves. High tide: she crossed the sand, stood watching the sea. The waves ran up over the toes of her boots.

Far out she could just discern something breaking the surface; a fallen tree, she thought it must be, washed downriver and out to sea. But the longer she watched it, the more she was convinced that it was a dragon's head she could see, the frills of its spine wallowing behind it. 'Brindle,' she called, and he came and stood by her, watching too. He started to shiver, cowered, tucked his tail between his legs. He was obviously frightened. Animals can sometimes sense things that we can't, Elfie thought.

The dragon turned head-on to the beach; it's swimming to land, she thought.

She thought of the Viking long-boats with their carvings of dragons.

Dragons don't exist. But she couldn't believe this one wasn't real, that it wasn't at the least foretelling a danger that would one day come from the sea.

Snow in January. The buildings were wrapped in it; they were heaped high with it, piled up with white, inside they were like mole-tunnels or fox-dens. Refuges, with blue smoke rising through the holes in their roofs, the snow thawed around them so you could see the wooden shingles. Warm inside, a sanctuary against the bitterness of the wind. Snow lay along branches. Snow heaped against doors, blew in windows. Piled, unmelting, on earth floors.

Come the morning, you could decipher the claw prints of birds, the hoof prints of deer, the long lope of the wolf who haunted the homestead at night.

Easy to track the deer. They needed them for food. 'Who'd have guessed there'd be so many people here at this time of the year?' said the cook, scratching his head. 'At this rate, we won't have enough wheat to last us through to the end of February, let alone into the spring.'

'We'll go south,' decided Wulfrune, 'so you can conserve the supplies that remain for the use of the household.' She consulted with Aelfhelm and her sons, and two weeks after the thaw, when the worst of the flooding had run into the rivers, filling them to over-brimming, they trudged the drab muddy roads as far south as their Northampton estates, where they were made welcome and given their four-poster beds in a heated outbuilding.

Elfgifu unclawed her hand, stretching out her fingers which were cramped with cold. She held her hand out to the fire. 'My poor love,' said Aelfhelm, weighing her down with his arm round her shoulders. 'It's been a hard journey for my little one. But you and your mother can rest here at least. Tomorrow Wulfgeat and I must ride on. There's a meeting of the Witan.'

'You're not going to attend it?' said Wulfrune sharply.

'We have to,' he replied.

'For God's sake, no. The king has gone mad. All you'll do is put yourselves in danger.'

'How else can we bring the king to his senses, other than by talking to him?'

'If you think you can talk sense into him, you're a bigger fool than I think you are.'

He took his wife gently by the shoulders, he leaned forward and kissed her tear-stained cheek. 'What choice do I have?' he asked wearily. 'Somebody has to speak up for the people of our land.'

'We'll come and keep you company as soon as the roads are better, Papa,' said Elfgifu.

'Maybe,' he said. 'Let me assess the situation at court first. Then I will decide what is best.'

Elfgifu was never to go to King Ethelred's court again. Her brothers brought back word to her of how it was a sadder place than it used to be, more serious, with Queen Emma replacing its former good comradeship with stale ritual and formality. There seemed no affection between her and the king; she often wore bruises on her cheeks, tears in her eyes. So fearful the court was: spies kept bringing reports that King Sweyn of Denmark was assembling forces in order to avenge the death of his sister Gunnhild. Spear and sword practice were carried out daily in the palace grounds. It was said that Sweyn's forces had been spotted sailing off the coast.

9. Emma, Winchester 1003

When her nine months were up and the baby came out from between her legs, Emma could not love it, this tiny wrinkled screaming thing, the product of so much pain. 'Ah, what a bonny baby,' cooed Mildred, who'd been nursemaid to Ethelred's children by his previous queen. It had long been a source of sadness to her that she had never found the body of her late mistress to wrap in her winding sheet, to say farewell to in a proper manner. 'You will be servant to my new queen now,' Ethelred had ruled. So now Mildred was a nursemaid again, and couched Emma's baby on her shoulder and wrapped a shawl around it, and she sang to it, and rocked it with the swaying of her body. As if by magic, the thing stopped crying. 'You hold him now,' she said, offering the bundle to Emma.

'No,' Emma said. 'No, I hate it. I don't want anything to do with it. The king hurt me so much when we made it. How can I love something that is born of the king's violence?'

Ethelred came and saw his child. It gripped his hairy finger with its tiny hand and that pleased him. 'Ah, little one, you have a warrior's grip already,' he said.

Mildred had the wise woman come, and she massaged Emma's breasts and burned sweet herbs in the close chamber with its fire of birch logs, where she was kept prisoner for a month. She wrote to her mother saying she'd performed her royal duty and the child was well, and asking, would she send fine silks in bright colours to work a tapestry with. And Gunnor sent Emma back a basket of the best silks, and needles, and also a small Book of Hours, beautifully gilt, and an ivory teething ring, and a letter which said not to be afraid, child-bearing was a woman's role and function, and maybe she had been at fault in not teaching her daughter that, rather than how to read. And she prayed she would find herself filled with love for her child. 'What is its name?' she said.

Emma wept because she'd hoped her mother would take ship across the Channel. She longed to have the comfort of her presence, to feel her arm around her shoulders, to be able to curl on her lap like a small child and cry into her bosom. Unburdening all the shock of living in this strange, uncouth court.

But the truth was that she had no-one: no friend, no comforter. So when her month was up she summoned all her courage and dressed in her best clothes, shawled her hair and pulled on her boots, and walked tall and straight as she could (feeling dizzy from her long confinement, but not wanting anyone to sense her weakness) to the palace chapel, and there she knelt and prayed earnestly to the Virgin Mother for comfort. And presently a ray of sun fell through the window and touched the back of her hands, and hope for the future crept into her heart. It was a warmth in her chest where before her feelings had been frozen. When she hadn't been able to see how life could proceed.

Hope, and with it a renewal of strength. An understanding that all trials pass: that she was Queen of England, and would be strong again.

She picked up a pen and wrote to her mother, 'My child's name is Edward. It is the name of a great English king of a few generations ago. It is our wish that in time he too will be great.' She didn't think she could love anything that was born out of the barrenness of her relationship with her husband. A horrible animal act, like dogs copulating under the table in the great hall, their baby's conception had been, a brutal act without emotion, quick, not since repeated, a duty imposed on her by her role as queen. When she looked at the mewling scrap in its crib, or being fed by one of its wet-nurses, she could imagine no great future for it, albeit it was son to the king and queen of England.

At the baby's baptism, as the nurse comforted the crying child, Emma had softened to the consolation of the bishop's hand on her arm. It seemed to convey sympathy for all the horrors she had gone through in performing her royal duty. When she turned to him, how comfortable she felt with his respectfulness and the solemnity of his demeanour – the same behaviour that the monks in the abbey at home had displayed. She remembered their patience in teaching her Latin; their instructions in the rules of the church. She needed a life with order at its heart. She could not countenance the sudden rages into which Ethelred flew, his refusal to heed advice on matters of state. The way he tried to appease the Vikings by buying them off from ravaging his kingdom, doling out huge payments of Danegeld, when experience showed that they would just come back again demanding more money. The way he was constantly at war with the members of his Witan when they did not concur with him. His animosity in particular towards the Northumbrian eorl Aelfhelm and his two sons when the fellows had what he saw as the impudence to argue against the national slaughter of Danes that he ordered – something she too felt strongly about, how could she not, when her own mother was Danish? – but she had by then discovered that arguing against Ethelred only made him more determined in his folly and wanton capriciousness. The members of the Witan had at least managed to limit the killing to what could be done in a single day – the thirteenth of November, St Brice's Day – how would the venerable St Brice have felt to have such murder committed on his holy day?

Emma knelt in the chapel and let the amber beads of her rosary slip through her cold fingers. This bead was the disturbed nights that her crotchety baby caused her, this bead the exhaustion from which she suffered, this the prickly bristle of her husband's moustache on her cheek, this the rotting meat in his beard, this the way he belched, this his farting, this his drunkenness, the way he fell headlong on the floor...

Holy Mary, Mother of God, what can I do? she prayed.

The divine answer came in the revelation that she should order to have built her own separate palace quarters. There must be a great central fireplace to heat the hall. Edward was to sleep in a distant room so that she would not be disturbed by his crying, it being furnished with benches whereon his nurses might sleep. For herself she had a private chamber with thick Norman tapestries hung on the walls, where the bishop was always welcome: a chamber where Ethelred, coming in booted from hunting, would stand stock still and stare around him, sniffing the effete scent of warm wax, dried lavender and rose petals as if he were a hound seeking the trail of a wild boar. Then he'd demand to see his son, and she'd say, he's in his nursery, and he'd say, you should be looking after him, and she'd say, his nurses are much more skilled at childcare than I, and excuse herself to pray, because it was always, in her ordered world, time for Matins or Lauds or Nones or Compline: her day busy with devotions. Seeking to attain a blessed life in Paradise to compensate for the raw unpleasantness and brutality of this one. From under her lowered lids she would watch Ethelred bite his lip, and frown; not knowing how to take his wife when she was at her prayers. He'd exclaim with impatience and stride out and she'd relax and sigh.

10. Elfgifu, Wolverhampton, 1003

Elfie's dog Brindle fathered puppies. One was sent south to her, a dog with a sweeping tail like a feather, whom she named Smokey and house-trained, who was her devoted companion all spring and summer, Elfie wandering in the orchards and meadows, climbing trees, swimming in the river and pools among the dragonflies, under the overhang of willows. Until in the autumn Aelfhelm decreed she should be sent to Wolverhamton Abbey which her grandmother had founded, to practise her reading and Latin, and learn to copy neatly and to do accounts, all skills her father believed she needed if she was to be able to run an estate. 'There's no call for that,' countered her mother. 'I want her to stay here with us. She will always have a husband to do things like that for her.'

'I don't want a husband,' said Elfie, kicking a pebble, sending it flying into the long grass.

'Don't look so sour, little one. You're a pretty girl of good birth. You might even aspire to the hand of one of the princes. You could in due course become the queen. Think how you could help your father then.'

Elfie leapt up to an oak branch, swung from it by her hands. 'The last queen wasn't happy,' she observed.

'Nonsense. She had three sons and all the riches she could have wished for.'

'We must make the best provision we can for our daughter,' said Aelfhelm sadly, caressing the back of his wife's neck. 'Nothing in this world is certain. You, my dear …'

'Don't start on that,' said Wulfrune. 'You know I've never wanted to learn to read. Besides, I don't need to be independent. Nothing is going to happen to you. I hold you safe in my prayers every night.'

'Yes, dear,' said Aelfhelm. Nevertheless he commissioned leather saddle bags to be made in which Elfie might carry her dresses and aprons, parchment, ink and pens, and in the autumn he sent her off to study at her grandmother's convent.

It came as a shock to her, the stillness, the order and discipline of it. The loneliness too, the quiet hooded figures of the nuns walking the cold cloisters, herself walking separately, hands clasped, no one to chat to or laugh with; her cold cell, the icy chapel. She suffered badly from chilblains in the winters, got used to the sores. Her isolation made her stronger, more self-dependent. *This is a time I have to endure*, she thought, *a passive learning time*. Watching, absorbing. She maintained her dignity, her pride in her family. *I am distant from the nuns*. They were all older than her. She walked tall, she opened her books, she tucked a stray strand of hair behind her ear, she dipped her pen in the ink. Every day, over and over. At night sometimes she cried herself to sleep.

Elfgifu, the nuns called her. Her proper name. She was not Elfie any more. She felt older, isolated. An island.

Then at Yule it was amazing to travel home to Northampton and to revive her old self and ride like a wild child through the hamlets and fields and forests of the estate, remembering its layout well, making friends with those who worked the land, with the millers and the potter and Johann who was in charge of the mint, turning silver fragments and ingots into buckets of bright silver pennies, all with the king's image on. And then when her brothers and father Aelfhelm came home from the king's court she had all the pleasure of hunting and hawking with them. The exhilaration of the outdoors, the sheer freedom of it. When her mother gave her embroidery to do, she dropped it on the earth floor, kicked it under the table; said she had to go outside.

Out with the stars and the moon and the wind and the sun. Outside with all she loved the most.

11. Elfgifu, Northampton, 1006

For Elfgifu, three years followed the same pattern: the straight ribbon of the convent, the wild loops of being at home. It seemed as if life might go on like that for ever.

But in 1006 a messenger came to the convent, demanding to speak to Elfgifu alone. She met him in the stone cloisters. Grey rain slanted in on the square of grass at their centre. His face was pale and weary, his cloak sodden and mud-spattered. What now? she wondered. Stared up at him. 'Eofric, is it?' she asked. 'Your father is the miller at Dallington?'

He said: 'Your father.'

'What of him?'

He brushed the raindrops from his face. Not raindrops, tears, she realised in a moment of sudden intuition. 'What is it?' She grasped his arm, stared up into his eyes that were red with grief and fatigue. 'What news do you bring?'

'Eorl Aelfhelm has been murdered.'

'No.'

'It is true, madam.'

'My father?'

'Yes, madam.'

'It cannot be true.'

'Indeed, madam.' The deed was said to have been done on the orders of the king, at the hands of the king's adviser Eadric Streona. 'You must come home to be with your mother,' Eofric said. 'She has sore need of you.'

She reached for her cloak on the back of the door, she swung it round her shoulders, she saddled her horse in the stables. A long ride home. When at last she pushed open the door to the hall her mother was in a terrible way. Distraught with grief, she was screaming uncontrollably. Her dress and apron were dirty and torn, her hair tangled with ash, dirt streaks down her cheeks. She threw herself flat on the earth floor, she curled up on a bench by the fire; she lashed out with her fists. She screamed in her sleep.

Elfgifu didn't know how to deal with her. She put her arms around her but her mother pushed her away. She fetched her young dog Smokey who was soft and friendly but her mother in her distress threw him off her lap into the fire. Oh, the terrible yelps of his pain and his fear. Elfie grabbed him out but he was burned so badly that Elfie had no choice but to kill him, to put him out of his pain. He lay whimpering and he thumped his tail feebly at the gentle sound of her voice, and she couldn't do anything to help him, so what she did was seize a heavy stone and crush his dear head with it. 'Oh, Smokey, no!' she cried. She had burn marks on her hands from the fire. She laid her head on his flank.

She was ashamed that her grief at the loss of her dog was greater than her grief at the loss of her father. Even though she had loved her father so much; she had always adored him. Perhaps it was because she could make better sense of the loss of her dog, it was more comprehensible. She longed for some sort of comfort, an arm around her. She touched her mother, but her mother didn't respond. When she looked at Wulfrune, she saw that grief had translated her into a different person, an alien being, her face was ravaged with distress, such desolation in her eyes that she was almost unrecognisable.

Then came the news that her brothers had been blinded. They had had their eyes gouged out, on Ethelred's orders. Who would be so base as to obey such a cruel and unjust order? The boys were brought home by their servants, but they were so mutilated, so ugly that their mother could not bear to look at them, she threw her apron over her head and wailed and trembled and beat her head against the wall and could not acknowledge them.

Elfgifu did her best to settle them into the comfortable familiarity of the small hall, she told them where they were, she said, here is the bench, here is the table, here is the door; sit on this cushion, she said. Feel, she said, feel, you can feel the rough blue linen cover. Blue as the sky in which the sun still shines. Come outside, she said, feel the sunshine on your bare arms, she said, soon it will be evening, the silver moon has no warmth. No more warmth.

She walked them in the courtyard on the cobbles. *Oh my lovely boys.* She bit her horror into herself and nursed their wounds with boiled water and comfrey poultices. She appointed men to care for their every need. To help them eat; to help them defecate. It broke her heart to see her brave, handsome beloved brothers so disabled and disfigured. Her chest was choked, her head ached with her anguish.

She had to take over the roles that her brothers and her parents had had in the running of the Northampton estate. She laid out before herself the simple, practical tasks she had to do each day. 'Tell me what I must do,' she said to her brothers and her mother again and again, breaking into their misery. 'Tell me how to manage the land. I don't know how. You must help me. Tell me, tell me what to do.' The Northumberland lands she had to leave for the time being in the hands of the steward her father had appointed there.

She couldn't believe how much she missed her dog Smokey running at her side. She ached for him. He was so companionable, she thought. He always made me laugh. With him these terrible things might have been more bearable, she thought, and she imagined sitting beside him, her arm around the soft fur of his neck; him turning to lick her hand with his rough tongue.

One day Wulfrune disappeared from the hall and was brought back by a peasant in the evening. She was bedraggled and damp from the drizzle. She couldn't tell her daughter where she had been. 'I was looking for your father,' she said, 'in case he is coming by boat.'

'My father is safe in Heaven,' says Elfgifu. 'You will not find him here on Earth.'

In the autumn Elfgifu wrote to her grandmother: I will not be returning to the convent, because of the pressing needs of my family. I beg you, tell me if you can see anything now that is of any good in this whole mortal world. Because I cannot.

Her grandmother sent a message to her uncles Morcar and Sigeferth, and they rode together to visit her. She met them on the borders of her family's land, where she was checking with her steward Edward Little on an incident of stolen sheep. How good it was to see them riding on their sturdy horses toward her, their ordinary, reddish faces, their squat stout build, their gruff manners because neither of them was used to the company of young women. 'Hail, Elfgifu, Aelfhelm's daughter!'

Within a week they had dispatched Wulfheah to a monastery where the monks would give him sanctuary in a cold cell, and would feed and guide him. Wulfgeat who had been the more handsome could not bear witnesses to his disfigurement, and he chose to live alone, with servants to attend him. The uncles ordered Elfgifu to return to the convent: *It is what your father would have wished.* But she would not go. 'I have to run the estates,' she said.

'We will appoint a steward for that.'

'I wish to do it all myself.' She was fourteen, not yet grown to her full height: skinny and straight and determined. She was of noble family; she had a duty, a tradition to uphold. She stood square in the hall of her father's palace, the great wooden walls stout about her, the beams of the roof vaulting high over her head. A sunbeam falling through a high window gilded her pale hair like an ephemeral crown.

'You have your damned father's cussedness,' Morcar complained. And her uncles washed their hands of her, and left.

Days later Wulfrune disappeared from the hall again. This time no one brought her back. Her body was found in the river Nene ten days later. The men who found her partially decomposed corpse nailed her up in a narrow coffin; Elfgifu never got to see her mother again. In the chamber where the coffin lay they burned rosemary – the dry dead branches from the underneath of the bushes that grew on the stone wall in the garden. The room filled with remembrance, the twigs crackled as if she were trying to speak. That noise was amplified by the echo from the timber walls, and Elfgifu listened hard to the sound, as if it were her mother's voice, but she could not make out any words. The flames flared yellow and died, and her father's men came to drag the coffin on a sledge pulled by four horses (Wulfrune had barely eaten in months; she had become very light) to Ely Cathedral, where her husband Aelfhelm was buried. Elfgifu followed the cortege on horseback, her two brothers beside her. Each of their horses was led by a warrior armed with a spear, who held the jingling reins along the track through the forest.

At Ely they were joined by their uncles Morcar and Sigeferth, and by their grandmother. The monks chanted the mass for the dead. Elfgifu stood with her grandmother and attendant nuns in the church, their stern habited figures like tall fence posts imprisoning her. A bristle of propriety, of dignity, of control. She couldn't bear it, it was all too much, her eyes stung, she couldn't contain her horror and grief any longer, she was blinded by tears, she had to break free, she dived between two of the nuns, she broke away, bursting out of their outstretched hands, running off down the nave through the crowd of mourners come to lament the passing of the last of her distinguished family, the end of an era: out to the sunlight and down to the pond.

Autumn sun low in the sky turned the yellow hornbeam leaves to gold, a weird radiance that in a shiver of wind fell on her hair and her shoulders. A kind of spotted halo. She turned up the palms of her hands to catch the leaves but the wind had stopped. She stood empty-handed a moment, then picked the leaves off her sleeves, shook them off her skirt, shedding them into the dark water of the pond. The pond full of reflections of sky and of trees... had her mother been searching out her own reflection when she died? So lonely she had been trying to find someone, anyone to share the extremity of her grief.

Her grandmother came running toward her, she threw her plump arms around her, clutched her to her bosom. 'Oh, Elfgifu,' she sobbed. 'There's no life here for you any more. You must come back to the convent with me.'

Elfgifu pulled away, wouldn't look at her. But her grandmother laid her arm across her shoulders and drew the girl to her side. The smell of the old woman's soft linen was that of sun-dried lavender. She was so solid, so dependable when the whole world was uncertain that Elfgifu instinctively nestled against her. 'Do not be afraid,' her grandmother said. 'Come back to the convent with me, I will keep you safe.'

When Elfgifu glanced up she saw her brother Wulfheah stumbling along beside their uncle Sigeferth. 'I cannot go,' she said. 'I have obligations here.'

Her grandmother followed her gaze. 'You can do nothing for your brothers,' she said coldly. 'Best to look after yourself. Come back to the convent. You'll be safe there if the king decides to pursue his vendetta against your family against you too.'

'No. No, I can't. I must help my brothers. I must look after the land – fill my father's place...'

'My dear, it is best for you to continue in the course of life that your father mapped out for you. You should respect his will, his knowledge of what would be best for you.'

Elfgifu hesitated. She was weighed down with the losses she had suffered that year. Losing both her parents, and her brothers, who, blinded, had given up on life. She was alone. She had such a headache, felt so disconnected from the world. She couldn't plan, she didn't know if there was anything she could hope for. She gave in to her grandmother because her grandmother was strong and there was comfort in strength, in resting one's head against a resolute shoulder.

Back at the convent Elfgifu found her old cell again, her hard narrow bed, her place among the nuns processing in to Matins and Lauds, to Vespers in the evening. The tinny clang of the bell summoned them to do their duty, over and over and over. The repetition gave form to the days. The soft words of the evening prayers became soothing to her as her mother sitting on her bed at night time had been. *Domine, ad adiuvandum me festina.* The ritual of the repeated words calmed the fears that welled up in her head. *Lord, make haste to help me.*

Her grandmother set her the task of copying out verses from Psalm 119. Elfgifu concentrated, forming her letters with care, the flames of three candles lighting the parchment on which she wrote that dark winter with great care. She wanted to do the best that she could. She concentrated on her task: on every elaboration of each letter, on bringing the script to a state of beauty and grace. The steps of an *M*, the flow of an *S*, or a capital *T*. The way you can ornament the script with carmine and indigo, brightening it with gold leaf. Everything else was wrong in her life, and she wanted to create something that was perfect. *Teach me knowledge and good judgement,* the psalm said. She concentrated hard. *I will get this right,* was her one aspiration.

Elfgifu's eyes ached. She rubbed them, she flexed her shoulders. She had been working too long. She stood up and stretched and stared out in the yard. Who was that there? A familiar figure. Not from her present life in the convent, but from her childhood. Edward Little, her father's steward, whom she'd grown up with, he'd always managed the estates around Northampton, it was him, surely. How much older he looked now, his face lined with worry and sadness, his shoulders slumped. She went out to him, she took his hand. 'What's the matter?' she said. It felt strange to be taller than him now. 'What are you doing here, so far from home?' she asked.

He bowed to her. 'Madam,' he said. 'I seek to know your will.'

'My will...' She stood there blinking. It occurred to her that she had forgotten how to wish for anything, for so long had her every wish been violated, firstly with the loss of her family, secondly with the way the convent constantly demanded obedience of her: you shall rouse yourself in the dark, get up and file into chapel in the bitter cold with only a weak taper to light your way, sing, and pray on your knees on the icy stones, cold seeping into your bones, and process out again. *You will forget the people that you love.*

Those daytime hours of meticulous copying in the scriptorium, her hand guiding the quill into the tall shapes of the letters, concentrating so hard on each task that it was only when she came to finish for the day that she realised how the cold had seeped into her belly and thighs and the muscles at the tops of her arms, her neck was aching and she realised she felt too sick to move…

'Your will, Madam, I mean,' said Edward Little, 'with respect to the upkeep of your hall in Northampton.'

So focussed had Elfgifu been for so long on her life in the convent, so conditioned was she into a pattern of obedience, that it took a moment for the image of her family's palace to build in her head – log piled on log to make the thick walls, the oak beams vaulting the wide space between them, the roof of birch shingles in rows like notes of music – plainsong they would be, sung to the harp, a minstrel chanting a saga of loss…

Edward Little coughed to attract her attention. 'Your hall has been empty so long, Madam,' he said, 'that the townsfolk are saying that you have abandoned it. They have started to steal logs from its walls. They say your family is done for, that you are only a girl, you will never return. Madam, I have spoken to your brothers, but they will give me no guidance. Madam, I beg to know, what should I do?'

Elfgifu bit her lip. She brushed loose hairs back from her forehead. The hall seemed so remote from the course of her life. It belongs to the past, she thought, it's nothing to do with me any more. My past is as remote to me as the moon. A shimmering star. I can't touch it. But then she thought: No. I am responsible for the hall. It belonged to my family. I cannot let everything from my past be destroyed. I have to stand by it.

It would be easy, so easy to simply turn my back. To pretend I haven't heard.

I'm safe here in the convent. What difference would it make to me if my family's heritage were destroyed? And yet…

The timber palace of Northampton was new-built, but the land that went with it had been in Elfgifu's family for generations, all the estates, some of them won by her Viking ancestors, some the gift of the king, some that her father had bought, some that were her mother's dowry.

If she were to go on as she was – if she were to become a nun, for that is what she had been planning to do, isolating herself from the world – her estates would enrich the convent where she lived. They'd enrich her grandmother. Had the kind old woman perhaps had this in mind all along? *No*, she breathed. *No*. She rubbed her hand across her eyes.

She couldn't betray her family. She had a duty to them. To uphold the dignity that they had held. 'I have to go home, don't I?' she whispered to Edward Little.

'Madam, that would be most welcome.' He stood looking up at her earnestly, turning his hat in his hands. 'Madam, in the hope that you would return home with me, I took the liberty to bring you your mare.'

'Well, then. I will come with you now. Nothing is served by delay. Are the horses in the stables?' She spoke to him over her shoulder, already striding ahead out of the courtyard, and it felt so good to be certain, and to be filled with purposefulness, and energised, not to be cowed. No one was in the stables, and deftly, while the chapel bell rang out to summon her to Nones, she harnessed her grey mare and tightened the girth on her saddle. She swung herself up. She laughed out loud; it was so good after so long to feel the warmth of the mare's back between her legs. 'Let's go, Edward Little.'

'There's nothing you wish to bring with you, madam?'

'Nothing.' Her pens, her paints, the gold leaf she had loved to work with, that had controlled her life, she was happy to abandon them all.

The two of them galloped out of the gate and past the ploughed fields and the green pastures with hedges dizzy with spring blossom, cattle out now, grazing on the new grass, the sun slanting and warm on the meadows, on into the forest where the bare trees were beginning to unfurl their leaves, hazels shedding catkins like worms on bare earth, a shimmer of underwater green in the encroaching dusk. Elfgifu was feeling awake and alive, herself for the first time in months, and, drunk with the pleasure of it, she was laughing out loud, and Edward Little was looking back over his shoulder and muttering, 'Your grandmother will certainly follow you,' and Elfgifu was saying, 'She likes her home comforts too much, she won't start in pursuit of me till the morning.'

Come the dark, when unseen branches hung low and dashed against their faces, they curled in blankets on the cold earth, and then at first light, when from below the horizon the sun burned the sky yellow, they rode on, and reached the Northampton palace around midday.

So strange to go in and find it empty. Fireless. A cold space. Silent. No one around. Long table and benches unoccupied. A couple of benches missing; stolen, no doubt. Elfgifu stared about her and shivered.

'We must set the ghosts of the past to flight,' said Edward Little.

But how to do that? Here, at the head of the table, was where her father had sat. He'd been happy with his house carls and his kinsfolk around him, he'd been proud of his sons, his legacy to the world. He'd held hands with his wife and the harpist had played and she'd sung a song of her childhood, a fair maiden overpowering a dragon, and then a storyteller told a saga of magic events in Iceland, and an Irish minstrel sang... Here her mother had sat, here her brothers, her cousins, her uncles... Here was the harpist, here the teller of sagas. Elfgifu was walking round the great thick boards of the table. She rubbed a patch of roughened oak at the edge where meat must have been spilt and its fat soaked into the wood. 'Mouse toothmarks,' she said.

'Nothing stays the same, ever,' said Edward Little.

Elfgifu stared around her. 'We can build good times again,' she said resolutely. 'We will hold a great feast.'

'A feast?' said Edward Little, shivering sharply in the chill of the hall. He shuffled his feet in the dead leaves that littered the floor, that had blown through the door last autumn. He stared at the festoons of spiderwebs on the beams and the walls, wiped off a patch of dust from the table, looked up at the roof where a patch of shingles had rotted, or maybe blown away in some winter storm. A hole through to the blue sky. A fleecy cloud sailing over.

'What else can we do?' asked Elfgifu.

'We need time,' said Edward Little. 'The land hasn't recovered from the famine of '05. Two years ago. There wasn't enough seed last year. It should be better this year. Then of course your father's murder - your tenants have lost heart, they haven't known what to do.'

The spring was always the lean season, when stocks of food – wheat, barley, dried beans – were running low. When cattle, sheep and pigs were needed for breeding rather than butchering. When everyone worried when the warm spring weather would come and start the crops into growth. A bad time for a feast. 'The autumn then,' said Elfgifu. 'We'll hold a feast come Michaelmas.'

'You need to speak to your tenants,' said Edward Little.

'Can't you do that?'

'If you are to take your father's place, madam, you need to do as he did.'

It felt strange to go in his chamber, to lie down on the bed he and her mother had shared. But her feelings of intrusion and grief were shattered when she heard a scuffle in the feather mattress and realised she was sharing it with mice. Mice, or rats maybe. She got up and beat it hard with a broom. Turned it over and beat it hard again.

She lay down, pulled the blankets over her, and gave a great yawn.

12. Emma, Winchester, spring 1008

Godgifu, *the gift of God.* This tiny blue-eyed child with blonde curls. The most beautiful child in the whole world. Queen Emma rocked her little daughter in her arms, she kissed her forehead, she cuddled her against her chest, she sang to her until her darling fell asleep. So wonderful to have a daughter at last after those two miserable mewling sons, Edward and Alfred, both the image of their father and their stepbrothers, skinny and dark-haired half-wits who liked to hit each other with wooden swords and float toy boats in puddles. You'd never imagine that she'd had anything to do with their birth. But Godgifu – this dear sweetheart – she wasn't talking yet but you could already tell she loved music, the way she waved her arms around when the harpist was playing in the great hall, the way she'd close her eyes and feign sleep while monks chanted in the chapel. 'Great things await you,' whispered Emma, and kissed her little daughter on her plump cheek. 'My clever child.'

She carried her on her hip, wrapped in her shawl against the April breeze, out into the sunshine of the spring garden, and sat for a while on a bench beneath the white blossom of the cherries. '*The Lord's my shepherd*:'

she sang the psalm right through to the end. She was comfortable in her uninterrupted solitude. The women of the household were off who knew where. King Ethelred and his older boys – his sons by his first wife – were away trying to deal with a Danish fleet off Sandwich. The longer they were away the better; their aggression and warring spirit wearied her. So tedious... The peace of the palace suited her; she could do just what she wished.

The sleeping child had become a weight, a strain on her arms, and Emma laid her on her back on the bench beside her. 'Little one,' she said fondly, tucking in the shawl around her body. Then she noticed petals had drifted from the cherry trees on to her silken skirt. She stood up and shook them off, bent and dusted a couple off Godgifu's shawl. She was still thinking of Ethelred being away, and the pleasure of his absence, and her feet took her into the great hall, beside the long table, past the red embers of the fire, up to the dais with its carved chairs. Too big for her: it made her feel like a child to nestle in King Ethelred's throne. She swung her feet above the floor, wrists on the carved arms, curling her gold-ringed fingers round the smooth snouts of the dragons.

She smiled. She was a woman with power. She struck the gong and a servant came running.

'Mistress?'

'Wine,' she commanded.

She sat in the big chair and watched dust-motes tremble in the low sun's rays; listened to an ash-log collapse. She grew restive; servants wouldn't make her husband wait like this. No, they were frightened of his rages. She struck the gong again.

The girl returned, a goblet of wine in her hand. A fine glass goblet of Syrian workmanship, very rare; Emma turned it in her fingers, holding it high to catch and refract the sunlight. It coloured her silken sleeve with a rainbow, and she laughed out loud at the beauty and the strangeness of it. But the wine, when she tasted it, was sour. 'What do you mean, bringing me this rubbish? Fetch me fresh. Quickly, or I'll have you whipped.'

'Summon Archbishop Aelfheah to me,' she said to the girl when she came back, and off the girl scuttled to do her bidding.

But the next person to enter the double doors at the far end of the hall was only her children's nursemaid, Mildred. She bent her knees. 'I beg your majesty's courtesy,' she said. She was blubbing, tears coursing down her flushed cheeks, her voice jerking with distress.

'Compose yourself,' said Emma.

'Godgifu….'

'What?

'Madam, your daughter…'

'Well?'

'I left her in the nursery, ma'am, but she's no longer there.'

'I took her in the garden, fool.'

'Madam, where is she now?'

'Still there, unless she's learnt to walk since None.'

'Madam, thank you. Oh, thank you, madam.' Mildred jumped up and rushed down the hall.

'I never said you could go,' Queen Emma shouted, but the Anglo-Saxon peasant was deaf as well as stupid, and paid her no attention. If it weren't that she was excellent at caring for the children – the miserable little boys as well as Godgifu – Emma would have got rid of her long ago. All the children doted on her. They'd hang on her skirt – Edward and Alfred would hide from her, their mother, behind the woman's skirt, they were so timid – Godgifu was the brave one, the best by far. *My fine daughter, you take after me. I will teach you all I know.*

Then Archbishop Aelfheah came in the hall. He was good-looking in spite of his age, tall and blue-eyed in spite of his Saxon name. Shoulders just a little stooped. He was meticulous in how he shaved and dressed and combed his hair. Well educated: she could speak Latin with him – such a civilised, precise language, the language of the intellect – and he would fluently reply. She was inclined to look favourably on priests because her beloved brother Robert had chosen the priesthood, and was destined to become Archbishop of Rouen. So civilised, these men: nothing of the warrior in them. They lived in the mind.

She wished to discuss with Aelfheah the changes he'd proposed to the liturgy. She gestured to him to sit on the end of the bench nearest her. 'My lord Archbishop of Canterbury,' she murmured. Aelfheah had a presence to him, no doubt. A purple cloak would suit him well. She would commission one woven of silk. 'Aelfheah.'

'You wished to speak to me, your majesty?'

'You serve me very well.' She extended her right hand.

He bent and kissed it. 'Madam,' he said reverentially, 'it is an honour to be permitted to serve a queen as beautiful and as wise as you.'

Her plump lips curved into an acceptance of his tribute. She liked the prickle of his moustache on her soft skin, she liked the elegance with which he dressed. She slid down from her throne and raised him to his feet. 'Let's go to the chapel,' she said.

At the altar rail she prayed alone beside him, their upper arms and thighs touching. How warm his body was. She smiled.

When they came out she put her hand on his arm, she wouldn't let him leave. 'My daughter,' she said, 'as she

---

67

grows older she comes more and more to have a look of you.'

'Then I am blessed indeed, madam.'

'I love her for it. But I don't know what the king will think.'

'The king and I, we have this in common, we are both Saxons. It's hardly surprising if there is some similarity to me in her appearance.'

'You and the king don't look the same.' Emma paused. 'I've heard it said,' she added carefully, pressing herself against his side, 'that if one spends time in someone's company, that empathy can cause a kind of spiritual conception.'

'Be careful what you speak of, madam. It's not a saying that we have in this country.' He pulled away. 'My lady, take care that you say nothing that should be spoken of outside the confessional.'

She averted her face. 'You know, don't you, that the king and I don't... Godgifu is her name. The gift of God. The name was my choice, not Ethelred's. He places no value in daughters. I know that if he suspected, his anger would be swift and terrible.'

'Indeed, madam. So silence must be the guiding will of God. Bless you, my child.'

When Emma returned to the great hall, Eofric the goldsmith was waiting for her. 'Madam, you asked me to attend you at noon,' he said.

'It's long after that,' she said. 'Look how low the sun is now.' She gestured towards where its rays were gilding the dragon carved on the upper part of the eastern wall, webbing its outstretched wings with light.

'Madam, I have been awaiting you many hours.'

'You are still welcome. Have you executed the commission I gave you?'

'Madam.' He extracted from a leather pouch a fold of green silk, and unfolded that to reveal a pair of brooches of carved gold: on each a cross caught in an interlace of thorns.

'They will do very well,' said Emma, pinning them to her dress.

'Madam, my payment...'

'Oh, the king will pay.'

'Will you speak to him on my behalf, madam?'

'You must sort it between yourselves. I am a mere woman, I have my little daughter I must care for.'

13. Elfgifu, Northampton 1010

On the last Wednesday of each month Elfgifu would go to read his steward's accounts to her brother Wulfheah. His little sister was the only person he truly trusted at this time when he feared that men would take advantage of his blindness to cheat him: some thought his blindness and his deformity had made him a fool. But his brain was sharp, he could remember every transaction, he could sense if things were not as they should be. At each quarter of the year he and Elfgifu would go through the figures again, checking every addition and subtraction. Laborious, painstaking work. 'This is so tedious,' she would sometimes complain.

'It's essential to get things right,' he insisted. 'Read that page again.'

He carved a statue.

At the summit of the hill above the abbey where he'd sought refuge stood a great rock. Nobody knew how it had come there, whether it had been brought laboriously on a cart pulled by eight horses, then abandoned, not required for building, or if it was something the ground had heaved up and spat out of itself, or if it was simply part of the skull of the hill, where its blanket of earth had been washed away by years of winter rains and snow.

But what was certain was that Wulfheah liked to sit there in the summers, his back against the sun-warmed rock, the gaze of his empty eye sockets journeying across the rounded tops of trees and green forest, across barley, rye and bean fields as the crops sprang up, ripened and were harvested. He listened to the come and go of travellers on the road – *Good morrow*, they would say to him as they passed, and touch their caps, and cross their hearts (*Lord save us from a fate like his, poor mutilated useless fellow,* they would think) – and Wulfheah's gaze, unlimited by sight, would travel back through time to the joy and purposefulness of life in the palace, and the trust he had possessed among men, and his strength and certainty – the *togetherness* of life in the hall, that protected them all against the lonely wilderness beyond its walls, that lonely exile in which he now dwelt – that sureness of strength, rank and place they had then, which guarded them all against the randomness of life, that meant they had no need to think for themselves. They were a group then: secure.

Elfgifu's brother spoke to her often of the times of joy; only once of the bad times, the sad times. It was the anniversary of their father's murder. He and she sat side by side, their backs to the rock on the hill. He fumbled towards her; she took his hand, held it pressed between her hands. 'If I could understand any reason for it...' she murmured. 'If only I could make some sort of sense of it. When they had been friends so long, him and the king, how could he...'

'Our father was always one to speak his mind. He spoke in front of the Witan of the famine the peasants were enduring. Pleaded that more food should be given them. That wheat should be distributed from the royal barns – that for a short time they should be allowed to hunt in the royal forests. Ethelred didn't want to listen. He didn't want to *throw away his money*, is what he said, I remember. Emma – Queen Emma...' He stopped.

'Queen Emma,' Elfie prompted after a couple of minutes' pause. She'd learnt to take her time with her brother.

'She agreed with him. She'd do nothing. Do you remember – did you notice – how unhappy she was at first when she became queen? She – I was the same age, or a little older. We were little more than children. She – she conceived a fondness for me. I – I was flattered. I thought I loved her. I've not told anyone of this before. You mustn't – you won't, will you? I can trust you?' He paused, swallowed and went on: 'We – the queen and I – we would spend time together. She wanted me to help her escape back to her family in Normandy. Ethelred was cruel to her, she said. I said, that is the nature of any king. I wouldn't help her. Ah, she said, but I thought you said you loved me. I said, I cannot, however much I love you, I cannot break my oath of fealty to the king, I cannot do it. *I need your help*, she said, *I will die if I go on living with Ethelred.* Still I would not help her. She got up off her knees, she brushed her skirt down. She stood tall as she could. You know how little she is.' His half-smile showed his fondness for her. '*I will exact terrible vengeance on you then,* Queen Emma said. *I will destroy you utterly,* she said. *Don't doubt me.* She walked away with her head held high. I have wondered if this – my blindness...' he gestured at his eyes – 'if this was done at her command.'

'She could not be so cruel,' Elfie said. 'No woman would ever be that cruel to someone who loved her.'

'No, no indeed,' agreed Wulfheah. He never spoke of the matter again; instead sat, seemingly content, there against that sun-warmed rock three fine summers, wearing a brimmed hat in the heat of the day, his skin browning like that of a peasant or a sailor. Each morning his servant would guide him to the top of the hill, and fetch him down at even-tide.

Mostly Wulfheah would just sit; but often he would stand and feel his way around the rock, so that he wore a smooth earth path at its foot, and he would run his hands across the rock, feeling its texture, learning every bump and crevice, every pit and extrusion and fault in the irregularity of its surface. When Elfgifu came she would see him there, fumbling pitiful and blind, uncertain. She would say, 'Wulfheah,' and he'd say, 'Is it that time again, my sister?' and he would give her his hand, and they would walk together down to do his accounts in the abbey.

The third autumn came. Elfgifu rode from the east, hooded in her cloak, the chill wind at her back. At the foot of the hill she heard a sound she had never heard there before: a banging in the air, a metallic hammering, irregular, as if pausing now and again for breath. She thought at first maybe a blacksmith had built a smithy there; but there was no smell of smoke. When she neared the top of the hill she saw Wulfheah with an iron hammer in his hands, a row of chisels neatly ranged in size laid out on the ground. He was reaching up (he was a tall man, her brother) to work at the rock, with blind fingers feeling for the place he wanted, and selecting the chisel the right size for his task, and hammering it in. Fragments of stone flew out. His hands and face bled red from superficial cuts.

Elfgifu stood in silence and watched him a long time, seeing how he felt again and again for the result of what he had done, watching how he changed the size of chisel several times. He was developing a ball shape with a moat around it.

'What are you carving?' she asked him eventually.

'You're there?' he said.

'Yes.'

'Sometimes I believe you're there when you're not. You have a kind of calmness about you. Your presence can make a windy day seem still.'

'I don't know what it is that you're carving.'

'You can't tell?'

'No.'

'You will.'

The next time Elfgifu rode that way it was early December and the hooves of her mare cracked the ice on the frozen puddles, and she reared her head, searching out the road through the thick fog that lay across the land. But Elfgifu saw the stone, up above the fog. Wulfheah's work was done, and a great eye – a giant's eye – huge and lashless – stared out of the stone. A mirage, a ghost of great power, it stared through the fog over the vast tracts of land Wulfheah had inherited from his brother, his father and his uncle.

Elfgifu rode Tempest up to it, she ran her hands across the cold eyeball, felt the chiselled smoothness of the stone. 'What are you watching for?' she whispered.

Condensing fog dripped from the bare branches of the trees below her.

The eye was huge, powerful and elemental. It frightened her. There was something of a god about it. She shivered.

'It's amazing,' Elfgifu told Wulfheah, down in the guest room of the abbey. 'That eye you've carved. It holds so much power. It dominates the land.'

He ran his hand across his wounded, eyeless face.

'Oh, Wulfheah,' she said. 'I wish I could do something for you.' In general she never displayed pity for him, believing it would serve no purpose but to reinforce his sense of weakness. This time, though, she reached for his hand. 'Heavens,' she said. 'You're hot.' She felt his forehead then: 'What's the matter with you? You're burning up.'

'I can't be. I have no fire in my cell,' he said. He coughed. He had on a novice's brown robe.

'It's December now. You need some heat.'

'Monks thrive on abstinence.'

'Are you going to take your vows?'

'Sister, do you think I am cut out to be a monk?'

She thought of the Wulfheah that she used to know: the bright-eyed boy flying falcons, racing horses, at sword practice with the princes Edmund and Athelstan, singing, dancing, playing the lyre; or he'd be taming himself to take part in meetings of the king's council. 'We all change,' she said. 'We have to change to adapt to the pieces life throws for us. We have no choice.'

'But I don't want to accept my circumstances,' he said. He coughed again.

She reached out a hand for his and took it. He was quivering, with heat and with some strange intensity of emotion. 'You have an infection in your left eye,' she said. The lid was red and swollen. 'Let me wash it,' she said.

He shook his head, coughed again.

'I don't know how else to help you.' Her own eyes were brimming with tears. 'I will wash your eye with my tears,' she said.

74

'Don't talk such nonsense. I am my own master. I will decide all things for myself,' he said. His voice was for that moment arrogant as it was wont to be.

Before Christmas word came to the convent that Wulfheah was missing. In March, after the snows had cleared, came word that his drowned body had been found in the River Trent.

Elfgifu rode to his funeral past the carving he had done. The hilltop was bathed in sunlight above the bare branches on the oaks and ash on the plain below. This will be all my land now, she realised, as far as the eye can see; Wulfheah has left it all to me. For her other brother, Wulfgeat, had died two years before. Of that close family of five only Elfgifu still survived. She was tall and thin and alone, buffeted by the storms of her life.

The rock was huge and elemental. That strange eye had a majesty and power that dominated the land.

14. Elfgifu, Northampton, 1013

'Stand up straight, girl,' hissed Elfgifu's grandmother.

Elfgifu bit her lip, leaning back against the pressure of her cousin Morcar's hand in the centre of her back. She felt it firm and square, pushing her forward. But she didn't want to move from the doorway. She didn't understand how the present situation had come about. No one had consulted her. They had simply summoned her here. *This is what you must do*, they had told her. She was used to being in charge, to managing her estates, was not accustomed to do anyone else's bidding.

She touched her blonde hair that Margaret, her former nurse, had combed until it gleamed, she steadied the gold circlet she wore like a halo, that used to be her mother's, she shook out her skirt.

Morcar exerted more pressure on her back. She stumbled forward into the hall. The grand hall of her family home. Her own home. So familiar.

There they stood, the hallful of men, all waiting for her, part obscured by swirling smoke, the downdraught from the fire. Strangers, all of them. King Sweyn's fierce warriors were to her left, her cousins' ill-armed farmers to the right. In front of the warriors stood a stocky, muscular man who, to judge by the jewelled hilt of his sword and the heavy gold torc around his neck, could be no other than Sweyn the mighty king of Denmark himself. His hair and beard were touched with grey. A bright scar across his cheek, a crippled left hand, indicated he was a seasoned fighter.

Beside him stood a tall boy in a blue tunic and wide silk trousers; boots of brown leather, gold arm-rings, golden hair that was a bit fly-away: newly-washed, perhaps. A crooked nose that might have been broken in a fight. Elfgifu glanced nervously sideways at her grandmother. 'Canute?' she whispered, and, 'Down,' hissed her grandmother, and the girl curtseyed deeply, bowing her head.

The king took her hand to raise her up. 'Well, you're certainly fair enough looking, as your cousins said. The lands you own are very extensive. What I have in mind is this – you and my son will marry as witness to our alliance.'

'Marry?' The word jerked up in Elfgifu's throat, making her gag, making her feel faint. 'Marry...' She'd never had this in mind.

But Sweyn was continuing with his speech, ignoring her. 'It must be long-lasting, this alliance...' he had turned from her, was speaking to her cousin Morcar now... 'You must understand that. A true partnership, without delay.

No shilly-shallying. I cannot defeat the king of England without the support of the Northern nobles. Unless I have a firm pledge of your support I won't place my men's lives at risk.'

'My men are even now marching to Oxford to join your forces,' said Morcar. Her cousin – her cousin with whom she'd played as a child, he was proposing to rebel against his king, his true anointed king Ethelred...

'And my men too,' said Sigeferth. 'Six hundred of them.'

Elfgifu glanced over at him, thinking how he had always been kind to her. Surely she could trust him. He was just a little older than her. In former days they had been companions together at the English court, him and her and the princes and her brothers, the six of them hawking along the river bank, and fishing, and studying Latin with the bishop in the afternoons; getting their fingers inky.

That had been only a few years ago, yet so much had happened. Elfie had turned from being a bright laughing girl into a dullard in a convent, and then into the mistress of extensive estates. Now she seemed to be about to change again, into being a mere chess piece in a men's game of power. A political pawn to undersign an alliance. Surely she didn't have to accept this. To become of no value in herself. Of as much worth as sealing wax on a letter.

Like wax, she began to melt.

'Oh, for God's sake, Elfgifu, dry your eyes,' snapped her grandmother. 'This is your wedding, not your funeral.'

With her sleeve Elfgifu scrubbed the tears from her cheeks.

'Elfie,' he said. Him. Sweyn's son. The boy with the wide silk trousers. It was the first time he'd spoken to her. Her husband to be. Canute. 'They tell me you like to be called Elfie.'

He was looking at her; he wasn't dismissing her as a cypher, an object of no import. She liked his voice. His eyes were blue and smiled at her. She began to feel warmer. She had grown so cold, waiting for him and his father through the torrential thunderstorm on this July afternoon in the chill company of her cousins, their frowning, pallid presence. 'You must do it,' they had said to her when they rode up, when they fetched her home from the apple orchards. They got her alone in the garden and told her of their plan. 'There's no one else,' they said. 'We have to form an alliance with King Sweyn to keep him on our side. You are the only single female in our family with the looks, the land and the money to attract a young man.'

'I don't want to marry anyone,' she had said. 'I am perfectly happy living quietly here.'

'You have to marry him, for the sake of the family. For the sake of the country. An alliance with King Sweyn is our only hope of defeating King Ethelred. Ethelred is evil. Think what he has done to your family. You must want to take vengeance on him for that.'

'They say Canute's only eighteen. I can't marry a child.'

'Five years,' said Morcar. 'Five years between the two of you. What difference does that make in the lifetime of a marriage?'

Now she noticed the rich twisted gold of the heavy arm-rings Canute wore, standing out on the tanned parchment of his arms like the haloes of saints in an illuminated gospel, thick and bold. She glanced up at his thin face, saw he was studying her with a slight frown as if he were deciphering Greek letters on a parchment. She lowered her eyes, afraid he might read her too well. 'Are you willing?' he asked.

'Willing?' she queried.

'This alliance my father and your cousins have concocted – are you content with it?'

'It has to be my pleasure to do as my cousins wish,' she said demurely. She had come to accept that on her compliance might rest the future of her people. The whole nation needed this alliance. They needed to be rid of King Ethelred.

'I don't want to force you. I don't want an unwilling bride.'

Elfgifu shifted from one foot to the other. She wished she were back in the leafy stillness of the orchard, working with the ewes and their lambs.

'If you don't marry him, Elfie,' a voice at her shoulder – her cousin Sigeferth – said, 'you'll regret it for ever. When we were children together, you were always the bravest, the most adventurous, the one who swung furthest out on a branch over the river, you can't be a coward now – Elfie, Canute is a good fellow, I've fought beside him, he's brave and true – you must marry him.'

'I must decide now?'

'Life is too short and uncertain to countenance delay,' said King Sweyn. 'We make for Oxford in the morning.'

'Very well,' she said resolutely, making up her mind. 'I will.'

'You're sure?' said Canute.

She hesitated, thinking of the scriptorium in the convent, her days of painstaking copying, her inky fingers. What life was offering her must be more interesting that. She smiled up at her suitor. 'I am certain,' she said.

At the centre of the great assembly of men were just she and Canute: the two of them, an island. Two strangers to be yoked together. A two-yolked egg contained in a single shell. A kind of horror. Or a love. Whatever they chose to make it. All she could see was him, all she could hear was him. This blond stranger, her future life. He reached for her hands. She drew back, she clenched hers tight as if she wanted to fight. No one had touched her meaningfully in the years since her mother and her brothers died, and she had grown into this habit of shrinking away from all human contact. It was an abhorrence to her. That heat, that dryness of another person's skin, their touch was like a parasitic worm seeking to crawl under her skin. Unclean. She felt sick, she jerked away.

Elfgifu shivered, naked under the sheet. Under her pillow she had secreted the knife she had taken from the kitchen, hiding it beneath her apron; a carving knife used to cut slices from roast boar and oxen. She had watched a boy sharpen it, listened to the sing of it against the whetstone, she knew the point and edge were keen. The handle was bone, snug to her hand. In her head played the song a Danish poet had sung in Ethelred's court when all was well, when life was good: the song of Gudrun, daughter of Iron Beard, whom King Olaf Trygvesson of Norway undertook to marry in compensation for his men having killed her father. The song told how Gudrun, the first night she and the king lay together, tried to knife him; but he wrestled the knife off her and she got dressed and fled with her men.

I can try the same trick, Elfgifu thought; but if I do, I will succeed. I'm not given to failure. She got up and checked that her clothes lay ready on the stool for her escape, so that she would be able to find them even if clouds covered the moon. She had told Margaret to be ready. 'Ready for what, mistress?' she had asked her warily.

'I do not know what will befall.'

She drew the linen curtain round the bed, she couched herself on the feather mattress. She felt for the knife, pushed it up to where he would not feel it. She waited for him.

Then he came. Through the fine linen, like a slight mist, she saw him in a sideways shaft of moonlight take off his clothes. He was young, younger than her; he reminded her of the princes, how they had been; of her brothers, what they had been like at his age. Full of promise.

He pulled the bed-curtains aside. He was beautiful. Like a kind of heathen god. He held out a golden goblet to her. She reached out to take it. How heavy it was in her hand. Heavy and the metal cold. She put it to her lips.

How sweet the mead was. How sweet.

'Elfie,' he said, and he took the goblet, and bent to kiss her with his warm lips.

When Elfgifu woke beside Canute in their wooden lodging the full moon, the huge round glowing face of it with its mountains and lakes, was shining in the unshuttered window. She pulled back the sheet and stared at his naked side, his taut belly, the thing that hung beneath.

She reached for the knife under the pillow. She stroked the blade. She turned it over in the moonlight. *I can do it now. Quickly, before he wakes.*

Then she sighed, and leaned over the edge of the bed and slid the knife as far under as she could stretch her arm, gave it a tap to slide it further. *I don't want to destroy the political union my cousins have planned,* she thought, *it is the only way for me to get vengeance on King Ethelred for the evil he has done to my family. The injustices he inflicts daily on the people of this country.* And further she thought: *I don't want Canute ever to guess what I have half had in my mind to do.*

For the truth was that what he had done had wrought some kind of magic in her, some transformation. She was changed by lying with him last night. There was no doubt of it. Made contented in a way she had never conceived of. She kissed his hair, his forehead, touched her lips to his.

He slept on. She pulled herself away, got up and wrapped a cloak around herself, walked out through the sleeping hall, waded into the chill river. Water ran off her skin as she emerged. Each water drop was silvered with moonlight, it was a mirror of the stars. The beauty of it. She stretched out her arms. Then he came to her through the half-dark under the moon like a mirage almost, or a ghost, and they lay on the cloak on the cold grass and made love once again. 'What have you done to me?' she whispered to him. 'You have changed me. You have spoken with a herbalist, you have drugged me with a magic potion. I am not like this. This is not me.'

In a strange way she felt he had completed her. Before, she'd always thought it was her grief and losses that made her incomplete, always wanting more. But now she was not so sure.

I don't want to be dependent on anyone.

I have depended only on myself this long time. I am weary of it.

Morning. In the great hall Canute was laying out his bride price on the long table, in front of Elfgifu's grandmother and cousins, and his father King Sweyn and all their men. 'Silk,' he said, letting the vivid green and gold fabric unfold and drift, tumble in rich waves; light and shadow. The sun was low enough in the sky to shine through the open doors.

'Byzantine stuff,' said Wulfrune appreciatively. 'It'll make you a pretty gown, my dear. I always thought those dull rags you wear a waste of your endowments.'

'This necklace.' Graded beads of polished amber on a silver wire. He fastened it round Elfie's throat. She had to force herself to stand still; her instinct was to run away. I am not so easily translated into a wife, she thought.

Silver arm rings on her arms.

Rings of twisted gold.

'Canute...'

'Hold out your fingers.'

'I am not used to such pretty things.' They were like a prisonment, the shackles of slaves. They made her skin itch. But she had to accept them. It was part of the social contract of their marriage.

A chatelaine, a gold chain that ended with filigree dragons' heads with open jaws and staring eyes, he fastened at her waist. 'To keep your keys safe around you.'

Keys imply a house, a home of my own, our own, she thought. A treasure-chest, maybe. A storage room. She touched his arm in a kind of wonderment. 'Where will we live, Canute?'

He looked to his father.

'For God's sake, boy, it's up to you to decide! I'll need you over in Gainsborough to maintain our fleet in readiness once our campaign starts in earnest. But for the moment why don't you stay here, or go to some other place of the girl's? She must have somewhere you'd like, owning all that land. These earrings... they're pretty things.' He dangled a pair of gold serpents from the tip of his fingers. 'I picked them up when we were looting Southampton. Meant to send them to your aunt, but never got round to it. Would you like them for the girl, Canute?'

'Thank you, sir,' said Canute. 'These oval brooches – gold filigree. See how the dragons on them curl and interlock in an intricate puzzle, Elfie? So will our lives meld together, my beloved.'

What fine words he had learned to speak, although he was still a boy. She took the brooches and fastened her apron with them. She held the earrings in her hand. Then he had nothing else to give her. There was a silence. She did not know what to do or say. She looked up at him, and saw he was looking to his father for guidance. She felt the need to fill the quiet. What could she give him in return? 'All my lands around Northampton,' she said, 'the villages and farmsteads, the managed woodlands and the forests, all these I give to you.'

'No,' said her grandmother, suddenly animated. 'No, you can't, Elfgifu, you were going to give them to my convent.'

'I never said...'

'Ha,' roared Sweyn. 'So that's why you're all honey-sweet to your grand-daughter, is it? That's why you insisted on being here? Trying to trick her out of her land, were you?'

'I'll have you know I don't hold with these Germanic marriages,' Wulfrune snapped back. 'Rape the girl and then pay the bride-price for her – what kind of contract is that?'

'It was good enough for me and the boy's mother, when we married. She's the sister of King Boleslav of Poland, she is, and if this kind of marriage is fine by her family, it's fine for a common woman like you. Avaricious old crone. Be ready in an hour, dame. I'll give you a safe-conduct to Oxford. That's where I'm headed next.'

'But the children's wedding feast...'

'In an hour or never, dame. I can't stand your English yearning to procrastinate. And I'm not leaving you around to spoil the children's fun.'

Alys, her maidservant, packed up Wulfrune's things, while she walked with her grand-daughter in the sunny meadow below the hall, the long grass licking at their skirts, darkening them with the heavy dew. Sweet honeysuckle twined up a young oak, scenting the cool air. Blue sky; puffs of white cloud swept along by the steady breeze. All was calm. But Wulfrune was like a spitting fire, jabbing out hatred of Sweyn – 'Who does he think he is? King of Denmark he calls himself. He's nothing but a jobbing pirate, a thief, a looter with upstart ideas. King of England, pah! He has no rights. Let him sail back to his own country the very soonest. What are your cousins thinking of, dreaming up an alliance with him? All right, King Ethelred's a vicious bastard, I'll admit, a fool, corrupt, treacherous, a thief, a destroyer of men's lives – but at least he's our legitimate king, isn't he? And English. Ethelred speaks our language, not the guttural rubbish that spills from this fellow's lips!'

'Oh Grandmother, you know you speak Danish as well as I.' They used to, in their summers at the castle in Northumberland. So many of the local people were Danish in origin. As children they mixed with them freely and fearlessly, fishing, hawking, blackberrying, helping with the harvest, stealing apples, running on the sandy beaches, paddling in the rim of the sea, venturing out on calm seas in small boats... Elfgifu brushed away the memories that were leaking from her eyes.

'That's not the point! He has no right to be here. What profit will marriage to his son be to you? Your cousins are

---

85

out of their minds. You should have married some good Englishman.'

Elfie had plucked a piece of long grass, she was stripping its leaves off it, sucking its juicy pith. She was thinking, in truth, what good Englishman would have been willing to marry a solitary orphan, the daughter of a nobleman whom King Ethelred had had murdered, whose family he destroyed? Haven't my cousins rather hoodwinked King Sweyn into believing that I have political value, as the daughter – the only one left, truly, of a family once honoured and noble, now disgraced? 'No suitors have ever come in search of me,' she pointed out, 'in spite of all my lands.'

'You only had to say the word and I'd have found you one,' said Grandmama. 'Not all Englishmen are scared of the king.' She tutted at a wild rose whose thorns had snagged in the fabric of her apron, she bent down and unpicked it carefully. 'One good thing,' she said. 'That young man of yours is bound to get himself killed pretty soon. Real hothead, I can tell. He'll be out to establish a reputation for himself. He's the sort that comes unstuck in battle. Trust me in this.'

Elfgifu was riding through the beech forest beside Canute, she on her grey mare and he on his bay stallion. The green leaves made an awning over their heads, golden shafts of sunlight struck through into the shadows. Behind them rode Margaret and a troop of some thirty men-at-arms. Their horses' hooves crunched in last year's dead leaves, their harness jingled. They burst out now and again in snatches of song. Elfie said: 'My brother used to live quite close by. He's dead now, though.'

'What did you say?' He reined in his horse, rode closer to her.

'What?'

'I didn't catch what you said.' He leant toward her. Sunlight, suddenly, in his blond hair, so it shone like a halo. She stretched out her hand to touch it, sharply reminded of the gold leaf work she had done in her copy of St Mark's gospel when she lived in the convent; how the gold lit up the black and white text of the pages. These last few years my life has been smudged dark grey, she thought. Maybe my marriage with Canute will light it up like gold leaf, provide opportunities I never dreamed of, if I choose to take them. 'I was just saying you'll like the farm we're going to. It's only a couple of miles off now. I know the way well, I used to ride this way often, before I went to live at the convent.' And she thought: forget my brother, forget my grandmama, forget them both, I have had enough of being weighed down by my family, by the sadnesses of the past. I can step away from them all, I can start a new life, begin again, if I choose. This marriage will be a new start for me. I can choose to be happy. It's my decision. It's up to me. She rode close to Canute, she touched his elbow. He smiled at her, he blew her a kiss, she reached for his hand.

It didn't come easy to her, behaving affectionately. Life had been very hard for too long. She shivered as he locked his fingers in hers. 'Over there,' she said, pointing (thus forcing him to release her hand), 'just over the hill, there's a grove of mature oaks. That's where I had timber felled to build lodgings close to my farm, a couple of years ago. You and I will sleep there tonight.'

'Sleep?' he queried, smiling.

Her cheeks flared with embarrassment.

'I'll send a messenger ahead to warn your people of our arrival,' he said, and wheeled round, back to his men.

How long was it since Elfie had been there? Fifteen months perhaps. The Easter before last, when she had appointed Ralph, Edward Little's half-brother, as her steward here. As she rode over the hill and out of the woods (great muddy hogs snorted and wallowed in the puddles in the shade of the oaks at the edge) she could see that Ralph Little shared his brother's passion for sheep. The home meadow where in the past cattle had grazed was dotted with ewes and lambs, a cacophony of bleating youngsters gambolling under the standard oaks and the ash. Two scarved women crouched on stools, milking the ewes. For cheese, the milk would be; Elfgifu nodded in approval.

The farm lay on the far side of the meadow. Smoke curled up from the centre of its wood-shingled roof. Beyond the hall were two huge barns; and nearer were the two houses that she had had built to provide private lodgings for herself and guests. She had allocated one of them to Ralph Little and his family. The other, she guessed by the way four girls were shaking a great feather mattress out the front, was being prepared for herself and Canute.

'Yih!' yelled one of Canute's men, spurring his horse past her, galloping down to the hall with spear poised at the ready. She was scared, heart in her mouth, afraid he was going to attack one of the girls. 'Canute,' she gabbled, grabbing at his bridle, but he said, 'Do not fear.' The warrior hurled his spear so it landed head into the earth near the entrance to the hall, stopping vertical, the shaft trembling with the shock, fabric coiled at the handle end unfurling into the steady breeze: a white silk pennant embroidered with two black ravens. The god Odin's black ravens on a white ground. The pagan symbol was such a shock that it halted her breath.

'I thought you were a Christian,' she gasped. The faith she had been brought up in was deeply engrained in her.

'Oh, I was baptised when I was a child,' Canute said, lightly, as if it were a thing of no importance. 'This is my battle flag, I take it with me wherever I go. Odin's ravens peck at the bloody corpses of my enemies.'

She was shocked at the disparity between their beliefs. 'My hall is a place of peace,' she said firmly. 'You have no enemies here. There will be no fighting here.' She dismounted and he dismounted too, and she led him by the hand down toward the wide-open doors.

Evening. Ralph Little's cooks had done him proud, conjuring up a feast for the Danish troop at a bare afternoon's notice. A boar was roasting on a spit over the long central fire, the scent of it rising to the high rafters, the crackling sizzling, fat dripping into the orange embers and making them flare; flames reflecting in the gold and silver torcs and inlaid buckles that the men wore, in the rings that spanned their muscular arms. In the silver rims of their beer horns. Their faces were young and stubbled, dirty from their travels. The room stank of their sweat, was rough with the shout of their voices. Elfie was beginning to know them by name: Hauk and Sigurd, Einar and Gudleif, Sigvat and Emund. They recounted stories of their travels from Spain to Iceland and north to the frozen sea; of blue icebergs and white bears; of great spouting whales, and seas silver with the curved backs of fish; of sledging across the snowy wastes of Russia; of the ease of their adventuring with King Sweyn in the equable climate of southern England over the last few years. They told of storms at sea, and waves rising high and cresting, trailing foam higher than the highest tree, as high as the World-Ash itself maybe, that had its roots in the Underworld and its topmost branches in Heaven; and of shipwreck, and drownings, and the grievous loss of friends. They told of battles, and crimson blood spilled on emerald grass; and of Odin's black ravens pecking out the eyes of the dead. The howl of wolves, the thin grey slink of them ghoul-like at dusk across the field among the lying dead men. Human flesh hanging from their stinking jaws.

A minstrel plucked the strings of his harp, began a song of requited love. Carp swam on the broad planks of the long table, baked with their tails pinned in their teeth. Unleavened bread fresh from the ovens was hot to touch. Roast partridges were piled up high. Little birds – lark and pigeon and blackbird – were threaded on skewers. Canute was eating one of them, his teeth biting through the crispy skin. He spat the bones on the earth floor, and a bitch squeezed from under the table to crunch them in her jaws. Elfgifu thought: how much greater is this world than the confined world I'm used to. And she resolved to open herself to it; to come fully alive.

Canute slept late the next morning. Elfgifu was restless and got up, summoned Ralph Little to her and walked around her land with him. He came only to her shoulder, she had to stoop to speak to him. His management of the sheep and hogs was excellent, but he had not readied the great barns to receive the harvest as he should, nor repaired the roofs, and one of the hay-wagons had a wheel slanted on its axle: 'Get that fixed at once,' she said. 'Think of the consequences if it comes off and a load of hay tips over. And the cattle, where are they?'

They were up in the forest with only girls to guard them. There was good fresh grazing along a valley by a stream, and the cows were healthy and round-bellied, but five calves had gone missing in spite of all the girls' efforts, the bells they clanged, their shouting, the heaps of stones they had piled up to hurl at wolves and bear. 'You must give them more protection,' Elfie told Ralph Little. 'Think of the winter. How will people manage when there is no fresh food? You must build a dairy up here, the cows' milk is going to waste, you must see that the girls make cheese and butter with the surplus. Winter will come only too soon. People must be fed.'

He had turned over the oat field, which was on a south-facing slope, to grapes. 'No fruit,' she said sourly. He said, 'Allow them time. All things need time to grow.'

She didn't know about cultivating grapes and so she took him at his word when he said how quickly and how well the vines had established. He showed her where he had had the forest cleared to make a new oat field. 'Hmm,' she said. 'It should be taller at this time of year. We'll need a good autumn for it to ripen.'

'Give it time, mistress, give it time. You are in too much of a hurry.'

In the apple orchards, sheep grazed beneath the trees. It was an idyllic scene, a sweet pastoral, the pale shorn creatures grazing in all that green, that dapple of sunshine and shadow. 'Leave me a while,' she said to Ralph Little.

When he had gone she lay under a tree, nestled in the grass – it was late morning now, the grass was dry – and she stared up at the apple branches, the green globes of the nascent fruit beginning to swell, the infinity of the blue sky above the leaves and interlace of branches, and listened to the munch of the sheep tearing at the grass, and the birdsong, the rich chirrup of finches and blue tits, thrushes and the coo of doves. A tiny spider was in her hair, it swung across her vision. A beetle on her hand – no, a ladybird, red spotted with black. When she moved her hand she found the ladybird had this rule: it strove always to climb upwards. She placed her other hand on top and it crossed up to it. White butterflies, red moths fluttered their dance above her face. She yawned widely.

'Sleepy?'

It was Canute. Her mouth slipped into a smile she couldn't prevent. She had forgotten it was possible to feel like this. Purely happy, she thought you'd call it. A simple, childlike state in which to be. Warmth in her chest, her head a simmering cauldron, bubbling with joy; the past all forgotten. Everything was new, an exhilaration, interesting, alive. She'd been reborn into *now*. This moment. The world was new and full of potential. Anything could happen.

'How did you find me?'

'I was exploring. It's a lovely farm. Very well cared for.'

'You have land in Denmark?'

He dropped down beside her, lying on his belly, laid his arm across her. 'Of course. More arable than this. Not so many sheep. We eat fish a lot.'

'Have you seen the stew ponds?'

'No.'

'Over there, the far side of the hill... carp and perch and so on, so many you can stand on the bank and catch them with a net.'

'Your English climate is so comfortable. Easy.' He rolled over on his back, yawned widely and stretched, arms above his head. 'Not surprising your people don't have the energy to fight. Always buying off the attacks of the Danes rather than fighting them. Lord, my father's grown rich with the tribute he's received from settlements along the coast.'

Elfie sat up indignantly. 'Your father's a thieving bastard. Stealing from people who have laboured hard to acquire what they have. Raiding their villages, pillaging, looting, burning their houses, murdering people who want to live in peace — there's nothing praiseworthy about that. What we have, hasn't come easy. Farming is hard work. Your father – he wants it all, but he's too lazy to work for a living.'

'Well,' said Canute slowly. 'That's a point of view I've not heard before. My father thinks highly of himself, you know.'

She felt abashed; she shouldn't have spoken as she had, she knew. Men had been killed for less. 'Sorry, I didn't mean...' she began to gabble, but then she thought, but I did. She needed to distract Canute from the anger she was sure he must feel; that she had certainly felt in the past, when members of her family had been criticised. She jumped up. 'Race you back to the hall.' She gathered her skirts high above her knees and ran as fast as she could. Through the orchard, down to the wooden bridge across the river, where, hearing no sound behind her, she stopped and glanced back, clutching the handrail, gasping for breath. He was leaning against the thick trunk of an apple tree, watching her. As she hesitated he gave a war cry, a fearful shout, and hurtled after her, so much power in his legs she felt weak as a cripple. She ran on again, but on this uphill stretch stones slipped under her feet, her left ankle twisted and she fell.

He loomed over her, square against the bright sky. He was barely panting. How aware she was of the strength of him. Like a great bull. A stag maybe. Or a poised snake. She was certain he would strike her. Her criticising his father had been unforgivable. 'I didn't mean it,' she said. 'Forget it. I'll go away. I'll vanish, I'll disappear. You'll never see me again.'

'Like Thyre,' he said.

'Thyre?'

'God, that was a mistake on my father's part.' He knelt over her, pulled up her skirt, inspected her knees. 'You've grazed yourself,' he said.

'It hurts,' she said.

He spat on it, he wiped the dirt away with the hem of his tunic.

He settled beside her, staring forward, hands hooked about his knees. 'Thyre's my father's half-sister. After my mother died, he and Earl Sigvald cooked up this marriage for Thyre with King Boleslav, so she'd get all the land my mother used to own. But Thyre didn't want to marry a lecherous old heathen. My father had to use force to deliver her into the old king's hands. It didn't do any good, though. Seven days after her wedding Thyre escaped and fled to Norway, where she married King Olaf Trygvesson instead. One of my father's direst enemies. Elfie, you don't feel like Thyre did, do you? I know you've had this marriage thrust upon you. A political arrangement between your cousins and my father to make their alliance secure. But you and I, we rub along well enough together, don't we?'

She leant forward, she put her left hand on his far shoulder, she brushed her cheek against the stubble on his chin. She coughed suddenly, taken aback by the huge wave of physical attraction that had welled up in her belly and throat toward him; she hadn't expected it. 'Sometimes your father's an effective matchmaker,' she said, lying back on the grass and pulling Canute down on top of her.

Some time later he hauled her to her feet. She tried a step and flinched. 'My ankle,' she said.

He stooped to feel it. 'Nothing broken,' he said. 'Bit swollen. A slight sprain, I'd guess. Be better soon.' He looped her up in his arms and carried her up the hill. She hung her arms around his neck so she didn't fall. He rocked her like a boat afloat in the North Sea in a storm, up and down, up and down on the great waves. 'Careful,' he said, 'keep your feet up, or sea-serpents will snap at them.'

'Love you,' she said.

Audrey Little was Elfgifu's housekeeper at the palace in Northampton. She had come with them to the small farm and now in the burning heat of late June – those kind of hot days that Elfie while still at the convent had spent skulking in the shady cloisters, or reading the psalms in the cool of the crypt – when her hands were too sweaty, too slippery to handle the delicacy of gold leaf, even with tweezers – when the weather was so hot that it was like in the psalm, *like grass on the roof, which withers before it can grow,* and she wilted rather than walked – even then Audrey Little set about washing all the household linens and wools down at the river, the fabric sudsing in buckets, left to soak overnight and then rinsed in the river and spread out on hedges and bushes, festooned like giant mushrooms over the prickly mounds of wild roses and hawthorn, so they were crisp dry and sweet-smelling by the end of the day. She had women sweep the earth floor of the hall, kept it clean, didn't spread straw on it until the arrival of Canute's warriors. Soon enough there'd be the sour smell from spilt milk and ale, boarskin and the bones of birds, rats' piss from the creatures hunting in the straw for crumbs – the occasional dead rat stamped flat by a warrior, or caught by a hunting dog –

Audrey had set the bakers baking and the sweet smell of fresh bread enticed everyone toward the hall. Roast boar too, cut in thick slices, and good ale to quench their thirst. Early purple plums and honeyed oatcakes were piled high in bowls.

After their meal Canute carried Elfgifu outside – 'I'm fine, I'm fine now, put me down, put me down!' – and he kissed her mouth and laid her in the shelter of an ash tree. Then he joined Rane the Far-Travelled in taking his hawks from their cages and tying them to their perches; giving them water to drink and checking them over. How like a boy he was still, in his enthusiasm, his eagerness to let them fly; in the way he stroked them, gently, with one finger, his hair falling forward over his face; the way he shook it back when he held the white gyrfalcon perched on his gauntleted wrist. 'Snowflake, her name is,' he called out to Elfie. He let her fly, soaring high into the blue summer afternoon; his gaze following her intently long after she was lost to Elfie's sight.

She had not flown hawks since she was last in Northumberland, before her father's death. Some six years ago. Unable to resist the lure of them, she limped over: 'Let me have a go,' she said to Rane.

'You're a woman,' he said. 'You can't do it.'

'I learnt to fly them with princes Athelstan and Edmund, when my father was King Ethelred's councillor.'

'Let her try the goshawk,' said Canute. 'We'll soon see what she knows.'

Hawks are strange creatures. They seem incapable of affection; a female gyrfalcon will kill any other bird, even her mate, so she has always to be kept tethered except when being used for hunting. Elfie didn't know a falconer who bred gyrfalcons; the ones she had worked with had all been caught in the wild, with nets, when they were migrating southwards from the bitter cold of the Norwegian winter. They were pricey, because of it. But they recognised when someone knew how to handle them; they responded to authority.

It felt good to have the little goshawk perched on her wrist, to stroke his feathers with one finger, to pull off his hood and let him drink, good to feel that mastery of a bird again; good, when Canute's gyrfalcon had returned, to let Fury fly and watch him dive on a pigeon. 'A mouthful for supper,' she said.

It felt good to have this shared knowledge with Canute. A place where they were equals. This shared freedom of the outdoors and of identification with a hawk soaring, hovering in the blue air above the valley and the woodland; a hawk diving, swooping, its quick, vicious kill. She gave back the goshawk, she stretched out her arms like a bird in flight.

'I shouldn't have doubted you,' he said. 'What else did you learn?'

'What princes do,' she said. 'I joined them for their Latin lessons. I can use a sword and spear.'

Only the Latin had she used in the convent, translating St Mark's gospel into English. It had been her intention to make a fair copy for use in the convent church; but now that she was married she never would. Her marriage would alter the set flow of the river of her life; she wondered where it might take her.

'Later we will have a spear-throwing match,' he said. 'I want to see how good you are.'

She laughed out loud. 'As if that would be fair.' She stepped close to him, felt his biceps, how strong the muscles were. He slid his arms around her waist, lifted her high. 'Don't, you fool! You'll drop me!'

'Will I, Miss Featherweight?'

'Oh, put me down!' But he didn't, he held her hovering powerlessly above him. 'I'm not... I'm not a *pancake*!'

'I could eat you up.'

'I could spit on your face.' She gathered spittle on her tongue.

'All right, all right.' He let her down.

She swung his hand; how much she wanted him. She led him back to their rooms, unbuckled his sword belt, laid it on the chair. He undid her apron, slipped off her shift. She lifted his tunic over his head. He laughed out loud.

'What I want,' Elfgifu said, lying on her belly, chin propped in her hands, 'is a wedding in a cathedral, with a crown and sceptre and all the royal trimmings. Cloth of silver and of gold. When Queen Emma married Ethelred, it was like that. Very grand.' She tickled his nose with a feather that had escaped a pillow.

He sneezed. 'When my father has conquered England, beloved, if I'm approved by the northern nobles – what he's thinking of doing, beloved, is handing the kingdom over to me to rule, he doesn't want it – Denmark and Norway, they're enough to keep him occupied – then we'll go through that rigmarole if you wish. Meanwhile...' he sat up and stretched – 'let's have that spear-throwing match.'

'Can't you just lie still for a while?'

'It's not my way, sweetheart.'

How well she was to learn the truth of that, in future years: he had so much energy that he could never keep still. Never would. What she wanted to do was doze in his arms, but he jumped up, pulled on his clothes and stood by the door, tucking the unkempt strands of his hair behind his ears. He put his hand on the latch. 'Are you coming, then?' he demanded.

Of course she went. She didn't want to be left on her own. She had had too much of that. His energy was making her feel alive again, making her feel that it was good to run and talk and laugh. Her quiet routine was at an end. It was good to feel the weight of a spear in her hand, to get the measure of its length, to find the exact point of balance where it was almost weight-free, when she should let it fly... it amazed her, how her arm seemed to have a memory of its own for the task. 'Hey!' she shouted triumphantly, staggering after her throw.

'Not bad for a girl,' he conceded, bettering her by twenty paces.

'It's not fair.' She ran after her spear and retrieved it. 'I haven't used a spear for years. And the weight is different to our English spears.'

'That's a hunting spear.'

She fingered the barbed head.

'Still, I can judge your technique. If I ever have to fight the princes, it'll be useful to know how good their tutor was.'

Elfie turned away, saddened. She had not thought of this. King Ethelred was her family's enemy; but his sons she had ridden and hunted and danced and studied with, she had no grievance against them. Now she was married to their foe. Whatever happened in the future, she would be pitted against her former friends. She could see no way to avoid it.

In front of her hall, on its spear-shaft post, flew Canute's banner of white silk, and when the breeze flapped it open the sun polished its sheen into rainbow colours, a flag of joy she'd have called it, save that a black raven was woven into the fabric, very lifelike, one of the god Odin's ravens, Memory or Thought, she didn't know which, and when she looked closely, she saw that the raven was flapping its wings, dancing in the wind with a ring in its beak, a ring of gold and silver plaited together, and she thought, this is a good omen, that his banner is so full of joy.

15. Emma, London, August to September 1013

The days were still warm; a heat haze hung above the houses of London, the great river Thames flowed wide and sluggish. Many boats upon it. Emma walked on its broad earthen bank each morning after chapel. Thistles pressed against her skirt, down from the spent flowers floated like angels in the wind. Her six-year-old daughter Godgifu chased after her. When she stopped and strained her ears, she could faintly hear the sound of fighting to the north – war horns, yells, the clash of iron. The two princes, Athelstan and Edmund, fighting the Danes. Upholding the might of their father Ethelred while he cowered in his palace.

'What should we do?' she said to Ethelred. 'What can we do?' So strange for her to ask his advice; it was her custom to tell him what to do. But they were both irresolute in the face of the might of King Sweyn's army. Over and over Ethelred's spies brought back reports of events going ill for the English.

'Why don't you ride north and rouse your men?' asked Emma. 'If they know you are cowering here, away from the fray, no wonder they are losing courage.'

'No point in riding into certain defeat,' he said.

'Well, what should I do? I and our children? Do you want me to stay here to be raped and murdered by the heathen?'

Ethelred shrank into himself. 'Retreat, then, retreat,' he cried. 'If that's how you feel. Safest to go back to your mother in Normandy. Take the children. Not for long. It won't be for long. Just till Edmund and Athelstan sort out this damned situation.'

'What will you do? Will you accompany me, to protect me?'

'I can't desert my country.' He had sunk to a bench, he was sitting hunched over, shivering in spite of the late summer warmth, head in his hands.

Each day Sweyn and his men drew closer. Each day Ethelred gibbered, irresolute with fear. Then London surrendered to the Danish forces. The only way out was by sea.

The river banks were lined with boats, boats with furled sails and sailors waiting, offering refuge in France for a fee. 'France, a safe passage to France,' they chanted. The estuary, blue-misted, stretched wide open to the sea beyond.

Emma summoned Elfsige, Abbot of Peterborough, to her, demanded that he escort her to Normandy. She climbed in her boat with her clothes and treasures – she wasn't going to leave them behind to fall into the hands of the enemy. Then she realised her two sons and daughter were still standing on the river bank. 'Bring my children and follow me!' she shouted to the Bishop of London. And at high tide, in the bright noonday, as the river waves lapped against the banks, the two boats set off, joining the ragtaggle trail of other refugees.

Ethelred, on the river bank, reined in his restive horse and watched his wife and children depart. An unpremeditated warmth spread through his chill veins; he drew himself up tall, straightened the gold circlet on his brow. His family were honourably disposed of, he'd seen them safe; he was now free to do as he wished.

He summoned his son Athelstan's wife to him, bade her await him in his chamber. How much he admired her beauty and biddable demeanour; he felt sure she'd provide him with satisfaction. Then he'd go to war.

16. Emma, Normandy, November 1013

'How lovely that the boys have settled down so well,' said Gunnor, Emma's mother. She topped up the sweet cider in Emma's goblet, filled her own, sipped it.

'I hardly know they're here.'

'When did you last see them?' Gunnor's blue eyes glittered with curiosity about her daughter's life; not able to make sense of her evident contentment when she had so recently had to flee from her husband and her adopted country; when she was a refugee in her birthplace with her children, for whom she seemed to have no maternal feelings at all – except perhaps for her little daughter, whom she liked to dress up as a doll, but was constantly forgetting, leaving her behind or not noticing when she was in danger. How close the child had come to falling in the pond, how close she had strayed to the huntsmen's hooves.

'That cleric you have with you,' Gunnor probed. 'What's his name?'

'Elfsige,' Emma responded, lingering fondly over the vowels. 'He is Abbot of Peterborough.'

'What is he doing here with you? He should be home with his friars or monks in their time of trial, not here.'

'Oh, I could not let him travel home when there was fighting on the road between London and Peterborough.'

'All the more reason for him to be with his monks, to give them guidance and keep them safe.'

'But I need him. He is my personal cleric. My confessor.'

'He has a taste for the best wine.'

'He is of noble birth. What else would one expect?'

'Indeed,' said Gunnor sourly.

Now that Emma's sons Edward and Alfred were close playmates of her brother's children, and staying with them on their farm, enjoying the freedom of the countryside, the chamber next to hers was empty; and what could be more natural than that she should invite her spiritual adviser to sleep there? No purpose was served by his being in a far-off room, a cold room with a hard plank bed and devoid of tapestries on the wall. Much better that he should sleep adjacent to his mistress, where he could offer her spiritual comfort at this time of trial whenever she needed it, with her royal husband still in mortal danger across the stormy sea. She was so afraid – the abbot's presence gave her comfort.

So the two of them sat on great woollen cushions close up against the logs that burned in the fireplace of her chamber, logs all orange embers and collapsing into grey ash. The plump abbot's face was red and shiny from the heat, and he was merrily recounting how poor the Norman harvest had been this autumn; how high the current prices were for food.

'Pity them,' said Emma lightly, not following his drift.

'Your majesty is not bereft of gold,' Elfsige pointed out.

'I thank the Good Lord for it daily,' she said piously.

'The local monasteries and convents hold holy relics. Maybe they will not be averse to selling one or two, in order to be able to buy food for the poor?'

'You think so?'

The first treasure that they bought was a tooth of St John the Baptist, a small tooth, scarcely bigger than a child's, encased in a gold casket set with rubies. The miracles of healing that it had wrought were well-attested.

'I will wear it round my neck for safe-keeping,' offered Elfsige.

The second treasure was a splinter of the Holy Cross itself, the old wood turned silver with age. 'It might be a splinter of oak,' said Elfsige. 'I did not know that oak grows in the Holy Land.'

'Olive wood, then, maybe,' suggested Emma, closing it into the gold box within which it lay, sliding across the tiny bolt that kept it shut.

'The little finger of St Clementine,' offered Elfsige.

'St Clementine?' asked Emma.

'She beckons bees to orchards,' explained the worthy abbot. 'She ensures good harvests.'

'She can't have done a very good job if they're selling her.'

'The error must lie in the penitents who prayed to her. They cannot have prayed with sufficient faith and belief.'

'Perhaps we should get her for half-price if she's not infallible.'

'Madam…'

'Tell them they are asking too much.'

The treasures stacked up in Emma's chamber. When she was in bed, preparing for sleep, she felt the holiness of the assembled objects falling like a sift net full of stars around her shoulders to protect her.

'The Norman air is so good for you, darling,' said Gunnor. 'No, don't turn away from me again. Let me look at you.' She took hold of her daughter's wrists, she held her firmly there. 'You were so pale when you came here, Emma, but now you have roses in your cheeks. You were so young when you left home, fourteen, was it? Now you have three children growing up, and yet you can't be more than – what? -– twenty-five. Little Godgifu is nearly half the age you were when you left home. I can't believe it. I don't know how I can have let you go. But the change in you this past month – it's as if you've recovered your childhood again.'

'You're imagining things, Mother.'

'You haven't forgiven me for sending you off to King Ethelred, have you? But it's what you yourself wanted at the time. It's what you begged for. It's what you seemed fitted for. I did not want to refuse you such an opportunity.'

'I am happy to be Queen of England, Mother.'

'You were always self-contained, my dear.' Gunnor released her daughter, who shook her wrists and turned abruptly on her heels, her skirt swinging out behind her.

Gunnor, left alone, let the tears that had sprung to her eyes course down her cheeks. She thought of how she had cherished Emma as a little child, nursed her at her breast, sung her to sleep, played tag with her in the garden, taught her her letters when she was still little. Oh, that tousle of blonde curls nestling under her chin when her daughter settled in her lap! The warmth of her little body. Wiry body. She was always springing away, even as a child. Always independent. Going her own way. Such a beacon of brightness, always out of reach. Remembering gave Gunnor an ache in her chest.

Emma looked at herself in the highly polished silver plate that hung by the door to her chamber. She saw what her mother saw; she did indeed look well, and happy. Laughter lines at the corners of her eyes and mouth, which weren't accustomed to be there. That weren't consistent with the dignity of being a queen. She contorted her face to try to dispel the happiness there, then, failing, laughed out loud. It was good to be here, to be away from Ethelred, away from the court; good to talk in her native language (how freely it flowed, how smooth it sounded!); good to be free of the responsibility for her children (let her mother cosset little Godgifu if she wanted, cuddle her, make her plump on peach comfits).

It was good to spend time with Elfsige, whose learning she respected; companionable to go riding with him, to visit sacred places and bend her knee in chapels where light fell through thick glass windows; greenish glass, underwater light, another dimension to these holiest of places, the holiness and happiness rubbing off on her. It was good to act with him in negotiating for the purchase of holy treasures, he always the enthusiastic one, she the more reluctant, holding the purse strings, the one more inclined to question the authenticity of objects; but the monks or nuns always wanted to sell, because of the high price of wheat due to the poor harvest, and they'd give way reluctantly. The skill was in assessing their sticking point. That bone from St Wilfrid's big toe, which was reputed to cure lameness: it was quite unreasonable of the nuns not to accept her first offer. She did increase it, in fact, because Ethelred was getting old, he suffered from rheumatism, he often limped, and she felt that that reflected on her own dignity as his queen, walking beside him. A ragtag progress they sometimes made, the pair of them, she felt. He let her down. Made her a laughing stock. She hated it. But St Wilfrid's big toe bone could cure all that.

Going in her chamber, she spread out her relics on the wide boards of the table and touched each one in turn, reciting for it the Magnificat, or Te Deum, or Lord's Prayer. Warmth filled her chest. With all this holiness, this healing power, around her, it was no wonder she was looking well.

A knock on her chamber door. 'Come in,' she called.

It was Elfsige. His solid presence always gave her comfort, his grey eyes, his slow smile. She smiled up at him, she reached for his hand. 'Where are we riding today?' she asked him.

Outside a light frost glazed the grass; a blue sky shielded Heaven.

17. Elfgifu, England, 4th February 1014

The warmth of the bed. The linen sheets, the woollen blankets. The prickle of it all. Cured sheepskins piled on top, faintly redolent of salt. The warmth of your lover couched against your skin. The dark of the overcast morning. No need to awaken. Nothing to do save take one's pleasure. Eat, laze on cushions, listening to the songs of the minstrels in the great hall. The old tales. Or just lie here and enjoy the warmth of your lover still asleep at your side.

Bur Elfgifu was restless. She wanted to move. She'd leave Canute to sleep. Slip out of bed, yawn, stretch. A cold draught blew round the shutters. She rang for warm water and was half way through washing when Edward Little burst in. 'Ill news,' he exclaimed, then seeing her naked stammered, 'Pardon, mistress,' and started to back out, but she said, 'Stay.' She reached for a towel and wrapped herself in it, rubbed the damp hairs at her neck, and said, 'It must indeed be urgent news for you to come in without knocking.'

'Mistress, a report from the camp at Gainsborough,' he babbled.

A wave of presentiment rushed over her, a shock, a sharp ache like a blow to her chest. 'Sweyn?' She rubbed her chest. 'Canute's father? All is not well? The Northern nobles have decided after all not to crown him king?' She was thinking how someone must have stirred up ill feeling against him, just when all things looked certain, when, with Ethelred having fled from his kingdom, the English throne lay empty, ready for Sweyn, with the backing of the northern aristocracy – the backing of Elfie's family – ready for Sweyn to take up the sceptre.

'Worse, madam. King Sweyn is dead.'

'No.' She stepped forward and grasped Edward Little's forearm, digging her fingers into his flesh, staring up at him wide-eyed. 'No. That can't be.'

'The messenger is here, madam. He wants to speak to Canute.'

'I will wake him, and tell him, and bring him to the hall. Make sure the messenger has refreshment. Give him a seat close by the fire.' She shivered sharply, suddenly aware that Edward had left the door open and that her bare skin was being washed by the chill draught between window and door. 'Canute will come to the hall,' she said. 'Go tell the messenger.'

She closed the door, she pulled the curtain across the window. Canute was still sleeping. She dressed in her grey wool dress, her dark apron, fastened it with her gold brooches with entwined dragons. How dark it was in that shadowy room this dull morning.

She laid Canute's clothes out ready for him, his woollen breeches and his shirt, his over-jacket of ermine, very warm. A cold journey he will have of it, she thought. A cold journey full of shock and grief.

She thought how it was when her own father died. When he was evilly murdered. The shock. Not being able to make sense of it. The grief. The disbelief. *This can't be true. Someone's making it up. It's make-believe.* The horror of seeing his poor slain body. How grief had made her physically ill. The terrible headaches, the raging fevers. She sat on the edge of the bed, gulped great sobs of grief. This is happening over again, she thought. Over and over again. When will people learn, when will they see there's no purpose to it?

Poor Canute, she thought. He's a boy still. He's seen men die on the battlefield, but it's not the same as to lose one's own father. How much a boy he looks, lying there. He could be fourteen. She knelt at his bedside; his face was softened by shadows. She laid her cheek against his. He reached out an arm to caress her. She wanted to protect him. How young he was; so full of the future. Not yet defeated by it, as she was. She couldn't bear to give him the news of his father. What would he do, how would he react?

'My dearest,' she whispered, taking his hand. 'My dear, there's business to attend to in the great hall.'

Canute had to leave; of course he had to go. 'Saddle my horse,' he commanded. He was too numb on hearing of his father's death to want to break his fast, as Elfie pressed him to. His men made ready; he dressed and buckled on his sword. His face still ash-white with shock, he sat on his great stallion before the hall; thin and shrunken back into being a vulnerable boy, in the fine cold snow that was spitting out of the dark sky.

'You can't manage,' Elfie said to him, clutching at his stirrup. 'I'll come with you.'

'So you're commander of the royal Danish army now,' Canute sneered, and snapped his bridle, spurred his horse sharply and led his men away across the stream and up the hill. Under the bare branches of the orchard apple trees, up into the jagged oaks that forested the summit. Out of sight. Elfie stared after them until the last echo of the hoof beats of the troop, the last call of the horn, had faded from the air. She stood there yearning after him.

'Mistress.' It was Marjorie Little. She had come up soft-footed behind her, she was reaching up to brush off the snow that had fallen on her mistress's shoulders, she was wrapping her in a cloak lined with bearskin. 'He is doing what he has to, madam.'

Elfie sighed, and rubbed her eyes. 'So do I count for nothing?'

'Mistress, come inside.'

These last few months the two of them had been so close that now Elfie felt a part of her had been torn away, she felt as if she were haemorrhaging from the loss of her lover. 'There must be something I can do. I remember when my father died...'

But then there had been nothing she could do; nor when her mother died. Her tears, her grief, could not bring them back to life. The ceremonies of the funerals, the fine words of the bishop, the eulogies of friends, the dark graves lying open, closing them up with cold earth crushed in the palm of her hand – the feasting, the drinking, and then the awful emptiness, left alone, the bitterness of the injustice of it all. How much she still wanted to avenge the wrongs done to her family by King Ethelred – that lousy coward who had fled to France to escape the might of King Sweyn who now lay dead – a sick man's death, brought on by a festering wound from one of the skirmishes he had fought – a surprise death, leaving no guidance for those he left behind him, his troops encamped at Gainsborough, the nobles starting to assemble for his coronation in York. Canute was still too much of a boy for them to place much reliance on him, for him to have the authority to step straight into his father's footsteps. The Danish army now had no clear commander; what would they do?

Elfgifu thought: King Ethelred won't be frightened of fighting an inexperienced boy. He will return to reclaim his throne.

She thought: I am Canute's wife, I must follow him.

She summoned Ralph Little to her and gave him instructions on how to manage the farm - the care he must take of the lambs and calves, the feed to give them: the oats and barley he must portion out among the poor who were always close to starvation at this time of year.

'Madam, I have been farming many years,' he protested. 'I know what to do.'

She walked the earth floors of the wheat barn and the barley barn with him, checking how many baskets of grain remained, letting the grain run between her fingers to make sure that it was still in good condition; ordering that supplies should be rationed right up until the end of June when the pea and wheat crops should be coming in. Still alive in everyone's mind was the memory of that terrible year of famine when the tall cliffs of Beachy Head had been lined with people who preferred to take their own lives rather than see their families starve.

'So – now I know all here is well, I will go tomorrow to join my husband,' Elfie said. She picked six strong men to accompany her, furnished them with spears and swords from the store; set out at dawn.

They reached Gainsborough after nightfall. A ragged half-moon, a high wind; clouds swept the sky. A chiaroscuro night, all sharp black and white. Closed houses; just a peasant boy whistling to call his dog. Elfie leaned down from her saddle: 'Where is the Danish camp?'

He pointed. 'Gone.'

'What do you mean?'

He shrugged. 'Gone,' he repeated. 'After they buried their king.'

The fields where the camp had been were indeed empty, the snow trampled into mud. A stink of latrines hung about the place. At the far side, by the river, rose a great mound of fresh earth; muddy-smelling, the ditch about it half-filled with water filmed with ice. On it stood a tall wooden cross, the deep runes carved on it cast into sharp shadow by the moon. Elfie dismounted, gave her reins to one of her men to hold and climbed the mound, her feet slipping in the snowy mud: arms reaching forward to maintain her balance. She ran her fingers over the splintery wood, but could not decipher the runes, not knowing the script. I should have asked Canute to teach me it, she thought.

Then she heard hoofbeats far off in the night, coming closer, and the jingling of harness; and she slithered down from the mound and remounted, rode forward to see who it could be. 'Canute,' she called loudly, hoping it was him.

'Elfgifu? Aelfhelm's daughter?' The voice that came out of the suddenly overclouded night was English, with a northern accent, and old – a contemporary of her father's, maybe. Who was there who lived in this area? The cloud swept past, all was clear, she saw a burly figure astride a heavy horse and shouted, 'Uncle Gabriel!'

He shouted back: 'The Lord save you, my dear. Come with me. It's no night to be out. Come back to my hall.'

His father's men would not listen to the young Canute, they would not accept his leadership. *Boy*, they called him. A kind of hysteria gripped them, from which he could not shake them. And maybe he too was so shaken by his father's death, his head so fogged with shock and grief, that he lacked the strength to impose his will on them. And so all the Danes had fled back home, with their boats.

'Even though they were in such a strong position militarily,' murmured Elfie. 'Even though they had forced Ethelred to flee to France, and were all set to conquer England.'

'There was no sense in what they did,' agreed Gabriel. 'But they had no one to command them. What motive would they have for staying on in England?'

Come daylight Elfgifu rode back to the campsite at Gainsborough. And what was there for her to find but the snow melted in the trampled mud under grey skies, and all the debris from men abandoning the camp in haste? Everything trodden into the mud: a blanket, a spindle with woollen yarn still attached, that, when she pulled it up out of the mud and followed it, led her to a flat circle that would have been where a tent was pitched. Gaming pieces were scattered across the floor of it as if men had been summoned to leave while still in the midst of gambling. She picked up the pieces, shook them in her hands, tossed them to the ground. Odds I try following Canute, she thought, evens I go back home and think this time with Canute has been merely a strange interlude in the weft of my life.

Evens, the pieces came out as. She slithered her way through the mud to the river bank, saw the tide was high and lashing in little waves at the edges, the grey river all turbulent rocking, a restless dapple of light and grey under the grey sky. She stared downriver toward the sea, but could see no sign of a boat, just the leafless willows at the river edge, a solitary lynx crouching to lap at the water.

She had no motive for staying on in Gainsborough, she knew: just the longing that Canute would come back to her. But his loyalty must lie with his men.

She could see now that the Vikings who had been camped here had laid waste the land, raided it for all the food it could offer, and she thought that she with her six men did not want to be a strain on the hospitality of her uncle Gabriel, when the Danes had left him with so little.

So Canute, whom she idolised, had deserted her. He'd run away. Such things happen. Nothing in her experience had ever led her to believe that life was perfectible. The opposite, rather. But still she couldn't stop herself from weeping as she rode back home, she couldn't stop her heart from aching. She couldn't bear to stay on at the farm where she had briefly been so happy. She returned to her palace in Northampton and there she collected up all the bride-gifts that he had given her and ordered Edward Little to pitch them in the fire in the great hall. 'No, mistress,' he said. 'No. Please, I beg you. You do not know the truth of what has happened. If Canute has indeed betrayed you, the least you can do is profit from your brief marriage and keep the goods. Think of their value! If he has rather been compelled by circumstance to behave as he has done, then it is only right that you should care for the gifts he has bestowed on you.'

Elfie brushed the tears from her eyes; she took Edward Little's outstretched hand. 'My friend,' she said. She went back to her chamber and wrapped herself in the green and gold silk Canute had given her, loving the smooth feel of it, so different from the rough wools and linens she was accustomed to wear. She fastened the silk with his brooches, pushed his bracelets up her arms, and lay on the bed they had shared, and dreamed of him, his pale hair threaded in the sea wind, his strong hand on the steering oar of his sea-dragon as it scudded across the dark water beneath a striped sail. The stars a bright glitter in the heavens above, a map to show him where to steer.

She set her women to making a copy of his raven flag, she flew it high from a pole before her door. This raven is *Hugin, thought* in our language, she told her women. When he flaps his wings in light winds, he will carry my thoughts to Canute.

Every day she waited for a message from him.

But no message came. Elfgifu pictured his fleet scattered by winter storms in the North Sea. She pictured the Dragon's hull upturned and empty, drifting over the waves. Canute lost and drowned. She longed to know what had befallen him.

A sickness came on her; she was sick every morning, she didn't want food. She thought it was from sadness but Marjorie Little told her it must be because she was with child. She locked her fingers across her belly, wondering if Marjorie were right, and wondering what a child of hers and Canute's would be like. Strong enough to take the throne of Denmark, she thought he must be; strong enough to take the throne of England too. How good that would be. The best way to avenge the wrongs done to her family by King Ethelred.

News came that Prince Athelstan had begun to march northwards into the country left empty by the departure of the Danish forces, claiming it for his father because there was no resistance. On, on toward Gainsborough. Nobody stood in his way. It was a slow progress. His army, unopposed, stopped at every great hall for celebration, feasting and pleasure. There was no hurry, with the Danish army gone. Prince Athelstan did his utmost to discredit them. Cowards, he called them. They'd run away. King Sweyn had not appointed anyone to replace him, he was

---

115

no soldier, Athelstan said. All mouth and bluster. The Dane had no comprehension of strategy, no ability to command at all. So witness the fact that he lay buried by his men under the Lincolnshire mud. But he didn't deserve to be buried there, in a Christian grave beneath English soil; Athelstan was going to dig up his body and behead it, throw the pieces in a bog infested with devils, where they'd be consumed by rats and snakes and crows as befitted the corrupt vermin that he was: no proper king as he had claimed to be.

Athelstan sent minstrels far and wide to declare his purpose. One came to Elfgifu's great hall in Northampton. She sat on her high seat and as she listened to his song her eyes grew bright with anger, her lips twitched with fury. And for the first time she felt her baby kick inside her womb, and was certain that Marjorie Little was right. Canute's child, she thought; it's furious at this talk of desecrating its grandfather's body, of not allowing him the honour of a grave befitting a king. I now have two loyalties, she thought, both to Canute and to our child. I cannot allow Athelstan to have his way.

But what could she do? She did not have an army to prevent Athelstan doing what he wanted. I could go to him, she thought, I could appeal to him personally because we were children at court together, because I sat beside him to learn to read and write. Be reasonable, I could say. You were always reasonable when we were growing up together. Don't listen to your father, if it is he who is telling you to do this. Don't desecrate King Sweyn's grave. It is a course that will bring you no honour. Throwing a dead man's bones around; what valour is there in that? I can't bear such dishonour to be done to the great king. But she knew the prince would not listen to her.

When it comes to the point, you do what you can. You identify what it is that you want, and you set out to achieve it.

What Elfie wanted was simply to ensure that King Sweyn, her husband's father, had an honourable burial.

Setting out after Athelstan, it was unlikely that she would reach Gainsborough before him. But if she rode back to the farm and then went by boat...

Elfgifu's steward Edward Little's cousin Alfred had a boat. 'I can take you to the coast,' he said. 'My wife's cousin married a Dane who is a merchant who trades in whetstones from Norway. He has a cargo boat, a stout seaworthy vessel. If he is presently at home he could go north to Gainsborough, he knows those waters, he could convey a body in a lead-lined coffin across the North Sea.'

How free Elfie felt, leaving home. Glad to be active. She took only her old nurse Margaret with her. She perched in the prow as Alfred's boat sailed downriver in the weak March sunlight, feeling the warmth of the approaching spring, celandines glowing gold with promise like stars in the wet fields. How excited she felt out at sea on the bucking waves, steadying herself against the mast and the hull of Stein's wide vessel; glad of the southerly wind that filled the sail and drove the boat north, tasting the salt on her lips, holding tight to her bench, hooded against the cold; feeling herself a different person on this Danish boat, afloat on this alien element, this watery ocean – she'd never sailed before – steadying herself, clinging to wood and ropes, knowing if she fell overboard she'd be done for, not knowing how to swim, relishing the excitement and the danger.

They travelled up the coast, past the great port of Dunwich, past Happisburgh and Skegness, and after she'd slept the night couched on a bench, comfortable enough under blankets and furs, a pale dawn came and she found herself sailing once again on a river, calm through flat fields, Stein's eyes bleary from his night's wakefulness, and the riverside trees were alive with the love songs of birds, and far off, faint, she heard the call of war horns, and she knew that Athelstan and his army must be within a few miles, to judge by the breeze that was presently blowing toward them. 'We must go faster!' she screamed at Stein. 'If we don't speed up we'll be too late!'

He set his six men at the oars, and the boat drove deep between reeds and the chirrup of moorhens ducking and diving in the brown water. 'Not far now,' he said.

'The camp is this side of town,' said Elfie. She reached down by her feet and unwrapped the long-handled spades that she had brought with her. She stared ahead, thinking, they will have laid King Sweyn's coffin on the ground, they will have heaped up the earth over it. She wondered how long it would take to dig it out, load it in the boat and make good their escape. 'Here,' she said, as Stein's boat bumped against the river bank and he leapt ashore to fasten the rope to a willow. 'Here.' She offered each sailor a spade, clambered ashore, knotted up her skirt and herself began to dig.

From far off came the drumming of distant hoofbeats. The English army must be galloping fast towards them. Elfgifu dug deeper, hurled the soft earth over her shoulder. Felt the thud of her spade against the oak of Sweyn's coffin. 'Quick!' she yelled.

It was months later that the minstrel Gudrod composed a song about the rescue of King Sweyn's body. He sang it in the great hall of the Danish kings, to the accompaniment of his gold-trimmed lyre. It was about an English woman

whose love for a Danish king was so great that she risked
her life to protect the body of his dead father against
being dishonoured and mutilated and cast in a bog where
devils dwelled. He sang about how the woman stood tall
with drawn sword at the grave-mound to confront Prince
Athelstan as he rode up on his great stallion. She slashed
at his sword arm and cut it; blood from the wound spurted
on her garments and stained them. As children at the
English court he and she had been boon companions, like
brother and sister, and he could not with honour allow his
vast army to attack her and her seven sailors. He clutched
at his wound and said she had beaten him in a fair fight,
and if she cared for it so much, let her depart freely with
the dead king's body. So the king's body in its lead-lined
coffin was dug from the mound, and placed all muddy in
the hull of the woman's boat. No dragon ship this, but a
clumsy cargo boat. The oarsmen rowed away as fast as
they were able. Athelstan, repenting of his generosity,
ordered his men to fire, and they shot up a host of arrows
that fell like hailstones in the river all about the boat, the
sailors meanwhile rowing as fast as they were able, the
woman standing, balancing, wielding her shield above
them like a turtle shell to protect them, deflecting the
arrow blows so that they might pass in safety to the sea.
After journeying through tumultuous waves against
contrary winds the cargo boat at last reached Hedeby in
Denmark. The captain would carry the late king's body no
further, for he had his own trade to attend to, he had
whetstones to fetch from Norway and carry to Britain. The
woman persuaded Danes to carry the coffin to Roskilde,
where they threw up a mound over it, and priests buried
Sweyn as befitted their Christian king; and then she set off
with only her nurse to attend her, no money nor fresh

clothes in search of the Danish noble that she loved. And so Gudrod concluded his song, and laid down his lyre.

'This woman, Gudrod,' Canute said. 'Can you see her anywhere?'

'She sits beside you, sire.'

Canute took Elfie's hand in his and kissed it. She was robed in blue silk overlaid with a finely embroidered wool apron. Her blonde hair was confined in two plaits. 'You are braver than I,' Canute said. 'You have saved my honour by ensuring my father had a decent burial. All I was able to do at that awful time was to make my way home and disband my army and order them to return to their farms and families. Since then I have sat here and done nothing. There is no glory in that.'

'I am glad to be with you, sir,' she said. 'Glad you are well. That is all that matters to me.'

'My father's campaign in England,' Canute said later, when he and Elfie had walked side by side to the coast, and were watching the ships moored at the jetties bobbing up and down on the Baltic waves, the sun's rays bouncing off the water to throw on their hulls a dancing, restless pattern that pulsed with restrained energy. 'All that fighting, what did it lead to? A few bags of silver, and a great deal of bloodshed. My father's death. There was no purpose in it. It is time to put an end to war.'

His words shocked Elfie, made her tighten her grip on his hand to such a degree that he looked down at it in surprise. 'You – my marrying you,' he said. 'That was supposed to bring about an alliance of the northern nobles to support my father. But it didn't do any good, he died anyway.'

'They did support you,' Elfie asserted angrily. 'Your father's forces almost captured London. King Ethelred fled to Normandy. All your father had to do was to defeat the king's sons. They would have listened to me, you know, they would have come over to our side, we grew up together, they would have wanted to negotiate with me...'

'I don't want to fight, Elfie.'

'You don't have the choice. That's not how the world is. You have a duty to avenge your father. It's a matter of honour. When I think of the wrongs King Ethelred did to my family, murdering my father, blinding my brothers – I couldn't bear for him to be free to do that to other families. Your own aunt, Gunnhild, your father's sister, Ethelred had her killed in that awful massacre on St Brice's Day. Ethelred is evil, you must understand that, you cannot allow him to behave as he does, you must defeat him...'

'Oh, let me be.'

'Oh, Canute.' This was said in the blackness of despair; she didn't know how to reach him. She saw how his father's death had changed him, touching him as the run of battlefield deaths hadn't; she saw how young he was, and how his father's strength had provided guidance for his life and now he was lost. She grasped his hand, unfolded his fingers to place them flat on the apron covering her belly. 'No – leave it there. Feel.' She was very serious. 'Feel. Our son, can you feel him kicking?'

Tremulous movements under the palm of his hand, that he did not know how to interpret.

'Our baby,' she said.

He kept his hand there. A slow smile on his face. A question. 'Our baby? Mine and yours...I... I never suspected.'

'Your father died, our baby will live, God willing.'

'There's so much I don't know. Don't understand.'

'You have to build a sound future for him. It is incumbent on you. He is our hope for a better world. A more just future.'

Pine trees grew in the sand dunes at the head of the beach. The warm sun heated their needles, their scent filled the sea air. Canute had a small hall built here. A safe place for Elfgifu to bear their child. He furnished it with cushions, with soft mattresses of feathers. The windows were eyes open to the sea. Elfgifu yawned in the shade under the gaze of the wise-woman Canute had had fetched.

The baby came quickly, without fuss. Elfgifu lay on clean linen sheets with him in her arms, marvelling at the miniature perfection of him: his blue eyes, hair so pale as to be almost invisible, tiny toes, tiny fingers that gripped his father's finger tight: 'We'll call him Sweyn, after my father,' said Canute. 'He will be a king, too.' He bent his head to kiss his son's forehead. The three of them were lapped by the autumn breezes, by the singing of the breaking of waves on the shore.

18. Emma, Normandy, spring 1014

Richard II, Duke of Normandy, to his sister Emma, Queen of England, when they were walking in the orchards, petals from the apple blossom fluttering around them like snow flakes: 'Emma, I've had as much as I can take of your husband throwing his weight around the place, trying to order me around in my own home. If he won't leave, I'll have no choice but to murder him.'

'Don't be ridiculous, Richard.'

'I've told him it's high time he returned to England. My spies tell me there's little danger there now the Danes have gone back to Denmark. They've stopped their raiding parties along the coast. Ethelred is left with just a few rebel nobles to mop up – nothing serious. A single march north and everything will be sorted. I spoke to Olaf Haraldsson from Norway when he rested up his fleet in Calais last week, and he's promised to give Ethelred support – he's a ferocious fighter, he's bound to bring your husband success. I tell you, in no time at all peace and happiness will be breaking out in England for ever and ever.'

Emma looked at her brother doubtfully.

'Well, maybe Olaf didn't quite have that in mind,' Richard admitted. 'It may be that he was thinking more of the loot he might win from plundering a monastery or two.'

'I'd be glad enough to be at home,' said Emma. Elfsige's archbishop had summoned him back to Peterborough to govern his monks, who had been consorting with the local townswomen – several pregnancies were imputed to them. Without him, Emma was finding life in Normandy boring. She felt she was considered a *nothing*, with no role in the household – not even meals to command – and her children taken off her hands, so she didn't need to care for them at all. And her mother did tend to lecture her on how to behave. She had been so shocked by Ethelred and Emma sleeping in separate quarters that she had now lodged Ethelred in Elfsige's erstwhile rooms, so that Emma could not avoid her husband invading her nights. Emma was not sure if it was thanks to him, or to Elfsige taking the majority of the holy relics that they had collected together back to Peterborough with him, that she had been feeling queasy the mornings of late: whatever, she thought she would be better off at home in England where she was queen and could control her own living conditions.

If Elfsige is too far away, she thought, or too preoccupied with looking after his monks, I'll seek consolation with the Bishop of London, or the Archbishop of Canterbury. They both owe attendance on their queen. Not like the local priests here who hold me in no respect – are antagonistic to me even, believing I have profited from my wealth and the good harvest in England to deprive the local abbeys of their greatest riches. To buy their much-loved, long-held relics. When all I was doing was assisting the religious in keeping their vows of charity.

She had her daughter Godgifu arrayed in blue linen and a sable cloak and had her nurse carry her before her on her saddle to the harbour. Her little boys she left to be taken to her brother Robert, who was archbishop of Rouen. 'It is so much better for them to be brought up in a different household,' she declared. 'They will learn much more than they would with me.' Her sons Edward and Alfred came out in the courtyard and bent the knee to her, she bade them rise and they kissed her hand and promised to be good and dutiful. Their father touched them on their shoulders with his sword, bade them learn battle-prowess so when their time came they would know how to be good princes of England. He bent down and kissed them, tears in the corners of his eyes. But Emma showed no such weakness. She watched unmoved. Any children she had by Ethelred would be tarnished by the bloody nature of their father whom she hated. She would never be able to love them.

Home in England, Emma settled back into her palace. Her servants had all left her because of the whippings she used to give them, her non-payment of their wages. She had to engage new ones, but when you are queen that is easy enough to do. She summoned the Bishop of London to her, and bribed him with holy relics to be her spiritual adviser.

Ethelred assembled the ragtag of his army from the streets of London and the nearby villages. They were glad enough to join him, to shout *Huzza!* and to have their stealing of food and raping of women legitimised by following the king, especially as the word was that the princes Athelstan and Edmund, his sons by his first wife, were doing well in their skirmishes with the northern nobles and that peace had nearly been agreed, with Olaf Haroldsson of Norway's forces providing a warlike backbone to the royal army.

But Ethelred refused to accept a settlement with his nobles – his sojourn in Normandy had refreshed his energy and vindictiveness. He ordered the execution of Morcar and Sigeferth, who were Elfgifu's cousins, and held authority over the boroughs of Leicester, Lincoln, Stamford, Nottingham, Derby and York. They were long-standing companions of the king and princes; erstwhile members of his council.

'You can't execute them, sire,' his son Edmund told him plainly. 'There's no justification for it at all. They are good men, they want the best for the people. Executing them will build up unrest in the land.'

'They are traitors, they have been disloyal to me.'

'In Heaven's name, sire, what were you if not disloyal to your country? You ran away, hell bent on saving your own skin, and now as soon as you are back you want to kill nobles who have stayed on here and tried to stabilise the situation.'

'Don't you dare speak to me like that. If you were not my own son, I'd execute you too.'

The executions went ahead. The northern army, leaderless, demotivated, disbanded and retreated.

Prince Edmund travelled to Morcar's hall, with a force of twenty highly-trained soldiers; though he and Morcar had been friends a long time, he was not sure of his reception. 'I share your sadness at the loss of such a good man,' he said to Morcar's family, speaking clearly, standing at the high table in their great hall. 'I did what I could, but I could not make my father listen to reason.' In response Morcar's eldest son whistled for his hunting dogs, and set them on to him. Edmund sprang on to the table and ran the length of it, finding his footing between the wooden platters and the loaves, dodging the hands that made a grab for his ankles, inches ahead of the slathering mouths of the hounds. Outside, he vaulted on to his horse that a mounted soldier held ready for him, and he and his men made good their escape.

When there was no more pursuit, Edmund reined in his horse, dismounted and led him to drink from a stream. Primroses bunched on the banks, the sky was soft blue, a cool breeze blew. The forest sang with birds. 'Our fair land,' he said. He was still shaking from the closeness of his escape. 'Now to Sigeferth's hall,' he ordered.

But his men refused. 'No sense in putting your head in a hive of angry bees,' Brian said.

'Leave me then,' said Edmund.

So it was on his own that he rode to Sigeferth's hall. He tied his horse on a long rein to graze in a clearing in the forest and walked alone, humble as a peasant, through the lanes. He came to the church, a tall narrow stone building, and joined the procession of dull serfs who had come to pay their respects to their dead master, hats clutched to their chests.

Close to the coffin stood Aldgyth, Sigeferth's young widow. Edmund pulled his tunic up around his neck and kept his face averted, not wanting to be recognised. But

still she cried, 'Edmund!' and stepped toward him; he
started to run, he had to escape; but he couldn't, in the
press of the people. She grabbed hold of him, she had her
arms around him, he tried to move toward the door but
her hold was too strong, and suddenly she was sobbing on
his shoulder, and what could he do but pat her on the back
and attempt to console her? Say, 'Aldgyth, Aldgyth, I'm so
sorry, it should never have happened, I tried my best to
prevent my father. Sigeferth, your husband, he was a good
man, what my father did was wrong, I can't bear it, he has
started to speak ill of Uhtred now, his friend Uhtred who is
married to my sister, the king is his father-in-law, how can
my father threaten his own son-in-law? The king is in the
grip of some madness, evil spirits possess him, some priest
must exorcise them. It is so terrible to be the son of a
madman.' And Edmund was sobbing too.

Aldgyth recovered herself first and drew back, said,
'Come. You must come to my hall and take refreshment.'

'No... no, not after what has happened.'

'I wish you to come.'

He did not know how to refuse her. How wary he felt
with her men all around him in the hall. This is a trap, he
couldn't help thinking. She has trapped me, I cannot
escape. He had only the knife at his waist to defend
himself with. He looked at the door, at all her men
between him and it. He tore at his bread, his throat dry
with fear, he supped ale.

She said, 'Edmund, there is the old way to make peace.'

'What do you mean?'

She leaned toward him, she grasped his arm. 'You have
no wife. I am a widow. We could marry.'

He stared at her in astonishment. He recollected how in
the old carefree days at court they would flirt together,
joking, knowing the king would never allow them to marry.

That was before her marriage to Sigeferth. How her union with the older man had made her solemn. He thought how now if he and she were to marry, it would unite the divided factions in England. He thought how angry it would make his father, and he smiled. 'If you are willing, yes. In a few months, perhaps.'

She stood tall and slender. With her serious face, still pale with the horror and shock of her husband's death, in her white silk girdled with a silver chain, her hair braided back, she looked like a spirit, or a ghost; a link between past and future. 'Let the marriage be now,' she said.

'Not in the midst of your grief,' he said.

'My grief has given me such a headache,' she said. 'I feel as if my head will burst. Oh, life is too uncertain, Edmund. We must take hold of it while it is still with us. I know it would please Sigeferth if we wed. He wanted peace. No more fighting, he said. England has had enough of fighting. It has gone on too long. Marry me, Edmund. It's the only way I know how to achieve peace.'

'You need time to reflect. How can you marry the son of the man who killed your husband?'

'Edmund, we are a new generation.' How earnest Aldgyth was, how utterly serious. 'It is still the new millennium. We can do things in a new way. We can set out to build peace.'

'You think that is possible?'

'We have to try.'

Edmund took the ring from his little finger, he slipped it on her ring finger. 'My pledge,' he said awkwardly. 'My promise. We are the new ones. We will do things better.' He bent his head to kiss her.

19. Elfgifu, Denmark, 1015

Spring. Blue skies, warm sun: the energy it gave. The hopelessness of Canute's mood had lessened with the birth of his son; now it dissipated in the soft breezes, the colours coming into the world: wood anemones, wild daffodils, bluebells and golden celandines starry in the thawing mud. The yellow-green of new leaves. Elfgifu, leaving their son with his nurse, rowed Canute gently along calm rivers, they paused to watch goldfinches and nuthatches in overhanging ash and willow, the flash of the kingfisher, in the cool evenings the pale swoop of the barn-owl as stars brightened to speckle the sky. The scream of bats. He taught her to find the North Star, showed her how to navigate at night. 'We'll sail together,' he said. 'I'll take you back to England.' He laid his arm around her shoulders.

Canute was recovering his energy after the shock of his father's death, starting to spend time with his men. He commissioned the making of swords: spent hours at the blacksmith's forge, within the dark heat of the log walls, the only light when the door was closed the fire and the red-hot iron that the blacksmith taught him to beat out with a hammer, bending wire into patterns on the blade while an old man pumped the bellows.

Word came that Ethelred, certain now that he would be safe, had returned to England with his queen; he had assembled his forces and was marching up to Lindsey to confront his northern nobles. 'What will you do?' Elfgifu asked Canute. He was lying on his back in the dappled shade of an old apple tree; she was tickling his nose with a jay's feather.

He reached out and grasped her ankle. 'Must I do anything?' he said.

'Yes,' she replied. 'You are a king, you have no choice. You owe it to your father, you must avenge his death.'

'Oh, later,' he said. 'Let me love this summer first.'

'Well, you must prepare.'

Canute to the blacksmith: 'I need a strong blade. It must not shatter in battle.'

'It will not shatter,' said the smith; and in the darkness and smoky enclosure of the smithy, in the orange glow of the fire, he chanted incantations over the steel, invoking all the strength of the old gods, marking magical runes into the blade which he then melted out, for though Canute had been baptised a Christian, they both still respected the power of the old beliefs which had protected their people for many hundreds of years; and which besides took account of all the unknowables of the earth, which explained the seasons, and war and seedtime and harvest, and understood the spirits that inhabit a place.

Fire spirits in that dark hut: sparks that shot out from the hammer blows and then faded. Green spirits when you walked through the forest, the liveliness of the young silver birches, the solemnity of the older, taller trees that looked down on you as you walked between them, protective in daylight but when night fell often threatening, talking to each other through their roots, angry with you for disturbing their world, ready to trip you or snatch at your eyes or your hair, so you had to weave for yourself an invisible cloak of courage, of *not feeling*, to wear when you were forced to travel alone; better always to be in a group, because a group could laugh and sing and scorn and fight – it was easy to have courage in groups. Noises in the forest. Robbers in the forest. Bog spirits that would try to draw you under, suck you down into the darkness under the mud.

20. Elfgifu, Denmark, after 8th September, 1015

Elfgifu waited down by the jetties, in the salt sea smell, the smell of rotting fish. Boats from Norway and Sweden, as well as Denmark, were moored in the dirty mouth of the river. War ships they were, long ships, not fishing boats. Metalworkers were busy plating the wooden figureheads, sailors knotted the rigging, carpenters smoothed the oars and the benches. Hammers rang out, saws sang amid a ragtag jumble of shouted languages; not many that Elfgifu could understand. The ships were filling up with goods; skins of fresh water and ale, bows, quivers of arrows, trembling bundles of spears. Salt fish in boxes, baskets of apples, vast hard cheeses.

At last Canute came striding toward her. She went toward him, put her hand on his arm. 'So you are going?' she said. 'You are leaving me and your son?'

'That's what you wanted, isn't it? Haven't you kept telling me to go? Wilfrid, where in damnation is the salted meat?'

She bit her lip. In the past, she thought, I wanted you to leave, I wanted you to avenge my father's murder, to avenge your own father's death; but now I have a child I simply want for him to grow up in peace, and be happy. Beginning again. Setting a new pattern for living. Now I want you to stay here forever with me and our baby. This has been the happiest summer of my life, and I don't want it to end.

The jumble of accents of the men on the boats rattled in her ears; the loud babble of their talk. The wind stirred up the sea, the waves swelled and crashed on the shore. She put her fingers in her ears. Grey clouds darkened the sky. Dusk drew on. *Everything changes.* Why can't things stay the same?

Little Sweyn could sit now, she propped him on a cushion so he could watch his father's preparations. Elfie caught Canute by the arm as he passed close. 'I don't want you to go,' she said. 'Please stay.'

He shook her off. 'You've kept on saying it was my duty.'

'Maybe the world has moved on, and changed. Maybe I was wrong. Your son...'

'I can't disband my army now. They are worked up to going. They have gathered here because they know there will be rich pickings in England. We sail tomorrow, if the wind is favourable.'

'No, Canute, no. Don't. No. Please don't go.' It would not be just her own loss, she was thinking, it would be all the men needlessly killed, all the children fatherless. Can't you understand that men are necessary as part of a balanced society, she was thinking, they're not expendable.

But he ignored her, strode in among the houses to meet the smith to demand if his new sword was ready forged. He weighed it in his hand, he swung it back and forth.

The wind swung to the north-east. A cold wind. Out beyond the river mouth the sea swelled up into great waves that crested in white foam, rolled over and crashed against the shore, raced up upon the sand. Elfie polished the blade of Canute's sword, she slid it in its sheath, she sang incantations over it as she buckled it at his waist. She reached up to kiss him. 'Farewell, dear heart,' she sighed.

The boats rocked queasy in the muddy river mouth.

21. Emma, London, 24th April 1016

'You would choose *now*,' Queen Emma complained out loud to her late husband's coffin where it lay in state in the dimness of St Paul's Cathedral, a tall candle in a great silver candlestick at each corner, the flames flickering in the chill spring dusk, the sweet scent of bluebells drifting in from the churchyard, the breeze rustling in the new leaves and doves softly cooing. '*Now*,' she repeated. 'Now of all times. The moment of maximum inconvenience to me. I ask you, why now? Our sons still little, and the two of them left in Normandy for their safe-keeping while you pursued your feud against those damned invading Danes.' She was still addressing the coffin. 'You, Ethelred, you could have just bought them off as usual, you could have given them chests stuffed full of newly-minted silver coins, that would have bought us time, that would have given us six months or so of peace and quiet. Six months for things to calm down. I couldn't get my brother to intervene, he said Canute was a law unto himself and he had many grievances to avenge. I kept saying to you, Ethelred, you've got to sort out your inheritance and ensure that it is our sons, the sons born of my loins, not that terrible ragtaggle trio left by your first wife, who will inherit the throne, but oh no, you wouldn't do anything, you insisted on behaving as though you were immortal. You carried on fighting. You eternal fool.'

She sighed, and pushed back her veil. Her face was pale and weary, dark circles under her eyes. Weary, or angry, or frightened-looking? It was hard to tell. She knelt at the end of the royal pew and recited three Hail Marys and two Lord's Prayers at high speed. Her heart wasn't on the words. Her hands were steepled in prayer in front of her eyes but images kept flicking into her head through the gaps between her fingers – the throne of England overturned, its carved arms escaping her grasp, the riches she'd accumulated tumbling into pirate hands, the power she'd acquired falling away from her so she'd be like a common person – her, Emma, Queen of England, reduced to a zero. No, it was impossible. She could not accept it.

'You know who the Witan will elect king as your successor, don't you, Ethelred? Edmund. Prince Edmund. Your son by that so-called queen you had before me. That weakling they think took her own life rather than rule royally. Edmund is young and well-built and handsome, he's one of the lads, he can take his drink, he knows how to fight, he's a lusty so and so, he married Sigeferth's pretty young widow a couple of days after you had the old man murdered – don't tell me it was me who egged you on to that, I know it was, but it was necessary, wasn't it? It had to be done. Sigeferth and Morcar had a lot of support up north, they were bound to go over to the Danes if they invaded again, and we couldn't have that, could we? I've always been better at the political arithmetic than you. You gormless so and so. Food for worms, that's all you are now. You were always gung-ho, you never stopped to think too much about things. Witness how when you'd alienated the Church with your high taxes, I softened them up, I brought them round to support you.

'And now – now, as a thank you for my support, you've gone and died at this most inconvenient of times. The Witan is bound to elect Edmund king, Edmund who can't stand the sight of me (well, I can't bear him either, him with his talk of goblins and elves still thriving in the Thames marshes, I ask you! Talk about childish! Such pagan rubbish! Does he not understand the nature of the true Lord?) You – you've deserted me, Ethelred. Abandoned me. Me. The Queen of England.' She stood up tall as she could on her pattens with their thick wooden soles, shook out the folds of her dress.

'I'm respected,' she said loudly, adjusting the gold circlet that held her veil in place. 'Everyone respects me. Except – Ethelred, now you're dead, what am I? I'm a cypher. It's only my marriage that made me a queen. You've died to spite me. Now you're dead, what will become of me? Edmund resents me. If the Witan elect Edmund king, as I believe they will, his little upstart wife, Sigeferth's widow, will become queen in my place. What will become of me then?

'Banished to a nunnery, perhaps. Humbling myself to the cloistered life. No, that's not for me. I enjoy the exercise of influence and power.'

'Madam.'

'What?' Emma had been so immersed in her thoughts that she had not heard the new arrival come stepping up behind her. She turned around. There the Bishop stood enfolded in his purple cloak.

'My lord.' She stretched out her hand for him to kiss.

He bowed, but didn't take it.

She bit her lip at his quick recognition of her loss of status; his forgetting of the intimacy there had been between them, that had benefitted him so much. Oh, the ingratitude of men!

'We are all set for the morning,' he pontificated. 'Consigning our great king to the earth from which we all come, to which we all shall return. Dust to dust...'

'Indeed.'

'For thirty-seven years he has ruled, madam. A goodly time. A worthy king indeed.'

'May he rest now in peace.'

The Bishop crossed to the royal seat, placed his hand on its back that was carved like a great dragon. 'Prince

Edmund will sit here,' he said, 'and his wife Aldgyth at his side. You...' He gestured to a seat behind them.

Emma picked up the soft peacock-woven silk cushion from the queen's seat and moved it back a row. 'It's said that Aldgyth is with child,' she said. 'She won't need it, she is well-padded enough.'

'The cushion belongs with the rank of queen,' said the bishop – he who up to now had always been eager to do her bidding. He took the cushion from her and put it back to its original place.

'It is my own possession,' snapped Emma, snatching it up, tucking it beneath her arm and marching off down the nave with it, her wooden soles clacking on the stone flags. She must gather up all the treasure that she could, she realised, before Aldgyth got her sticky fingers on it. It was a great shame she was in London rather than Winchester where the royal treasury was locked away. Still, she would go to Ethelred's rooms and collect up his riches, his gold arm rings and his sword with its blade inlaid with silver and scabbard purple with garnets, his gaudy gold and garnet buckles and his great helmet; she would preserve them with all the other treasures in her safe-keeping.

Then where would she go? In a nunnery she wouldn't be able to keep her riches. It seemed she had no choice but to return to her family home in Normandy near where her sons resided. Her sons who were rightful heirs to the throne of England, whom when they came of age she could present before the Witan and push forward as the true inheritors of the kingdom of England. And then she would take up her proper role as queen mother.

She remembered the story of what King Ethelred's own fierce mother Aelfryth had done for him when he was but ten years old. His half-brother Edward had been king of England then; and Aelfryth wanting the honour of being the queen mother had held a great feast at which she leaned across to distract Edward by offering him a bowl of honeyed sweetmeats, pink and yellow jellies rolled in raw sugar and served up in a silver dish; and meanwhile her servant dove in under the table and stabbed him in the belly. It had been neatly done, Edward's death almost instant. Ethelred, his proper heir, was immediately made king.

Emma stumbled on the stone step going out of the cathedral, grasped the door jamb to steady herself. For the moment I must be patient, she thought, there is nothing I can do for now. I must paint myself with ashes and tears, must play the role of grief-stricken widow for the time being. But an opportunity will come, I'm sure; I'm not by any means defeated. She had her two sons by Ethelred, children still, and they might well be a powerful throw in any game of dice for the throne of England she was to play in the future.

She would leave Edmund to be king for the moment, let him battle it out with the invading Danes. The odds were that he would be killed in the conflict. She would work out what to do once the fighting was over. Then would be the time for her to come back to England with her two sons. How happy the people would be to see their former queen restored to power, she who was renowned as a peaceable, honourable and strong Christian ruler, whom they could count on to bring order to their troubled land. When she returned they would come out to greet her, they would wave broken-off oak branches and acclaim her as their present and ever queen.

22. Elfgifu, England, 1016

'Can't you and Edmund settle matters without fighting?' Elfie asked Canute. They were out with the falcons, flying them on the plain by the sea, that dull cold day.

'You mean, I could just say, I want to be king of England, and we'd shake hands, and Edmund would say, here, take my throne, and welcome?' he said.

'Edmund - you know, I grew up with him, he was like a brother to me, we were children at court together, I learned to read and write with him, I learned Latin with him, my father was his father's councillor, I learned to fly a hawk with him. We were good friends. He is the legitimate king, his father's successor.'

'He murdered my father.'

'You know that's not true.'

'Edmund shouldn't have fought against him.'

'What else could he do? He was honour bound to defend his father's kingdom.'

They stood and in silence watched the hawks for a while: the way they soared, and hovered in midair; the way they rested in a tree, weighing down a slender branch, the way one flew again and plummeted on a dove. A broken neck; a puff of feathers on the grass. Elfie ran to retrieve it; tossed the warm body to Canute who slipped it in his bag.

'I wish I could prevent the two of you from fighting,' she said. But she knew that was impossible. 'When you married me,' she tried, 'it was to make an alliance with the Northumbrian nobles and get their support against Ethelred, so...'

'Not so quick,' Canute interrupted. 'That was my father's purpose. But as for my intention – I married you because I loved you at first sight, sweet heart.'

'You'd never have met me if your father hadn't...'

'Destiny brought us together, Elfie. It was meant to be. We are right for each other.'

'Why can't it be like that between you and Edmund?'

'You want me to marry him?'

She tore a clump of moss up off the ground and tossed it at him. They collapsed together, laughing. But still she wished with all her heart that there might be peace between Canute and Edmund. There must be a way, she thought. I don't know what it is at present, but peace must be possible. Somehow I will bring it about.

23. Elfgifu, England, 17-18th October 1016

Elfgifu urged Delight on, shaking the reins, clenching her knees on the saddle. With every step Delight took, their names throbbed in her head: Canute, Edmund, Canute, Edmund, Canute, she beat out their names with each step like drums upon the earth, Canute, Edmund, do not fight, my friends, do not fight, in a rhythm that travels this long earth road to wherever you are, where you have gathered your armies around you, have made ready to fight this fine morning when the sun sends its long rays across the land, its fingers of light to touch sea and sky, field and forest, sword blade and axe blade, to make the silver glitter on helmet and shield-nails. Canute my lover, Edmund my old friend, do not fight, stop your fighting, listen to me, let my name come to you in your dreams, see, I send you my name from the tips of my fingers – I am the peace-weaver, I am Elfgifu the peace-weaver, peace will fly to you from the tips of my fingers, it flies through the air – you are my brothers, let there be peace between you, listen to me and I will bring reason, I will make peace between you, there will be no bloodshed in the fields where you are, no one will die, no one will die at all.

Listen. Listen to me. I send you my thoughts on this slight breeze, let it reach your ears and whisper, *There will be peace. Know it in your hearts.*

She had outpaced Cedric and Margaret, she had flown like an eagle on the brushed back of Delight through the forest.... *Peace* was in the sigh of the leaves in the breeze. Let the word Peace enter your heads. Do not fight. There is no need to fight.

I will make peace between you. There will be no dishonour to either of you in it. Peace, peace, let this day end in peace. Weave the word in your dreams.

Dusk fell long before Elfgifu could reach them. In the twilight Delight went slower, she shied at branches. Then she stopped altogether. Elfgifu tried to urge her forward, but she would not go. Elfie slid from her saddle, she intended to lead her mare by the reins. But then she heard wolves howling and knew there was no chance of her mare proceeding.

Grey wolves howled. *Let them keep away.* She thought of their thin hungry flanks, the way they twisted through the secrecy of the trees, the great yellow teeth in their gaping mouths, their red tongues that lolled. She thought of them slinking round the gathering of Canute's and Edmund's armies. Those living, vital men, flexing their muscles, laughing, eating, drinking, gambling, singing; men with families at home, with people who loved them, who would be devastated by the loss of them: what madness was it that overcame men, that made them agree to fight, that made them want to kill each other? There was no reason for it. *Let the wolves feed on rats and squirrels, not on men.*

She could not stay in the forest with the marauding wolves.

'Don't go,' said Audrey Little.

'Don't go,' said John Little. 'It's not pleasant, the aftermath of a battle.'

'He hasn't come home,' Elfgifu said, pulling tight the laces on her boots. 'I have to find him.'

'I'll come with you,' said Margaret.

'No. You must stay and look after Sweyn.'

'I'll come with you,' said John Little.

'No, your sheep...'

'I'll prepare your mare,' he said.

'Why is there no word?' Elfgifu asked Margaret. 'Why has no messenger come?'

Margaret hesitated. 'Perhaps he lost his way in the fog,' she suggested. But Elfgifu guessed: she's thinking, perhaps he was killed on his way here.

But when she went out of the hall she found there was indeed a low mist hanging in the air, that clung to face and hair and hands and cheeks, and blurred all distant hills and trees. 'I know the way to where they are,' she said.

John's pony was slow and when she set Delight free to gallop on the wide track through the forest she soon outdistanced him, and left him far behind. When he was lost to sight she reined in Delight, they went more slowly. There was no need to exhaust her mare. She thought the lack of messenger could mean only one thing: that Canute had suffered defeat. 'Edmund,' she whispered to the air, 'be merciful to the man I love. I have tried so hard to make peace between the two of you.'

Toward noon the mist lifted. When she stopped to rest Delight the sun was a blaze in the vivid yellow of cherry leaves, in the gold of hornbeam and the browns of oaks.

The sky was a brilliant blue. She thought: this must be a good omen. And then as she rode on cloud swelled to curtain the southern sky, rising to veil the bright sun so it was translated into a silver disc, a ghost of itself, that was soon swallowed up.

The day grew colder. She shivered. She drew her cloak tight around her.

There came the caw of ravens. They are not done yet, Elfgifu thought, with pecking out men's eyes. And there was the howl of wolves. They must still be feeding off the slain, she thought.

What she hadn't expected were the human predators: the dark-hooded women stepping from body to body, stripping the armour from the dead: tossing knives and swords, axes and helmets into the baskets that they carried. The almost merry ringing of the metal that they'd retrieved.

Arrow shafts lay across her path like twigs blown down by a storm.

She let Delight pick her way through the carnage. She tried not to look. She kept her gaze averted, focussing on a tall ash tree on the hilltop ahead.

But she could not stop herself hearing the piteous cries of the wounded, could not stop her nostrils burning with the stink of blood and shit. And of woodsmoke and boiling leek soup. Two women with bloodstained sleeves and aprons, blood-speckled cheeks, were feeding leek soup to the wounded, and going back to smell their bellies. If they could smell the leeks they knew the men's stomach wounds were serious, that they were mortally wounded. That nothing could be done to heal them. Just a hand under their head for comfort, strong mead to alleviate the pain.

On the slope below the ash tree men were shovelling the stony earth, digging great trenches in which to bury the dead. *Canute, this isn't the way,* she found herself thinking. How can this slaughter resolve anything? This waste of manhood when men are so needed to build a strong kingdom that can exist in peace...

Then the breeze swirled the mist and she could make out two figures standing by the ash tree. And, in an instant of sunshine, the gleam of Canute's battle banner, the white silk with the black ravens, and Edmund's stiff flag of scarlet with its embroidery of lions. It used to be his father's. She remembered as a child sitting with her mother and Ethelred's queen before Emma, persuading a needle full of gold thread through the thick fabric; with a thimble she had worked painstakingly, taking care not to loop or tangle her stitches. She had stitched a lion's whiskers in silver.

A woman shouted. A cloud of ravens flew up: the dark servants of Odin bearing away all thought and memory from the dead, leaving them empty. The woman cried out a name; she started noisily to weep.

Elfgifu didn't pause to comfort her. She dismounted from Delight and led her by the reins. She was trying to make out the figures by the ash tree. Who were they? She strained her eyes against the mist. The one of them was tall and straight: blond hair, that hooked nose. 'Canute!' she shouted.

'Elfie! What are you doing here? You should be...'

She dropped the reins, she ran toward him, she threw her arms around him, she smothered his mouth with kisses. She stepped back, she stared at him. 'All's well? You're not wounded?'

'Elfie, I told you to stay at the farm. You should not have come here.'

The other figure jerked a laugh. 'You don't know her well yet, Canute, if you expect her to do as she is told.'

She span round. 'Edmund! You are well too?'

His right arm was in a sling, his face was strained and very pale beneath his mop of dark curls. 'Oh, fine,' he said. Then he had his good arm round her, he was embracing her, he was kissing the top of her head. 'Dear Elfie,' he said, 'it's good to see you.'

'We haven't seen each other for so long,' she said. All the memories of her father's death, her brothers' blinding, rushed back into her head. She and Edmund had grown up like brother and sister, but his father's cruelty had driven a wedge between them. 'I didn't want you two to fight,' she said. 'I tried to stop it.'

'Fighting is a fact of life,' said Edmund. 'It's not a woman's concern.'

Canute called his manservant to him. 'Take her home,' he ordered, as if prompted by Edmund's words. 'She should not be here. Lead her round the side of the hill, don't go through the field of the dead.'

That night, and for many nights following, Elfgifu had nightmares of that battlefield. Though she had tried hard not to look, she had not been able to avoid seeing some of the carnage. She lit candles in the chapel, she prayed on her knees for hours for the souls of the dead, the lives of the wounded. And then at last Canute came home, and all was well. He and Edmund and their councillors had arranged to meet at Deerhurst to see if they could hammer out a peace agreement.

Sense at last. Happiness beat in her heart.

24. Elfgifu, Deerhurst, 30 October 1016

In the great hall at Deerhurst a feast was held. At the head
of the table sat Canute, crowned with a circlet of gold,
seated on the Prior's carved throne; and on his left was
Edmund, on the throne that was used when a bishop came
to visit; and on Edmund's lap, cuddled in his uninjured
arm, was his happy twelve-month bride Aldgyth, widow of
Sigeferth who'd been a victim, like Elfgifu's father, of the
late King Ethelred's random executions; and bouncing on
Aldgyth's knees were her and Edmund's tiny twin sons, full
of smiles. They made a lovely family, the future of England.
'How did you do it?' Elfgifu asked Aldgyth, stretching
across to kiss her cheek. 'Twins, I mean. It was all I could
do to manage one.' How alone she felt all at once, without
Sweyn with her; she wished she had brought him south,
but she had left him at home with his nurse Margaret.

This did have the advantage of leaving her free to talk
to the twelve eminent nobles who had witnessed the
contract between Canute and Edmund, their oath to be as
brothers, and to maintain peace in the kingdom as long as
they both should live, with Edmund controlling London,
Wessex and East Anglia and Canute in charge of the
Danelaw. And she met as well other old friends, who
came up and clasped her hands and said how good it was
to see that all was well with her, and that she was at last in
a position of power such as her father's nobility entitled
her to; and they talked about her blinded brothers, and
how sad it was that they had both died. Eadric her father's
good friend, an old man now, white-bearded, took her
aside and told her how she should be assuming the role of
head of the family that her brothers had been destined to
fill until fate in the shape of the evil Ethelred had deprived
them of it. She should, he said, perpetuate all the old

English traditions of hospitality and generosity, and she smiled and took his two gnarled hands in hers, and said, Sir, it is what I am determined to do, and, releasing him, she seized a drinking horn and filled it with mead and lifted it to his lips. 'Sweet,' he said, and she drank too.

Then Brother Magnus who had taught her Latin accosted her, and they talked about the old times in the palace before the Queen Mother died and broke those familial constraints that bound her son, setting him free to commit injustices without restraint; they spoke of the court pleasures of hawking, and boating in the summertime, the great Yuletide feasts and log fires that had been customary in midwinter. The long stretched-out springs when flocks of birds sang in every hedge and tree and yet food was scarce. A few loaves only on the table, that they ate hot with melted butter; every crumb.

And suddenly a young woman flung her arms around Elfgifu, and she backed away, bewildered, and the woman said, Elfie, don't you recognise me? It's been so long, it's so amazing to have this treaty uniting the kingdom, we'll have peace for evermore now, don't you think? And Elfgifu said good heavens, it's you, Gertrude, it's been so long, indeed, and they talked about how her grandfather the earl had been determined she should go to a convent and train to be an abbess, but she'd rebelled and married one of his men, and now had four children (four, Gertie, that was quick work!) and an estate in Dorset, where they had suffered for years from the Viking raids, the pirates demanding protection money in the form of tribute – it breaks your heart, Elfie, it truly does, to hand over hundreds of shiny new-minted silver pennies to those filthy thugs – so in a way she was glad that Canute was king because it would mean things would be more settled; and she said how good-looking Canute was, and how she envied Elfie, for her own husband was battle-scarred, and had lost an arm.

That made Elfgifu look at Edmund again, and she noticed how pale he was, how haggard beneath his dark mop of curls, and how he winced when one of his sons bounced against his injured arm; and she went up and talked to him and asked him how he was; but before he could answer one of his little sons grabbed at her finger, and she said, 'Oh, you, you've trapped me, sweetheart, do you know I have a son just a little older than you, his name is Sweyn,' and Edmund said, 'Oh, I'll bet he's crawling by now,' and she said, 'Yes, but I've left him home with Margaret,' and he said, 'Not Margaret who was your old nurse?' and she said yes, and he said, 'My father wanted the same nurse for his children by Emma as he employed for all of us, but Emma put her foot down and took on a Norman nurse. The poor little bastards have ended up speaking Norman French rather than English.'

'Where are your half-brothers now?' she asked.

'Back in Normandy with their mother,' he said. 'She's always been one to look after her own.'

Then a minstrel began to sing, a new song about the Battle of Ashingdon and how bravely Canute and Edmund had fought hand to hand, blade clashing against blade, and how first Edmund lost his shield and then hewed Canute's shield in two with a single hefty blow of his axe, and how neither was stronger than the other, so they made peace; and how this peace would bring joy, and last a thousand years.

A thousand years, Elfgifu thought; a whole millennium: the length of time from the birth of Christ to the childhood of Canute. And she thought how afraid people had been that with the year 1000, the new millennium, would come Judgement Day, and Almighty God descending in clouds of flames and ice to the Earth and pitching screaming sinners into the fires of Hell, and decking out the holy with white robes, wings and glory, and raising them up to the realms of Heaven. People had become obsessed with building churches and founding abbeys to have clerics pray for their souls. Not that that had made them behave in one jot a more Christian way.

A thousand years since the birth of Christ. She wondered what the world would be like in another thousand years; whether Canute's peace could possibly last that long. There was no reason why it should not, if people set their mind to it.

Just now Canute was busy distributing gifts to those warriors who had served him well in his campaign in England; gifts of land he had conquered, gifts of gold and silver arm-rings he had stolen. The hall bubbled with goodwill and self-satisfaction.

25. Elfgifu, 1st December 2016

Elfgifu was happy to be home in the farm, and to lie in the dark mornings in her bed of furs and wool blankets with Canute in her arms until little Sweyn escaped his nurse Margaret's surveillance and crawled in their room, where Canute lifted him up on his belly and rocked up and down as if Sweyn were riding bareback. He held Sweyn under the arms and heaved him over his head, shouting, 'Over the fence,' or 'Over the river,' or 'Over the fallen tree,' until Sweyn was giggling and dribbling.

Those quiet days were good. Elfgifu dared to hope they would never end.

But on the first day of December, while Canute and Elfgifu still lay abed, a messenger in black burst through the door. Canute leapt up and snatched the sword that he kept always by their bed and drew it from its scabbard. 'What news, Arnvid?' he demanded.

'Your majesty,' said Arnvid, bending his knee.

'Spit it out.'

'Twice majesty. King of Wessex and the Danelaw.'

Foreboding grabbed at Elfgifu's throat. 'Edmund,' she said. 'What has befallen Edmund?'

The infection in Edmund's arm had grown worse. He had had a high fever these last four days. This last night he had died, in Glastonbury, where he had gone because of the renown of the monks there as healers. Elfgifu thought about him and his wife and their children, how happy they had been in Deerhurst on the day of the feast. How glad she had been for the four of them.

'He is indeed dead?' said Canute. 'Edmund king of Wessex is dead?' He reached for his breeches, he pulled them on. The scratch he had sustained on his chest had almost healed up; the scab was peeling off. He ran his fingers through his hair, picked up his tunic. He seemed to be growing taller, broader-shouldered before Elfgifu's eyes: to be puffed up with air, floating almost on a cloud of elation. 'You are sure?'

Yes, nodded Arnvid. He was a Saxon, a messenger who had come to Canute many times before. There was no reason to disbelieve him.

'I must ride to Glastonbury to check this for myself,' said Canute. He picked up his sword belt and buckled it on.

'I'll ride with you,' Elfgifu.

He glanced down at her as if he'd forgotten her existence. 'There's no need.'

'I want to come.' But by the time she had dressed and carried Sweyn to Margaret, her husband had already left, had been swallowed into the mist of the valley beyond the hills that encircled the farm. But Elfgifu could not bear to be left behind. She was Canute's queen, deserving of respect. She ordered Delight to be harnessed, a troop of men to prepare themselves to accompany her.

It was a chill day in Glastonbury when Edmund was buried. A strong wind from the west whistled between the buildings and tore the last of the leaves from off the trees. It rained, intermittently; a thick biting drizzle. Elfgifu dragged Aldgyth into the shelter of the porch at the door to the nave. Raindrops were like glass beads upon their cloaks. They each held one of her sons. She had fed them and they were sleeping; they were swaddled in woollen shawls against the sadness of the day. Elfgifu pulled her cloak around the child she held, she hid the baby's warmth close to the chill of her heart, keeping him safe from the dreariness of the early December dusk. She kept thinking: it's Edmund we are burying, we are burying my good friend Edmund, the last of the boys to survive unwounded our carefree, happy childhood in the palace, back when his mother my namesake Elfgifu was queen, and when King Ethelred's mother was still alive to keep her son's wayward behaviour in check. Edmund was the last one of us to believe in the certainty that all would be well; that King Ethelred would defeat the Viking raiders and our kingdom be ruled in peace with justice. Banners in the wind; minstrels singing of his glory.

Beside her, Aldgyth had started to weep. Her shawled figure was bent double, her body racked by great sobs, she was retching as if she might vomit up her heart. Elfgifu didn't know what to do. Awkwardly, she took the infant Edmund from her, but he started to bawl and set little Edward off. 'Margaret,' she called to her nurse, but she was holding Sweyn. Elfgifu had to command a couple of the friars forming the guard at the door to step out of line and take the babies from her.

Elfie put her arm under Aldgyth's. She tried to raise her up and give her support so she could stand as her husband's coffin passed and bid him farewell with dignity. But Edmund was the second husband Aldgyth had buried in a twelvemonth and she had loved him utterly, and she had their twin sons to keep safe, whom she knew that Canute could not but see as a threat to his rule: a relic of the old order when he needed to instate the new. Once Edmund's coffin, draped with his banner, had been carried past, Aldgyth started to scream, and did not stop until her voice gave out. Elfgifu slapped her, trying to break her out of her hysterics. She put her arms around her, she held her tight. Only exhaustion put an end to her weeping.

Elfgifu was in bed with Canute. It was warm and comfortable in their bed of furs; from the great hall came the distant rippling music of the harp, the singing of the minstrel. They had made love and she was resting her head on his arm and he was talking softly about how under the treaty struck at Deerhurst he would become sole ruler of England: London, Wessex, the East and Northumbria. As well as being king of his native Denmark, of course. Though his brother Harald was governing that for the moment. 'Little Elfie,' he murmured, kissing her ear, 'you never dreamed you'd be such a queen, did you? Wife to the ruler of the western world...'

'I never wanted it,' she murmured back. 'All I wanted was you to be my lover.' And then Aldgyth's terrible grief came back into her head. 'You must be a just ruler,' she whispered. 'This land has suffered so much injustice, there has been so much mourning, we must make it a better

151

place. You are so strong, you can change how the country is run...'

He yawned widely, he fell asleep.

She watched the light of the moon fall slanting across the bed. All day the clouds had been thick and heavy, but now that night had fallen they had lifted and the full moon was brighter than the sun had been during the day. How the world has been turned upside down, she thought. Aldgyth, the mother of King Ethelred's grandsons, legitimate heirs to the throne of England, will be forced to flee with them into exile; while I lie in the arms of the man who has taken that throne by force, and I know that I will do everything in my power to ensure that our son rules after him. He is my child; he will share my compassion for the people of our land, he will do everything that is best for it. He will be a just ruler; there will be justice in this land at last. He will grow up on my farm, he will understand the earth and ensure that there is food for everyone. No one will starve. No one will fight. There will be peace throughout the land. Happiness and plenty. I have to battle for my son.

At the next meeting of the council it was formally agreed that Edmund's infant sons must be exiled. 'Fostered with my maternal uncle,' pronounced Canute blithely, but he might as well have said, *removed from harm's way.* The grandsons of King Ethelred of England placed where they could never be a threat to the legitimacy of Canute's rule, where they could not be a focus for dissension in his kingdom. When she heard the news, Elfgifu silently slipped her hand into Canute's because this was a contract for their son, this meant that their little Sweyn would be undisputed king of all England, and the child presently growing in her womb, if it proved to be a boy, would be a prince.

But still Elfgifu's heart bled with sympathy for Aldgyth who had lost two husbands, and now must lose her native land as well. She must go into exile with her sons, become a refugee. Not belonging anywhere. No loyalties, no allegiances. Elfgifu pondered what she might say to reconcile her to her fate. 'It will not be so bad,' she said in the end, taking Aldgyth's two hands in hers. 'Truly, Aldgyth. Do not fear. I've been there, to King Boleslav's court, I mean. Where he lives, it's closer to the East, you know. Close to the overland trade routes. Silks are imported from China. Brooches and necklaces are hung with dirhams, silver coins from the East with holes drilled in them – the women wear bright silks and make a tinkling sound, as of small bells, as they walk around his court. It's strange at first.' She said nothing about how she loved silence, and so how angry the noise made her, as if she were a pet cat or lap dog that needed to be kept track of at all times. She said nothing about how authoritarian Boleslav was, how violent, how he dominated everyone at court. How he was still a heathen, and practised heathen rites. 'Aldgyth, my dear friend, I'll miss you,' she said. 'I'd hoped our sons would grow up together.'

'They will meet when they are older,' Aldgyth said, folding her arms around her.

Elfgifu nodded uncertainly, thinking how unlikely that was.

So maybe it was guilt that made her take the time to ride with her friend to the coast. Fear also perhaps in case one of her husband's more ardent followers might decide it would be expedient to deprive Aldgyth and her sons of their lives. Elfgifu wanted to see her safely shipped.

The last day of their journey was overcast and rainswept, but as they neared the estuary the clouds lifted and the pale sun came out; blue sky, a bright sheen on the wide stretch of rippled water. The bow of Aldgyth's boat was a dark silhouette against the brightness of the sky: a sea-serpent figurehead. Gulls screeched; a heron paddled in the mud. Five wide-winged birds flew in a dark line. 'Is something the matter?' Aldgyth asked Elfgifu.

'No, nothing. Just that I'm so sorry you have to leave. Go. Your boat is waiting for you.' She kissed her on both cheeks. Then she stepped back and watched as Aldgyth and her nursemaid went through all the awkward business of carrying the babies and their belongings along the plank that ran from the shore to the boat. The sailors helped, they stowed the luggage in great baskets in the footwell by the mast. Seeing that Aldgyth was being well looked after, Elfgifu turned away, she started her ride home. On a slight hill she paused and swung Delight round to face the coast, she watched the men rowing the vessel out toward the sea. They hoisted the sail, and she waved one last time.

26. Emma, Normandy, 1017

'You can have a room in my apartments,' Emma's mother said.

'Mother, I am a queen, I cannot live in a single room any more.'

'You were a queen,' said her mother.

Her brother Richard had dismissed her two hundred retainers, saying they were too much of an expense for him to feed. She was left with only the lady Elisabeth, and Elfsige the Abbot of Peterborough to act as her priest. Her sons had been sent to be fostered with her brother Robert in Rouen. They are too old to stay with their mother,

Richard had said. Only her daughter Godgifu remained with her mother; and she, when she was older, would go to a convent.

Of course she had hoped that Ethelred on his return to England would defeat the Danes. But that wasn't to be, even though her brother Richard had obtained for him the doughty support of Olaf Haroldsson of Norway, that fierce Viking. Trust Ethelred to waste such an advantage. When, after his father's death, his son Edmund had been elected king of England, Emma had hoped that he would find a queen-mother role for his stepmother, as was fitting, and had written to him to that effect. But he had ignored her letter, had been oblivious to the filial duty that he owed her and now he too was dead. Serve him right. Finally, with Canute king, the English nobles had confirmed the disinheritance of her sons.

If only she could see a way forward. How she should proceed.

Emma paced out of her chamber and along toward the chapel. She was thinking: I cannot live like this, subservient to my brother and mother. Not after having been mistress of my own court. In charge of a kingdom. It is too much of a change for me to take. But I don't know what I can do. How to move forward. If it had been from Winchester that I fled, rather than London, I would have raided the treasury, taken the English royal jewels with me. I could have bought vast tracts of land here. Had a palace. Been patron of abbeys. But as it is I have only my own jewels.

She unfastened the gold reliquary pendant from around her neck, and laid it before the solitary candle burning on the altar in the chapel. The flame flickered in the draught from her hands. She knelt on the scarlet cushion, she bowed her head, she closed her eyes, she prayed with all her heart that St John the Baptist whose tooth was contained within the reliquary would intercede for her and bring some relief for her humiliation. How terrible it was to have been a queen and now to be a poor, unwelcome widow dependent on her family. I will have no choice but to go into a convent, she thought. She should by rights become an abbess; but would that happen if she had insufficient riches with which to endow the convent? There was no certainty of it.

Oh blessed Saint John, have mercy on me. Have mercy on me. Holy Virgin Mary, Mother of God, have mercy on me. Lord Jesus Christ, have mercy on me.

Her prayers brought neither comfort nor resolution. She sighed, fastened the pendant once more around her neck, stood up and walked to the great hall.

Where a messenger had just arrived from England.

His hair was wild and windswept, his breeches were stained with a salt line from when he had jumped ashore from his boat. He spoke in Danish. 'My lady Emma-Elfgifu.' He bowed to her. 'Your royal majesty.'

He had come in haste from Canute, Sweyn king of Denmark's son.

Canute was now king of all England, he said. Canute had declared there had been enough of war there. He wanted his people to live in peace. And to that end – and having heard of your great beauty, the messenger assured Emma – Canute wished to suggest that an alliance be forged between himself and Emma. Between himself and the former queen, who had proved her abilities as an effective administrator, particularly with regard to negotiations with the rich English church. He believed it was prudent that they should marry. It was a resolution he was most desirous of.

Canute king of all England was suggesting that Emma should be queen of England again. A marriage whose purpose was to form a lasting alliance between the divided factions in the land. Will you marry me, the messenger said Canute had ordered him to ask.

Emma's heart jolted with excitement at the thought. And with fear. All the years she had been queen her husband had fought against foreign raiders. Mainly against Canute and his father. They had been the dragons, the ogres, the raiders who harassed and stole from the English people. Who murdered them, who burned the crops in the fields, who took them as slaves. Who were, on occasion, bought off with Danegeld. Could she possibly put all that aside?

In earnest of the seriousness of his intentions Canute had sent gifts: a thick gold armlet, a massive garnet brooch, a great length of silk cloth. Cloth such as had never come Emma's way before, thick and heavy as she unfolded it and let it run through her hands. It glistened with a soft sheen, ivory-coloured and with a cream pattern of lily-flowers woven into the texture of the fabric. She have never before seen anything so rare and beautiful; so wonderful, so lustrous.

She dismissed the messenger and paced the length of the hall holding the fabric bunched beneath her breasts, pushing its thick folds forward with her feet, the ends trailing behind her. The fabric was rich, and it whispered, and she turned, swinging the cloth around, and paced back again, to where her mother was coming in the door, stopping startled at the sight of her. 'My God, Emma,' she said, 'I thought you were an angel, robed in that,' and Emma laughed, and said, 'Should I marry the man who sent it to me, even though he was my husband's enemy?' and her mother said, 'Did you love your late husband?' and she said, no, he was a cruel man, he treated me ill, and her mother said, *What loyalty do you owe him then?*

Emma hesitated then said, I bore his children, and her mother said, your sons are safely fostered with the Archbishop of Rouen, what reason is there for their existence to hold you back? and Emma held up the rich fabric like wings and said, Indeed, Mother, I could be queen of England again. It would be ill not to take advantage of such an opportunity, would it not, Mother? If the good Lord has guided Canute to make such an offer, should I not accept it?

Her mother reached up to take her hands then; her mother clasped her hands over hers so they formed a vee of prayer, and she said softly: Emma, think how discontented you have been in your brother's court, how unhappy you have been here these past months. I always knew you were destined to live your life a queen, I felt it when I was pregnant and bore you in my belly and laid my hands across the top of you. I knew my child was destined for great things. If Canute indeed wants you…

'How do you know the fabric comes from him?'

'Do you think he would approach you without first speaking to your brother?'

'So I'm a pawn in a game of politics again?'

'No. No, how can you think that?'

Emma, longingly: 'The messenger said he'd heard of my great beauty.'

'My love, news of it is widespread. Your love for your children – that has softened you. Canute – he is now undisputed king of the entirety of England…'

'He is just a boy.'

'A boy with a great future, which you can help him build. He trusts in you to assist him. In your maturity, your experience as Queen of England, in the alliances you have forged.'

'I've heard he already has an English wife.'

'She's of no account,' her mother snorted. 'Forget about her. A simple Northumbrian girl whom he married only after the Danish fashion of taking hands. She is only his concubine. He will have no more to do with her once he is married to you.'

'Will her children have the right to succeed Canute?'

'That can be negotiated in your favour in the marriage settlement. He certainly won't want your sons by Ethelred to succeed him. You will be starting a new dynasty. Emma, queen of England – what more could you achieve in life than to be once again queen of such an affluent realm?'

Emma laughed out loud, she swirled the rich fabric around herself. She had the messenger summoned back to her. 'Give your master the answer, yes,' she said.

'Yes, mistress,' he said, and bowed, and left.

Emma stepped out of the silken pleats and left them crumpled on the floor for her servant Elisabeth to fold neatly. She reflected that she was thirty-three years old now. Middle-aged. Life proceeds at a pace; it never stands still. Her sons by Ethelred could have no power because their father was dead and Canute had usurped his throne. I must breed a new batch of children if my inheritance – my family line, my values, the things I care about – are to live on, Emma thought. I must move on, I must adapt to this changing world.

'Emma,' her mother said. She did not touch her; it was not their way. She made a nervous gesture as if to brush the hair back from her forehead, though it was, as always, neatly confined by her scarf. 'Emma, can you take this step? Do we expect too much of you? It is only just over a year ago that your husband died. All his reign he was at war with Canute or his father. How difficult this must be for you. This transition.'

'I hated Ethelred,' Emma confessed, for the first time ever. 'Marrying his enemy will make all things right.'

27. Emma, England, 1017

Emma wondered if the sailor had dropped her in the sea on purpose. That great brawny lout with his uncombed crest of thick ginger hair sticking out from his head at right angles, his vast unkempt beard with seaweed and glittering scraps of oyster shell caught up in it. 'Do you use it for catching fish?' she'd asked him. 'It stinks as if you do.' His personal body odour was no better; she'd had the chance to savour it in full when he had rammed her face under his armpit as he carried her from the boat through the waves to the shore. She'd fought herself free and yapped, 'Don't think I'm going to give you a tip,' and then the fool had dropped her in the drink. Not too deep, fortunately – when she sat on the sandy sea floor blinking salt out of her eyelashes her head was well above the surface – and she had the satisfaction of hearing the captain berate the fool; and after that delay, he had helped her up. The sea was cold, falling in it was a great shock, but she was comforted by the thought that in the six iron-bound chests she had with her she had dry clothes to change into.

But one chest was missing; the chest that held her shoes. 'Where is my chestful of shoes?' she roared; but no one knew. 'I'll wager you left them behind in Normandy on purpose,' she shouted at the sailor who had carried her ashore. 'Cut off his right hand at once, captain.' But the captain said that the man was a useful member of his crew and refused.

So she had just the one pair of shoes with her. Beautiful Norman shoes that were made of soft leather that was now wrecked, salt-marked and sodden, tearing where the nails held it into the wooden soles. Tearing more at each footstep as she minced up the sandy beach and along the path at the beach edge toward her horse that was held ready for her to mount. 'I can't meet Canute for the first time wearing these disgusting things,' she complained. 'The very thought is obscene.'

A messenger was sent ahead, a shoemaker was summoned to meet her in Canterbury. He came to her the next day in the late morning, in a private chamber off the Archbishop's great hall, where she had rested the night. He brought samples of soft leather dyed red, black and green, cut garnets that glowed with a purplish light, gold orfrey fringing, ribbons of yellow silk. 'I've brought oak too,' he said, kneeling at her feet with his wares spread out about him. 'Perhaps your majesty might appreciate platform soles to augment your height a little?'

He was an older man, thirty-five or even forty perhaps, of slender build but square-shouldered, very clean, hands gentle as they wrapped leathers around her cold feet. 'Like this,' he suggested, his voice warm and intent. 'So – orfrey trimming the top, garnets twinkling on the toes, a great bow of silk on each foot – four-inch platforms to keep your feet out of the mud, perhaps...'

How lovely his voice was, how gentle his hands. How satisfying to have him kneeling at her feet. Serving her. In general, Emma was not keen on men (nor women either, come to that). Clerics she liked – good holy men – but none so far had given her that warmth in her chest and groin that this man had, that feeling of physical desire. Except maybe the abbot Elfsige... If I were not a queen, she thought. If I were perhaps some common person... like perhaps King Canute's reputed concubine. One could imagine a harlot like her, a common strumpet, consenting to have this lovely shoemaker suck her toes and run soft hands up her shins, caress her knees, let his hands run on up beneath her skirt... She groaned with the imagined pleasure of it.

'Did I cause you some discomfort, madam?' said the shoemaker.

'No. No indeed. Perhaps just three garnets on the toe. To have more might seem vulgar. But the silk bows – let them be extravagant.'

'I'll trail the ends over the platforms, so, to soften the transition from the uppers,' suggested the shoemaker.

'They must be ready by tomorrow morning.'

'Madam, I will not sleep till they are done.' He gathered up his wares, and out he went, backwards, bowing.

28. Elfgifu, England, late July 1017

Elfgifu's head rested in the crook of Canute's outstretched arm. Her left arm was around his naked body, his around hers. Their ankles were tangled together. They fitted together snug as pieces of a puzzle; as right as a sword in its scabbard, as an oar in its rowlock. It felt like absolute rightness. I will never move, she thought. We will exist like this for ever. He breathed softly in his sleep. She watched the bar of sunlight that fell between the shutters angle across the sheet until it reached his cheek. She put up her hand to shield him. Let today never come, she was thinking, let us be together for always.

She was thinking that she should shake him and say, Canute, you must get up, they will be waiting for you. But she didn't. She couldn't bear for him to go. She held him tighter.

A knock at the door. She didn't answer. The latch lifted and in came Finn. 'Sssh,' she whispered. 'Don't wake him.'

'Sir,' said Finn loudly, 'the congregation are gathering in the cathedral.'

And maybe Canute had been awake all this time, because he stretched and rolled away from his wife. His Germanic-law wife. Not by the law of the church. His concubine, churchmen might say. Whom he had married only by the taking of hands, the giving of bride-gifts. He stood by their bed. He was so tall, he was like a star or a planet.

He stooped to kiss her breasts. 'You must go,' he said.

She clutched his leg. 'I'll never leave you. Canute, I'll love you always, I'll never leave you.'

'I have to do this, you understand that, don't you? For the peace of the kingdom. I don't want to. What must be, must be. Kings don't have the choice.'

Finn held a bowl of water for him. He unpicked his wife's fingers and stepped away, washed his face, under his arms, between his legs. He dried himself on a towel. Finn gave him his shirt and he put it on, fastened the ties. Finn held out his breeches. 'For God's sake, man, I know how to dress myself! Go!' Canute snapped.

When the two of them were alone again he crossed to the window and opened the shutters. Light flooded in; he was a dark column against it, his edges swallowed by the brightness. She rubbed her eyes with the palms of her hands.

'Elfie,' he said, 'today... it will change nothing, you know. It will seem to change things, but it won't. Do not fret. I will always love you. This... today... it is only a ceremony, this formality in the cathedral, a show, a masquerade. A political act. It means nothing.'

Elfgifu lunged out at his leg and grasped it with both arms. 'Don't go,' she said. 'I can't bear it if you marry her.' She pulled him closer. 'I'll never leave you,' she said.

163

He tickled her until at last she couldn't help giggling and released him. 'Elf,' he said. 'Don't come today, will you. It will only hurt you. I will seem to make promises to another woman, but they will not be true.'

'You don't have to do this. We can run away, we can take ship, we can go to Denmark...'

'I've been elected King of England now. That gives me responsibilities.'

'You don't need to lecture me.'

'Then try to understand...'

Sadly, she did. She knew the way of the world. And, later, when he had gone, she got up and rang for Margaret, and had her bring her old clothes, peasant clothes, and she shawled her hair and went out in the street. Out in the press of people. They were all drinking and shouting, laughing and listening to minstrels singing Canute's and Emma's praises, they were gaming and eating, playing football and fondling and farting, as crowds everywhere are wont to do when they escape the drudgery of everyday.

No one recognised Elfgifu. The doors of the cathedral stood wide open and she squeezed inside and shoved her way to the front of those standing at the back. From there she could see across the top of the well-coiffed and richly hatted heads of the nobility of England, to where Canute sat elevated on a dais on a throne beside Emma-Elfgifu, who was soon to be anointed Queen of England for a second time. The two of them did not look real. They looked like statues. They sat very still.

Emma was like an angel in a robe of ivory silk that was obviously thick because it was pleated so full under her breasts that it looked as if she might be pregnant. Her sleeves swelled huge as budding wings, and the hem of her skirt flowed beyond her feet. She wore scarlet shoes.

One of them had come off and lay at the foot of the dais and Elfgifu could see it was thick-soled like the clogs they wore in wet weather to keep their feet out of the mud, but in this case it had to be to make her seem taller so that the height difference between her and Canute was not so great. The ceremony had already begun; the archbishop was blessing the oil, he was anointing the queen and the king.

Canute was utterly serious. With no animation in his face, he looked plain; almost as if he were suffering. He made the pledges he had to: to Emma, to his kingdom of England. He undertook to care for them both. To fulfil his duty to protect the Church and promote Christianity.

I know he means it, Elfgifu thought. I have known him long enough to be certain when he speaks the truth. Her heart sank. Whatever he says, this will change things. I am losing him for ever, she thought. He may not intend it, but that is how it will be.

Dread brought sick up in her mouth. She bowed her head, buried her face in her arms.

29. Emma, England, after marrying Canute 1017

Emma lay in bed. Her feather mattress cosseted her, a linen sheet lay light across her bare body. A shaft of sunlight sliced between the shutters. She yawned, stretched, felt replete.

She had assumed that one husband would be pretty much the same as another. When she had agreed to marry Canute it had been because she wanted to be Queen of England again – she loved the power and the riches, she loved that men kowtowed to her – whereas with her family in Normandy her living quarters had been cramped, her personal staff limited to two, and she had not even had the authority to order up the food she liked to eat. Peaches brought by boat from Spain, dripping sticky sweet juice down her chin; grapes and fine wine from Italy, had been no part of her diet in Normandy; only tart apples from the orchards in the autumn, that grew soft and wrinkled in storage over winter. She reached for the goblet beside her bed, but it was empty, the dregs having evaporated in the summer heat.

Canute had gone. She was sorry. He was young – twenty-two she'd been told. His body slender, moving lightly on top of her: but strong – she felt the muscles in his thighs, his arms and back. Alive with suppressed energy. She herself was soft and plump: her strength was in the rigour of her mind, she believed.

Canute was good to be with. He was well-educated; or at least he knew how to read and write. His knowledge of the Roman poets was sketchy. He was a second-generation Christian – his father had been baptised – he didn't follow heathen ways, but his understanding of the True Faith was vague. Obviously that was something she would have to take in hand. Meanwhile he had delegated to her all royal responsibility for dealing with the Church. 'They are the great landowners of the country,' he said. 'As such, I need to extract a fair amount of tax from them. You are used to consorting with them, you understand them. You will know how to achieve that and yet keep their goodwill.' She swelled with pride at his confidence and trust in her. Ethelred had had no respect for women at all.

There was only one thing that made her uncomfortable in her marriage. One wrinkle, one furrow that she had to smooth out.

She first became aware of it a fortnight after they were wed. He had to travel to Northampton on business. (They settled in Winchester, the city with two minsters; he was having a palace built there.)

When he came back to her he had a love bite on his shoulder. 'Oh, that,' he said, as if it were a thing of no importance. 'That's just a bruise. I walked into a door.'

She knew he had been married before he met her. Well, not married: he had a concubine, which was a marriage under the old Germanic laws, though not in the sight of the Church. Elfgifu, the woman's name was: that awful English name by which Ethelred's first wife had been called, by which Ethelred when he married her had had her baptised, being too lazy, too slovenly to bother to learn her true original baptismal Christian French name. Emma had met this concubine Elfgifu once or twice in the past – she was the daughter of a member of Ethelred's council who had turned out to be a vile traitor. Elfgifu had, too, while still a child, taught Emma to speak English in a basic sort of way. Elfgifu was taller than her, thinner, pretty enough in a wan blonde sort of way; she had a pent-up energy about her which was most unladylike, and during Ethelred's rule she had often consorted with the princes, Ethelred's sons by his late wife, and was accustomed to go riding and hawking with them, hoyden-like. Until the rumour surfaced about her father, of course. That he was a traitor to the king. Emma had insisted the rumour was true, she had encouraged Ethelred to have him murdered. That put a stop to Elfgifu's friendship with the princes, as it should. Then the girl had disappeared from court.

Now to reappear in association with Emma's new husband. Or so the gossip went. Occasionally, there were long blonde hairs – ash blonde, not golden blonde like hers (mouse-colour, her brother had once called her hair; she'd kicked him hard) – ash-blonde hairs on Canute's shirt. One wrapped about the pin that fastened his cloak, as if that woman had laid her head against his chest; one caught up in the golden torc that he wore. Emma said nothing to Canute about them, for she was certain those hairs weren't there by chance. That woman was out to create trouble, to ferment a dispute between her and Canute, to disrupt the harmony of the royal marriage. And Emma was determined that her marriage would be a success. She carved her husband slices from the breast of a roast swan, she made sure that his unleavened bread was fresh and hot.

She contacted Elfsige, Abbot of Peterborough, again, went to visit the scriptorium, saw the beautiful work that was being done by the monks. She ordered a St John's Gospel from them. The finest parchment, skin of young goats. Illustrated in gold, scarlet and blue. Garnets on the leather binding. It was hideously expensive, of course. But Canute was pleased about what she had found out about the Church's wealth, he didn't complain about her outlay.

Then Emma discovered that the woman Elfgifu had given birth to a second son. The first one had been named Sweyn, the same name as Canute's father; the second she had the cheek to have baptised Harald, the same name as Canute's grandfather. Those were the names that one would expect the legitimate heirs to Canute's two kingdoms of England and Denmark to bear: but one could not legislate as to what anyone might call their child. Their names alone did not make them true heirs. Their fathers could be anyone.

She longed to get pregnant herself, to have a son to establish a dynasty of which she would be the matriarch, the power behind the throne, the mother-figure. Those three children she'd borne to Ethelred whom she hated, they didn't count. She did not care for them at all. Let them grow up with her brother in Normandy, let them forge what future they could for themselves. They were not her responsibility. She'd cut them off. Their father dead, they were orphans, in effect. Her concern was only with her own future: in maintaining her authority and dignity as queen.

For which she needed a son. She kept welcoming Canute to her bed. How young he was, how strong. How lithe and lissom. He smelt so good.

Her little son came within a year. Harthacnut, his father named him, rocking him in his arms, and calming him, obviously more experienced at how to hold a baby than Emma was herself. In a sudden rush of jealousy, she said, 'Let's call him Sweyn, after your father, as is right for your true heir;' and Canute looked at her strangely, and said he already had a son by that name, and Emma said, Oh, Elfgifu's son, it's said his father was a shoemaker, the same man who makes my shoes; and Canute looked so sour that she amended it: well, maybe not a shoemaker, maybe his father was a priest, she said; and Canute looked at her straight then, and said simply, Sweyn is my true son.

There was nothing more that Emma could do. Harthacnut: a wise child. A strong baby. He liked to sit and watch with his blue eyes what was going on. She liked to have him with her, when she went on long journeys had his nurse accompany her, carrying him before her on her saddle. He had a Danish wet-nurse, appointed by Canute.

30. Elfgifu, England, late August 1020

Canute and Elfgifu were walking in the familiar beech woods, hip to hip and arms entwined, between the high trees whose leaves were an airy dapple against the blue of the sky, the ground beneath them a shuffle of last autumn's fallen leaves and soft mounds of moss. The two boys ran on ahead and it was good for once to feel like a family, all belonging together: father, mother and children.

'They've grown, haven't they, since you were last here?' She pulled him closer to her.

'So much, Elfie, I can't believe it. Elfie...'

They dragged behind and kissed deeply while the boys raced down into a valley where a tree had fallen like a bridge across a stinking, reddish bog. Sweyn stepped up on to the trunk and his mother broke away, instantly aware of the danger. 'No, not there,' she shouted, 'don't you dare. You'll fall in and get filthy. That tree up the top's much better for climbing on. You show your father.' Sweyn hesitated, then decided to do as he was told, jumped down and tore up the hill with Harald toddling after him.

'They're fine boys,' said Canute.

'Your sons,' Elfgifu said. They had a look of him, tall and thin, with his blond hair, blue eyes. Sweyn was the fairer; his hair was almost ash. Harald had his father's energy, his need to be on the move all the time. Sweyn was slower, more circumspect; more like his mother.

'Queen Emma...'

Her heart sank at the mention of that woman's name. 'Yes?'

'No matter.' Running his fingers through his hair, combing it back from his forehead, the way he did when he was worried.

'What is it?'

'You know I have a son by her?'

'Yes.'

'Harthacnut.'

He had called Sweyn by his father's name, Harald by his grandfather's. They were his firstborn sons.

'Harthacnut is like his mother. Small and plump. He cries a lot.'

Babies do. Canute had rarely been around when their boys were small. Whenever he came to visit, Elfgifu made sure that their wet-nurse Margaret cared for them that night. His visits were so precious she couldn't bear to share him.

The boys had reached the top tree now. This one, torn out of the ground by a gale last spring, lay flat, its roots rearing up in a tangle of earth, its long branches still green and leafy. Sweyn clambered along a branch, steadying himself on another branch until he reached the leaves, and there he started to caw in fair imitation of a crow. Harald pulled himself up to the mass of roots and poked at the dry earth around them with a stick.

'What are you doing?' Canute asked his little son.

'Find treasure,' the boy said, and laid a split stone in his father's open palm.

Canute smiled over at his wife. 'Oh, Elfie,' he said, 'I've sailed hundreds of miles in search of riches, but all I needed to do was stay here with you.'

She laughed. 'You'd never be content staying in one place.'

'You have a place in my heart that no one else can occupy.'

'I'm sure you say that to all your wives.'

'There's only Queen Emma, besides you.' And he frowned. 'Elfie...'

Harald started to cry; he had hit himself in the eye with his stick. His father swung him down from the tree trunk, told him there was dirt in his eye and he must blink to get it out. 'Keep blinking until you see clear, my boy.' Harald did as he was told. Dirt pooled under his left eye and Canute wiped it clean with his thumb.

'I never thought to see you so gentle with them.'

'I have been thinking how to keep you safe, you and the boys.'

'What are you worried about? All my retainers are loyal, I'm sure. We live quietly here.'

'You need to take care.'

'Care of what, my dear?'

'I fear for your safety here in England. There are people who are jealous of my love for you. Who claim you are not my legitimate wife. They would do you harm if the chance arose. Sweetheart, I've decided you must go to Denmark. My brother Harald was king there, but he caught a fever and died, and now dominion over Denmark falls to me. You will be safe there, in the East, in the land of the Wends, you can live happily there, you and the boys.'

'I don't want to leave you, Canute. Don't make me go.'

'It will be for the best, beloved. I want you to govern the land on my behalf.'

'No.'

'Oh, you will enjoy it. And the boys will love the journey! I will command my housecarls to escort you to Dunwich, and have the *Dragon* meet you there. She's a fine vessel, she will carry you safely across the sea.'

'But you – you and me – I cannot bear for us to be apart. The ocean between us. I cannot live like that.'

'I will come to you there, in Denmark. Do not think for a moment that I will ever forget you.'

'Canute, no, do not send me away. No, Canute, no. I love you, I need to be with you always. I cannot live without you.' But she knew even as she spoke that she had no choice, ultimately, but to do as her liege lord wished.

31. Emma, woods near Ticehurst, 1020

Woodland in late October sunlight. The low sun slanted into Canute's and Emma's eyes as they rode on alone. Fallen leaves obscured the track. Canute pulled on his reins and Serpent, his stallion, slowed. 'I don't know where we are,' he called back. 'Do you recognise this place?'

'No.' The trees pressed round them, their tall trunks hid the way. Emma was weary, frightened that wolves might emerge at twilight to follow them between the beeches. 'It was a mistake to ride out without an escort,' she said.

'Dammit, it's only a couple of miles,' said Canute. 'No risk at all. We need to head south-west, toward the setting sun, I reckon.'

'I'd rather ride to higher ground, from where we might enjoy a view.'

'Very well, we'll do as you see fit. This is your country, not mine – better to go by your instinct. I'll always be a stranger to England. I'll never feel at home here.'

'Nor me,' said Emma. 'We are both exiles from our native lands. We have that in common.'

'Indeed.'

The quiet forest. The thud of the horses' hooves in the soft earth, the jingle of the harness. Rattle of a blackbird in the leaves, the scamper of a pair of squirrels. A figure came toward them through the trees, hooded in rough wool. Emma reined in Constance, called out, 'Tell me, fellow, what's the way to Ticehurst?'

The figure stopped and stared at her: a skinny old man with a long wisp of white beard. He turned his head away and spat on the ground.

'It's your queen talking to you,' said Canute sharply.

'She may call herself that,' said the old fellow. 'But she'll never be my queen. She's a Norman and a Dane. The king's a Dane too. They've neither any right to be here in our fair kingdom of England. They're foreigners, both of them, they'll never be natives here, however much they pretend.'

'You deserve to have your hands cut off for your rudeness, peasant,' said Emma.

'A brave thing to do to an old fellow,' sneered the old man.

'Leave him be,' said Canute. 'He can do us no harm. Come on. This is fine woodland we are riding in; excellent hunting country, I'll be bound. I'm by no means inclined to give it away.'

'You said you would grant it to Archbishop Aelfstan of Canterbury,' Emma pointed out, catching up with him. 'You can't change your mind now, he's expecting it.'

'Oh Lord, these old churchmen, why do I have to keep them sweet?'

'They are the root of wealth and power in the land,' said Emma. 'Consider Archbishop Wulfstan of York – he used to preach so fiercely against the Vikings, and yet by your gifts – by the respect you've shown to his ability and position – you've turned him into a gentle lamb. Now he's one of your key administrators.'

'The only reason I sought to rule England was in order to own its riches. The richest kingdom in Europe by far, the most peaceful...'

'Peaceful because of its law codes,' said Emma. 'Archbishop Wulfstan understands all that. You need him to help you.'

'I'll take your word for it. You know how this blessed kingdom works better than me.'

Emma reached out to touch his hand. One of the things that constantly surprised her about Canute was the way he respected her advice on matters of state, and would take guidance from her. It was a relic of his good childhood relationship with his mother, King Boleslav's sister, she thought. Though his father had banished his mother from Denmark, Canute and his brother Harald had since brought her back. He was fond of his sister too; his family was important to him. And although he was so young he took his responsibilities to his new kingdom seriously. 'Remember what you promised at your coronation, Canute,' she said. 'You swore to maintain peace, good order and the rule of law.'

'I'm not one to break my oaths,' said Canute. 'I'll do my best.'

'Your proposal to allow everyone the freedom to petition the king - that's very popular.'

'I do want fairness and justice in this land. Oh, listen - I can hear voices ahead. We must be near a lane.'

A lane set deep within hedges and trampled by heavy mill-oxen. Muddy; their horses' hooves slid in the mud. But there ahead of them nestled the village of Ticehurst, where they were to rest the night.

32. Elfgifu, Denmark, 1021

Elfgifu stepped beside Canute on the sandy path between the stunted pines. The air was still and filled with the heat of the sun, the scent of pine needles. Their feet crunched the shed pinecones and the crisp grey lichens and mosses. He was tall beside her, and strong and carefree, glad to be back here where he'd often sailed as a child, steering his sailboat alone across the sea, escaping the royal court where his dark-haired Slav mother ruled from her great carved throne, silver earrings from Russia threading the dark mass of her hair, gold bracelets twisting round her white wrists, serpentine brooches from Ireland fastening the rustling Chinese silks of her dress. All her emphasis had been on protocol and rules, and he had loved to escape that formality. Hence his coming here. He was already an explorer, even then; already he had loved to be alone and stride soft-footed and certain. Not afraid.

That is how I want to be. Self-assured, certain of myself, was what Elgifu thought.

He led the way across the island to the opposite shore, to a shack where perhaps a fisherman and his family used to live, the timber of it sunbleached and patterned with lichen. He leaned, arms crossed, against the outer wall and she sat cross-legged on the sand at his feet. She stretched back to caress his ankles.

'Are you happy?' he said.

'Happy,' she confirmed.

They listened to the conversation of the blue sea with the rocks that lined the shore – all that repetition of shush and hush and suck and undertow. They watched blue wagtails hop from one rock to another and butterflies flutter over the spent sea campions and suck at a thistle. He slipped his arms under her armpits and hauled her up and turned her round, he kissed her deep and wondrously, and they made a bed of their clothes and lay on the crunchy lichen together. She cried out with pleasure, and he laughed, and later he fell asleep, cushioning her in his arms. She lay there a long time breathing him, and listening to his breath and the slight breeze in the pines and the crack of the lichen each time he shifted. His belly rumbled and the waves lapped and the sea-birds called.

At last she detached herself. The night was cool now and she shivered and walked down to the sea and squatted on a rock to scoop up handfuls and wash herself. As she turned to go up to him again she noticed a piece of driftwood among the debris at the high water mark. It was bleached and white, the grain weathered clean by the sea, every line and curve of it. A steering oar, she realised even in the half-light that it was, and she knew that some boat had foundered and its crew drowned. 'Canute,' she whispered, standing over him. 'Take care, my love. May the good Lord watch over you always.' She pulled on her clothes and he woke in the midsummer twilight, above the horizon the full moon rising fat and gold, he took her hand and pointed out the map of it, the mountains and lakes and eyes of it, and he said, we must all travel to new places, constantly. Every day is a new journey. Think of me as you travel.

She said, will you not stay with me?

He said, I have other responsibilities.

She could not bear to think of his going back to Emma. Lying in her arms. She would not give him any pleasure. 'I could kill her,' she said.

'No,' he said. She knew he understood what she meant. 'She is useful to me.'

They sat on the beach a long time together with their hands around their knees, watching the stars and listening to the soft breaking of the waves on the rocks, and she shivered with the chill of the night and he put his arm around her and it seemed that fullness, that completeness would go on for ever, and then he spoke in a quiet voice about the raids that the Norwegians were making on Denmark now that his brother Harald had died, and how he had to put someone strong in place to defend it, and it would be his brother-in-law Earl Ulf Sprakalegsson, but it would not affect Elfie and the boys in the East of Denmark, they would be fine there. And his mind wandered away from her, and he said that he was going to ask Ulf to foster Harthacnut, his son by Emma, because he wanted to get him away from his mother, he wanted a son who was a warrior, not an archbishop.

There was quiet a long time and then Elfie said, our sons, your and my sons, and then didn't say anything else, and he said, I love them. I love the way you are bringing them up to love what I love. And he said: you and they must go and live in the Wendish regions, to the east of Denmark. I don't want there to be conflict between you and Queen Emma. You can be regent on behalf of Sweyn until he is old enough to rule on his own. I trust you to do what is right, beloved. You have so much experience of governing land in England, you will know what to do.

And the two of them made love again and then they went back to the boat and Canute rowed them back to the mainland, and when they reached it the sun was well up, morning had come.

33. Emma, England, making plans for her son in early May 1022

A warm day in early May. A day so lovely, so new green and full of promise that Emma let Canute persuade her to walk with him and their children in the beech forest close by the palace. How bright they all were in their silks, like butterflies on the earth path, the pale trunks of the tall trees towering over them, the new leaves catching the sun, making a gold-green tent that shimmered like the rarest of fabrics. 'The tree trunks remind me of the stone pillars that are reputed to still stand in the ancient city of Rome,' Emma said, smiling beatifically. 'I have read how their beauty surpasses everything else that has ever been built.'

Boo went the children. They were playing hide and seek. Harthacnut was five, Gunnhild three. They chased over the dead leaves, wove in and out of the trees. In clearings bracken was springing up and unfurling; cow parsley floated its white froth of flowers. Birds sang in the branches.

'She's not playing properly.' Harthacnut came back to his father, complaining. 'She's not keeping to the rules. She was looking when she should have been hiding her eyes.'

'She's only little, she doesn't know any better,' said Canute. 'Be patient with her.'

'I'm not playing with her any more,' went Harthacnut, and, finding a straight stick, he hefted it up on his shoulder and threw it like a spear, ran forward to retrieve it and threw it again.

'She's not that little,' said Emma. 'She's nearly four now. We ought to begin looking for a husband for her.'

'Don't be ridiculous,' said Canute. 'There's plenty of time for that.' Fondly he watched his daughter, arms outstretched, balancing on the mossy root of a massive beech.

'By no means,' Emma declared. 'I have been thinking...'

From far off came the shouting of older children racing punts on the river across the valley. There came a scream. 'Someone's fallen in,' said Canute. 'I remember what fun that was, when I was a child.'

'What you must appreciate,' Emma lectured, 'is that because of your eminent rank Gunnhild's choice of a suitable husband will be limited. Only someone like little Henry, who is heir to the empire of the Holy Roman Emperor, would be suitable for her.'

'Little is the right word. He can't be any older than her. Fine to leave it for a while and see how he matures. I wouldn't let her marry a wife-beater.'

Emma snapped off a twig and tore the new leaves into shreds. She was thinking of her first marriage, to King Ethelred; how cruel he was; how much she hated him. The thought of him made her scowl – it was rare now for her to remember his existence; she had put that time almost totally behind her. And yet, she acknowledged, the experience had given her the strength and determination to become a powerful queen of England. You could choose how episodes in your life affected you, she believed. You could go under, or you could gain power. She tucked her hand in the crook of Canute's elbow and drew him towards her. 'There'd be no harm in sowing the seeds of the marriage in Henry's mind,' she said. 'You must travel to Rome and speak to his father. You, my dear, need to be conscious of your status. Now your brother Harald of Denmark has died, you are king of two nations. How many kings can claim that?'

'Maybe king of three, soon,' said Canute. 'I've a mind to rule Norway. The Norwegians are nothing but trouble at the moment. They keep on attacking Denmark without warning.'

'Of course,' said Emma, 'if Gunnhild is betrothed to the Emperor's son, it is only right that Harthacnut should have some privileges. Could he not be King of Denmark? Take that weight from off your shoulders?'

'I've been thinking of sending him to be fostered by Ulf. My brother-in-law; my sister's husband, their son is the same age, the cousins would make good companions for each other. Better for him than playing just with Gunnhild all the time. He needs to play with other boys, to learn how to be a warrior. Ulf is a good man and a wise regent, he will teach Harthacnut a great deal about ruling a nation. More than he'll learn as a pretty altar-boy. I didn't like to see him parading around in the church last Sunday. You should have requested my permission.'

Emma looked sideways at her husband. She had been living in dread of when it might come up, the Viking custom of sending sons away to be fostered. She had hoped to avoid it by having Harthacnut educated by bishops and monks; but book-learning bore no weight with Canute – what mattered to him were martial skills and physical strength, and wisdom in ruling. Harthacnut, king of Denmark; she could see that would be what men would call her little son soon. And she would be both queen and queen mother. She smiled with self-satisfaction.

34. Emma, England, 1022

And now farewell. Emma stooped to fold her son in her arms, she felt his bird-bones, the softness of his hair, the sweet scent of him. But he pushed back against her, rejecting her embrace. His age; his six years. Was this to be all she had of him? 'Ah, sweetheart.'

How independent he was growing. Wanting her neither physically nor emotionally. His bright intelligence burgeoning, his blue eyes already sharp to read a charter or to spot a songbird in the forest. His hands grown supple and adept at holding a pen, copying in black ink on to fine parchment, his letters not yet fully formed, his wrists flexible to wield a sword; fitting himself for the world of men. How reserved he was with her; he would never hug her as he did his nurse.

'My little one... my hope, how much you are my hope...' She was sobbing theatrically. She'd pitched all her hope for her future on this child. All her expectation as to what she was to leave behind her in this world. Her hopes for the future of the nation she had adopted as her own, to keep it great and make it greater. Her hope for – not eternal life, she didn't worry about that, she was confident that her religious observance would secure her a place in Heaven – but *living on* – she believed that after her death she would live on in her son – he would keep the memory of her alive, he would make her kingdom ever greater and keep it prosperous and at peace, all those terrible years of Ethelred's wars forever over – in a peaceful kingdom people would have enough to eat, they could plan, they could farm and build, never mind the prestige and drama of fighting, those would be things of the past. With peace, you could build a rich, cultured and glorious kingdom.

'May Christ go with you always.' Let Harthacnut never be a heathen, let him discard his heathen heritage, his Viking heritage that held that the only way to secure heaven in Valhalla was to die in battle – she felt that that legacy could be pushing from inside the boy's pale soft skin like the mythical crocodile, a monster that cracked through its translucent shell, and it scared her.

'Be a true son to me.' Believe in what I believe in – and yet, she thought, may you have that heathen love of treasure, because power and riches go together and I want you to have both, so that I can have a share of them too. Travel, that's important, trade – sail in the finest dragon-ship with a figurehead of gold that cuts the deep waves and rises above them to flash in the bright sun, and dips again – oh, bring me fine gifts when you're older, go to Greece and commission a gold cross of the finest manufacture, set with rubies. Together we will build up treasure in the treasure-chamber in Winchester. This will be the richest kingdom in the world so suitors will come from many lands to court your sister, offer her bride-gifts sumptuous and rare – and when she is married, and you are king, they will respect me for the queen-mother I am, though I will be old. I will not be discarded, I will still have power, people will kneel before me, seeking favours – they will respect me as a saint...

Go then if you must, my Harthacnut. Turn your back on me, but never forget me. Respect my wisdom, be ready to do my bidding. Because I am strong. 'Here, take this basket. There are sweetmeats for your journey. Slices of dried apple. Honeycomb. Hazelnuts.' Emma rubbed her eyes, turned and walked back into the palace. Never once did how she had said farewell to her sons by Ethelred come to mind. Her indifference to them.

Harthacnut's old nurse stayed with the boy. She buckled on his little sword, fastened on his cloak, helped him mount his pony that a groom held by the door. 'Whisper will go with you all the way,' the old nurse said. 'There's space for her on the boat. Your father commanded it. You'll have a good time with Ulf"s son, your cousin. He's the same age as you. You'll live by the seaside, you can swim, and sail between the islands. The winters are snowy – you can toboggan and go skating. It's the kind of childhood your father had, he wants to share it with you. Ah, here's your father. He said he'd ride with you, he didn't want you to be afeard.'

Canute on his great charger; Harthacnut little on his pony. 'Come on, my boy! Let's set forth on this adventure together!'

Inside the palace, Emma had turned her jewel-box upside down on the table within her chamber, spread her treasures across the bare wood surface; she was fingering through the heap of glitter. 'Here's my St Christopher,' she said, picking it out. 'I'll hang it above my pillow so that it may protect my son on his travels.'

35. Canute, Winchester and London, 1023

Outside the main doorway to the palace in Winchester, Canute's house-carls in their chainmail were gathered on restless horses that nickered and stamped in anticipation of their journey. Bridles and bits jingled, stirrups rattled as men brought their horses under control. Canute took his stallion's reins from his groom and swung himself high up into the saddle. How good it was to be outdoors, and among fighting men, where he belonged. When he was confined with Emma or in council-meetings his back and joints were laggardly and slow, they ached at their confinement so he wondered if he was becoming arthritic as an old man; but once on horseback he felt alive and free. He pulled on the rein to steer his stallion toward the gate, then with a touch of his spurs sped off along the road, the straight old Roman road to London where the boats that would carry his army to the defence of Denmark were being built.

His own dragon-ship was huge, with sixty benches of rowers. His good friend Earl Hakon's had forty benches, and the figureheads of both were gilded all over. Oh, they were bright, a dramatic sight in the sun, they promised menace and danger. Both vessels were painted above the water line, and the sails of both had stripes of blue, red and green. Such colour they would bring to the sea, such fear they would inspire!

The last time he had been to London the hulls of other great ships were being built. He loved the drama of their keels and ribs silhouetted against the dawn sky, he loved the smell of the newly-sawn timber, and the promise that it held. That magic transformation of a tree fixed in the earth by its roots into a vessel racing across the waves, conquering the sea. You could not but be excited by it. He shook the reins, he dug in his heels, and his stallion sped on, pursued by the house-carls toward the shipyard.

Soon he would lead the fleet in the defence of Denmark against the attacks of King Olaf of Norway and King Onund of Sweden. He would be properly a man again, no longer emasculated by his dominating wife and her precious clergy. He would fulfil his duty as king by restoring order to his world.

36. Elfgifu, eastern Denmark, 1027

Half way down the grassy slope below Elfgifu's hall a hedge cut across the hillside, a thick hedge of hawthorn and prickly sloe bushes interwoven with brambles and briar roses; good for fencing in cattle, for preventing them from straying. The path down to the well ran diagonally across the slope, breaking through the hedge between a tall oak and an ash tree, both arrayed in fresh spring green this lovely day. The trees leaned toward each other as if gossiping; and they cast a dappled shadow underneath the arch they made, which was like a tent, a kind of benison, a blessing on this unseasonably hot blue day; the branches carving an intricate fretwork of light and shade, such as, wrought in timber, might be used to ornament the eaves of a royal great hall; or like the cutwork embroidery on a cathedral altar cloth, or the delicate pattern on a brooch; its intricacy a gift that dappled Sweyn and Harald, there where they stood in the shadow, resting their heavy leather buckets. Elfie could almost see the tree-spirits slip from the hedge to help the well-meaning boys, taking some of the weight as the boys began again to toil up the hill, the water that slopped over the brims sparkling in the sunshine.

Pray God it will be like that when they are older, Elfie thought, that they will be given strength when they most need it. A man's life is not easy.

Nor a woman's neither. Thank God I have never had to fight in battle. She thought of the women she knew who tended the wounded and dying on the battlefield. How much do they do it through care for their brothers, she thought, how much do they do it to steal from the slain?

'Thank you,' she said to the boys; and she dipped her finished weaving into one of the buckets to rinse the natural oils out of the wool; squeezed it gently and spread the shawl she'd woven during the dark days of winter out on the grass to dry, careful to stretch the fabric to its proper shape. Women are the peace-weavers, she thought, that's what they say; and she wished on this beautiful spring day when all seemed perfect that that might be possible. But Styrr who had been a good friend of her brothers had written to warn her that he feared that Queen Emma resented Elfie's position as ruler with her son Sweyn of Jomsburg in Wendland, in the east of Denmark. 'Beware! Emma is like a she-bear defending her cubs when they have just awoken after the winter,' he had written. 'She is not to be trusted. King Canute has gone on a pilgrimage to Rome, and while he is away she may attempt to outdo you, and seize control of all Denmark for her son. Take care, and God be with you always.'

37. Emma and the royal seal, 1027

It was a mistake, of course; Canute would never have meant to leave his seal matrix on the table. It was a product of his haste, his eagerness to be off on his pilgrimage to Rome. Emma picked it up; she turned it over. She had an idea for a game she could play while Canute was away. She laughed out loud at the cleverness of it. She took Canute's seal matrix to her chamber; on her lectern she melted red sealing wax on creamy parchment. She pressed the walrus ivory matrix into the wax. It was a perfect impression.

With the royal seal, that assurance of law and of right, in her control, and Canute away, she could command anything and no-one would question it. The royal seal. The seal of power. *I can command anything, and no-one will doubt the authority of my command.* The royal seal, which Canute always kept on his own person, or locked away, was here for her to do with what she wished.

She could demand the cathedral roof tiles be plated with gold and no one would challenge her. She could order the finest embroidered silk cushion for her sole use on her wooden throne in the great hall. She could even make her young son Harthacnut King of Denmark. That would be one in the eye for Canute and his concubine. He'd always said that he wanted Denmark for his sons by Elfgifu – what a fool he was for believing they were his when everyone knew they were illegitimate, not his own sons at all! That lying, deceiving bitch Elfgifu – if Emma made Harthacnut king of Denmark that would put an end to Elfgifu's ambitions for her sons for ever. They would be the mean worms Fate had destined them to be, instead of having the glory their wicked mother had conceived for them.

Emma needed a letter. She could not write it herself, she had not the skill of a scribe. Ulf would immediately recognise that the letter had not been written for Canute. The king had his own scribe, Alwin, who worked in the cathedral scriptorium. Emma rang for Alwin to come to her at once.

'Write this,' she said. 'Address it to Earl Ulf Sprakalegsson, protector of Denmark, foster-father to

Canute's son Harthacnut. Write this: "The king commands..." Here. Start here.'

'I cannot write this,' said Alwin. 'I write only what the king orders me.'

Does he suspect me? Emma wondered; but she continued, 'The king left in great haste today. He was so eager to catch the tide that he did not have time to speak to you directly. But look, he gave me his signet, the royal seal, as assurance that I must act on his behalf. Even while he broke his fast in the great hall, among his men, he told me what he wanted to say to Ulf. His brother-in-law, his sister's husband, his dear friend. Write now: 'I, Canute, am king of both England and Denmark, but I cannot divide myself in two to fulfil my obligations to both. Denmark must of necessity have a king of its own at this terrible time when it finds itself under attack from two kings, Olaf of Norway and, as seems likely, Onund of Sweden. In former times Denmark had always a king of its own. Therefore I ask you to recommend to the people at their Parliament that they take my son Harthacnut as their king, with yourself as his protector. This I command, and hereto I set my seal.'

The letter was entrusted to a messenger. Emma went to the cathedral, she knelt in the royal pew, she bowed her head. The Virgin would understand her deception, she felt, She would condone it, as a mother. She must always have wanted what was best for Her Son. It was not Her fault if Her Son kept on insisting on the values of humility and poverty; just think what earthly riches could have been His if He had wanted them. 'Oh blessed holy Mary,' she began to pray; and then she began to giggle triumphantly, marvelling at what she had just achieved.

'Your majesty?' queried the bishop, coming in.

'Oh, nothing,' she said. 'Just I have played a good game.'

'Do you wish to confess it, madam?'

'It is of no import. Tell me, that land near Ely, have the monks received it as I willed?'

38. Elfgifu, eastern Denmark, 1027

'No,' said Elfgifu. 'No. That cannot be true.' She paced around her chamber, she tore at her hair with her fingers. 'Canute always promised – he promised it to Sweyn, his firstborn, to whom he gave his father's name – he promised him the throne of Denmark, from when he first won the throne of England for himself – Canute's father had been king of Denmark, you know – when Sweyn was but a little child Canute said, Denmark will be Sweyn's, and now you – you who purport to be a messenger, you whom I have always trusted to tell the truth, all through the years Canute and I have been apart – you come here and you tell me Canute has made Harthacnut, his firstborn by Queen Emma – you tell me he has made Harthacnut king of Denmark – and because the boy is so young Ulf will be his protector for the time being... that can't be true. I don't believe it. You must be mistaken.'

'My lady. It is no will of mine. The order came in a letter sealed with the great seal of mighty Canute himself. No one but the king may use that seal. That was how Ulf knew the order to be true. Why he obeyed its command. He recognised the writing, too, as that of Alwin, who is most often the scribe of Canute's official letters.'

'But Canute has gone to Rome. How can the order have come from him? Oh, I am sorry, so often messages are delayed by the sea or the wind, by storms, I cannot blame you – how will I break the news to Sweyn though? When it is something that has been planned for for all his life, when it's been a certainty. It will hurt me to tell him. Tell the servants I bid them give you meat and bread and ale. I must go in search of Sweyn.'

She found him in the garden, kneeling among the cabbages. A king's son in his early teens. He was collecting caterpillars from off the leaves, dropping them in a leather bucket. 'They will become white butterflies, Mother,' he said earnestly, looking up at her. 'Like angels. It is a magical transformation. Each of them will live only a few days.'

'Yes,' Elfgifu said. She loved the gentleness of her son. She ruffled his hair. She did not know how he would make the transformation from being a quiet nature-loving boy into being a commanding king, but trusted to time and his inherent nobility. Oh, how boys change as they become men. 'All will be well,' she murmured. 'Truly, all will be well.' How could it be otherwise? Don't goodness and right always conquer? She pushed aside the memory of what had befallen her brothers.

39. Canute, Rome, March 1027

Canute paused at the end of the street. Another of those damned statues was raised up there, a figure larger than life, made of the stone the Romans called marble which when it was newly sculpted was smooth and had a fine polish to it. But this one must have been outdoors much of its life, it was weathered and pitted by rain, its colours faded. A young man, a naked athlete. How strong he was, how supple. How still. The shadow of a tall poplar fell across him, the swaying of its branches in the breeze was all the activity there was.

The Romans found the marble underground, buried under the earth, in *quarries* they called them, they found it and dug the marble out of the earth and a sculptor would choose a piece and chip away at it with a hammer and chisel to make one of these amazing lifelike statues that were found all over the place in Rome, both out in the open and in the strange old villas that the rich lived in. You could imagine there were two species who lived in Rome, the flesh and blood people and the marble people. The marble people were less numerous. They were beautiful, handsome, idealised. Faded paint lingered in the crevices of their bodies. They had been created between a thousand and nine hundred years ago, so the old stories related. They dozed on in the warmth of the sun. The sun eased the aches in Canute's body; did it do the same for the statues? The nearest likeness to them that the northerner Canute was familiar with were the caskets sailors carved from walrus ivory; or ivory chessmen. The raw material for Viking carvings came from the sea; for Roman carvings from the earth. That exemplified the disparity between the two nations, the wide gulf between their cultures.

The language of Rome defeated Canute. He had to take interpreters with him wherever he went. He submitted himself to the Pope, he knelt before him, he kissed his ring that probably a thousand dirty beggars had already mouthed that day; he choked in the chapel on the scent of the incense that displaced the smoky air of the city. He didn't belong here. He longed to be home.

He attended the grand coronation of Conrad II, the new Holy Roman Emperor, drank from silver goblets in the vast painted rooms of the Emperor's palace on the Aventine Hill, spent hours in negotiations over customs and tolls; didn't forget to mention he had a lovely daughter of an age with Conrad's son, spoke of the benefits of uniting the Empire of the North of which he was ruler with Conrad's Empire of the South. Together their two children might rule the whole world.

At other times he walked the streets of Rome, often alone, escaping the courtiers. He felt comfortable with the marble people whose silence was a language he could speak, their youthfulness and energy – here was a fresco of a boy catching a prancing horse, his dog running after him, here satyrs danced, playing pipes in procession; their marble was warm to the touch in the sun, warm almost as flesh – here was continuity, time playing out over and over and over and over again.

He would run sometimes, to release his pent-up energy, in evenings tepid with the left-over heat of the day, the dark streets moonlit and rutted with horse-hooves and cartwheels, thick with the shit of horses and cattle, the odd drunkard fallen headfirst, children chasing each other or pausing to beg, the glimmer of flickering rushlights tumbling pallid through unshuttered windows, pretty girls silhouetted inside, all raven-haired; but he rarely stopped to watch them, he was too busy finding his footing in the half-boots Elfie had sewn him, she'd worked a spell into their soles as she'd stitched them she said, not royal boots but fighting boots that would serve him well in battle, that would give him energy and strength and see him safe home always, she prayed. He ran fast, his steps didn't falter, he was outrunning the politeness of each day, the restraint, shaking off the conformity of the court, his heart pounding, breath rasping, becoming himself again, the man not the king.

That was how he wished it might be. How it should have been. He was only in his early thirties. But in truth his battle-scars made him slow. That time when a churl lofted an axe up high to bring down on his head and he had thrown himself sideways but slipped on the bloody grass and rolled swiftly over out of reach – he'd severed the man's foot with his sword – it felt as if he had torn something inside the calf of his leg and his knee was still swollen and painful these years later. He still had a pronounced limp, worse at the end of the day when he was tired. He would not use a stick; he would make no concessions to the pain that he suffered. He longed to feel again that rush of energy, that thrill and excitement that came with facing danger, that coursed through his body and made him exhilaratingly alive.

But it seemed that was now in the past. He was middle-aged, a king with responsibilities, with a dignified post to fill. Emperor of the North, his wife Emma called him. The Emperor of the Holy Roman Empire had given him a silken peacock cloak as a gesture of his esteem. It was worth more than its weight in gold.

So when he was back at his lodgings he summoned his Irish slave Eithne, she of the dark hair, heaving bosom and laughter, and he had her wash him and rub his skin with perfumed oils to make him feel more supple. Then she would comb his hair and dress him in a silk tunic and voluminous silk trousers, and buckle on the jewelled scabbard of his knife whose blade was engraved with runes; and he would once more take his proper place among the dignified, the rich and effete. People would bow down before him. He would yawn.

40. Elfgifu, Denmark and Norway, 1029

The messenger had brought a letter from Canute. An official letter; it was obviously important. Elfgifu accepted it and laid it on the table. She poured ale for the

193

messenger and had bread and pickled herring brought for him. She picked up the letter again, broke the royal seal and unfolded the vellum. *To Elfie and Sweyn, my dear ones,* it began. She wouldn't read it without her son there; she had him summoned from his sword practice. She strode up and down the hall, wondering what news the letter would bear. Life had been comfortable here in Jomsborg for a fair while; she didn't want things to change.

'Ah, I'm glad you've come so quick, my dear. Here's a letter from your father to us both.' How her heart warmed to him as he came in. He was fifteen now, willowy and tall like his father. Ash-blond. He was her hope for the future, for a good England. She worried, though, that maybe she had infected him with her gentleness. How soft he was with his dogs; how he would spend hours watching birds in the estuary, or dragonflies over the pond. He could identify each bird by its song, he knew which dragonflies were the hunters. *You need to be bold and brave to achieve anything,* was often in her heart when she looked at him. Oh, such a sadness possessed her, such fear, knowing the trials that growing boys, young men must face as they emerged into adulthood, it sucked at the strings of her heart.

Canute's letter was short. Sadly, his close friend the Norwegian Earl Hakon, whom, after the defeat of King Olaf, Canute had appointed ruler of Norway, had fallen overboard when crossing the North Sea, and had drowned. 'He was a strong man whom I trusted, well-connected and popular with the Norwegians,' Canute had dictated, and Sweyn read aloud in his quiet voice. 'Now I must appoint someone else. I thought of you at once, my dear son, for though you are but young your rule over the Wendish regions to the east of Denmark, together with your mother, has been outstanding. The Norwegians will be more difficult - they are a warlike and troublesome people, converted to Christianity only in the last few years, and that by the wielding of King Olaf's blood-stained sword rather than by persuasion of the truth of Christ's message. But do not fear: I will appoint senior advisors from Denmark to help you in your task. You will be king of Norway, my son, and this I decree, that your mother will act as regent on your behalf. God bless you, my dear ones, and keep you safe.'

Sweyn blinked his pale blue eyes, his blond lashes spidering across his cheeks. 'Can I take Terror?' he asked.

'Your dog is your only concern?'

'I love him dearly.'

'Oh, my dear, when I was your age I had a dog I loved, his name was Brindle. I had him from a puppy, so soft he was, how sad I was to part from him every time the family travelled south.'

'Terror is used to always being with me.'

'You will need to tie him with a rope, so he can't fall overboard when we travel.' She bit her lip, knowing she was treating him too much like a child. How would he ever grow up if she did not treat him like an adult? 'How soon do you want to travel?'

Sweyn shrugged his shoulders. 'Tomorrow?' he suggested.

'Very well.'

They sailed to Denmark first, to meet the team of advisors that Canute had appointed to help them: a dozen sturdy older men with grey hair and greying beards, past fighting age, grown fat and solemn, well-used to drawing up and implementing Danish law. Successful, worthy men. Square-shouldered. Their sword-belts jangled as they walked into the great hall, their arms were weighed down with gold rings. Elfgifu had water and towels brought for them to wash their hands; she ordered a feast to be provided for their refreshment. But the sight of them instilled dismay into her heart; she was certain that the comfortable tenor of her quiet life was about to be disrupted. How would these successful bureaucratic men match up to the fierce lawlessness and piracy of the Norwegians?

A short trip across the sea between Denmark and Norway. But a sudden storm drove out of the west, driving rain that bit at their skin, great waves that curled over with green underbellies, a roaring wind that tore at the sail. The boat heaved up and down. Men grasped the oars, they held the boat as steady as they could. A priest, a Dane, clung tight to the bare mast and prayed loudly for their souls, his words ripped away into the air. Sweyn clung to his dog; Elfie held tight to her bench.

At dawn they came within a bay of calm water. Serenity. The local people met them, they gave them spring water to wash with, they brought them towels and dry clothes. At a meeting in the open air (blue sky now, fluffy clouds, a soft breeze and sunshine) the people assembled on the grassy area before the great hall, and agreed to take Sweyn as their king; loudly, with shouts of acclamation, they welcomed him.

Sweyn made a successful progress northward, being accepted as king and welcomed in every town he came to. In due course they came to a great hall that had been one of Earl Hakon's when he ruled Norway, before he drowned on his final sea-voyage, journeying back from England where he'd met up with Canute. Long-horned cattle cropped the green grass round about the hall which was built on a shelf of level ground half way up the steep side of a valley, overlooking a fjord that cut its way inland, its waters the deep blue of the ocean and filled with reflections of fleecy white clouds underlined in grey, that were swept inshore by the westerly breeze. Chill breeze. Elfie pulled her cloak around her shoulders, while her son ran on ahead, laughing, throwing sticks for his dog Terror to chase after.

The hall crouched almost invisible, its sturdy sod walls broken only by three doorways, its vast roof of birch shingles gleaming silver with age. Some way beyond it, the dark pines of the forest began their march uphill. By each of the three doors great heaps of birch logs were stacked, hewn ready for firewood.

Elfie glanced back to where her phalanx of Danish advisors trudged up behind her, pacing heavily in their great boots and long cloaks, solemn as dark shadows. Thore, the Norwegian earl striding at her side, showing her the way, was in contrast a golden staff of energy, the sun shining in his shock of blond hair, his walking easy and loose-limbed. She understood him easily enough after these few weeks in his company. There was not that much difference between his accent and a Danish one. Just the occasional confusion, when she needed to clarify things.

'Olaf, the former king?' she checked. 'He's returned home to Norway? You are sure? King Olaf?'

'Indeed,' said Thore.

'I understood he'd fled to Russia after Canute defeated him, and that King Jarisleif and Queen Ingigerd had offered to make him king of Vulgaria. Did that come to nothing? Why on earth would he come back to Norway when his people have rejected him? I thought everyone in Norway was in favour of the regime of peace and justice that Canute has promised them. That's what I was told.'

'Yes, in truth,' said Thore.

197

'So much blood was shed in Olaf's reign. What Canute wrote to me was that my role was to be a peacemaker. "Women are the peacemakers," is what he said.' She felt in the pocket of her apron for the letter that Canute had written her, which she kept close beside her for reassurance in this strange land. She unfolded the creased parchment. 'Here, this is what he says: "I will trust you to bring harmony to the land." He trusts me to bring peace and prosperity to Norway, to end all the terrible bloodshed there has been in recent years, with King Olaf forcibly converting his people to Christianity.'

'Do not fear, we will deal with Olaf.'

'We must gather a fleet to resist him.'

'Do not fret yourself, madam. You have no need to concern yourself, we will deal with the matter. Olaf is marching overland, through Sweden, through the forest and wild bogs. His plan is to accrue an army on the way. To gather to himself the disaffected. The lawless in search of excitement and the poor in search of loot.'

'How do you know this?'

'We have our spies.'

'I don't understand. Sweyn – my son – he has already been accepted in all the local parliaments where he has presented himself. No one has rejected him. If no one supports Olaf...'

'Do not fear, my lady. This is a little local matter. Nothing for you or King Canute to concern yourselves with.'

41. Elfgifu, Norway, 29th July 1030

To be still. To feel aloneness. This is good, Elfgifu thought. To have no demands made on you; no strangers to be introduced to, no having to interact formally with them, no pretences to keep up. No journeys to make.

Instead of the thud of horse hooves, the jingling of harness, the ribald laughter and loud singing of the men she travelled with, to have quiet. No demands upon her. Nothing she must do.

Elfie didn't know what to do with herself at first. Her body was still tensed to act, her mind to make decisions, her tongue to talk.

To be quiet in a green pasture where all there was, was sheep; this was strange. The mountains in the distance reared up their craggy heads, they pointed at the deep blue of the sky. Forests of pine and birch wrapped themselves around the lower slopes. And, nearer, the sun slanted yellow across the farmland, casting long shadows beyond every tree and bush.

Her body was not tuned to stillness. *I can't do this*. She itched to act.

She folded her skirt under her and seated herself on a grey rock. She felt the tenseness of the muscles in her arms and legs; she felt her heart thud in her chest. She made herself sit still, counted slowly to a thousand.

Sun in her hair. Soft breeze on her face. It was only the twenty-ninth day of July, but there was already a chill bite to the air. The promise of winter. Snows would bring stillness, wouldn't they? She imagined the black slopes of the mountain clad in white. Glistening with light in the short days, the bright moonlit nights. Reflecting the light of the stars in the glitter of ice crystals.

She watched a solitary butterfly. A goldcrest in a juniper bush. A wagtail pecked by her feet, darted off when she sighed and stirred.

In some meadows hay still dried, spread on strung-out ropes. In clearings in the forest, cattle grazed throughout the summer. Girls stayed with the cattle to milk them and to guard them against attack from wolves or bears. Stones were the girls' weapons to protect themselves; heaped piles of stones. The girls churned cheese and butter from the milk, vital supplies for the coming winter.

An old woman was rowing a small boat across the water of the fjord. She stopped and shipped her oars, heaved in the line she trailed over the stern. Even at that distance, the silver shimmer of a great fish.

The land was empty of men. It was paused on the brink of battle. Quiet, still. Waiting. Elfgifu wanted to step between the two armies, hold up her two hands and say *Stop*, *stop,* as if she were breaking up a fight between six-year-old lads. *Stop. There is no need for this.*

She felt useless. She wished she was at least one of the nurse-women who followed the army, who had the skills and knowledge to save the lives of the wounded, but she was ignorant of medicine; scared, to be honest, of the brutality of battle. The madness of it. She couldn't understand it. Why cause so much anguish and pain when talking was what would ultimately resolve matters?

She jumped up and walked across the fields to the vast barns where that summer's crop of oats, barley and rye was stored. Dusty-smelling, when she had succeeded in heaving open the great door. Stacks of grain that would enable survival through the long winter into spring, until the early crops of peas. Cabbages. Radishes and beans. How well-stocked the barns were. A sufficiency for everyone.

She swung the great barn door closed and wandered to the well, tugged up the bucket on its clanking chain and cupped her hands to take great sips of the clear sparkling water. With the back of her hand she wiped the drops from off her chin. She walked by a small stream up through the sheep pasture and into the edge of the forest, where on a boggy bank she found a few late cloudberries: she squatted to pick the lovely bulbous orange fruit; she curled her tongue around them and swallowed.

She wandered back into the great hall, into its empty cave-like dimness, where once her eyes had adjusted to the lack of light she found on the table bread gone cold, which she ate with cheese. She didn't know where her Danish advisors had gone, didn't care to search them out. When she went back to her chambers she found no sign of Sweyn or his dog, only his bed unmade. He'll have gone hawking, she thought. Earl Hakon had left a beautiful white gyrfalcon tethered there. 'May I fly him?' Sweyn had asked his mother. 'You are the King of Norway,' she'd replied. 'You may do as you will.' He would be up on the mountainside now perhaps, or out on the headland, hunting toward the sea. It wasn't the catching of birds he loved, it was the being in the wilderness, at one with wild creatures and the trees. His faithful dog Terror would be with him, she knew, and she didn't fear for him.

So quiet everywhere, as if every bird and animal had fallen asleep. She wondered if the household had gone to watch the battle. It would not be far away, according to her understanding. But, truth to tell, she had not paid much attention. *They are a fierce and warlike people*, Canute had warned her. *You must try to prevent them from fighting.* But there was nothing she could have done. She'd washed her hands of the whole business. Olaf Haroldsson, the former king, coming to reclaim his lost throne. Marching through Sweden with only four hundred men, Thore Hund's spies had said. Carrying their boats across the land, through forest and desert moors, rowing across lakes. His project was madness. How could he win over his disaffected people?

So quiet here. Alien-feeling. The sky was turning red, as was the sun. Though it was only afternoon the day was turning dark and red. Foreboding.

A storm approaching. But the air was still. The leaves on the trees hung down as if in fear or sorrow.

Dark and darker turned the afternoon, until the sun itself was extinguished, put out like a candle by something passing in front of it, or so it seemed. The moon maybe? Or some kind of magic. A heathen trick in this pagan land. Elfie shivered, she made the sign of the Holy Cross upon her chest, she knelt to draw it in the dirt. *Sweyn*, she was thinking. She set out in search of her loved son in this daytime night. She would seek him on the headland.

Sweyn had set free the white gyrfalcon.

'For God's sake, why? What were you playing at, Sweyn? It was a valuable bird. It wasn't yours. I'll have to pay Earl Hakon's family compensation for it.'

The round shutter across the sun was sliding away, the day was still dim and the boy's thin face was lit by a beatific expression, a glow. His blond hair a halo. 'It was so beautiful, the gyrfalcon,' he explained. 'Like a dart of light. He deserved to be free. I stripped him of his hood and jesses and he flew up and snatched a swallow from the sky. He brought it fluttering down to my feet and tore it apart and devoured it. Once he'd realised he was free he soared up again. Like a spark in the dark of the eclipse. He flew way over there, he was above the pine forest when I lost sight of him.'

Elfie said nothing. She felt often that her son was fey, more in tune with the natural world than with the world of men. Oh, she loved him, she loved him with her whole heart, she wanted the very best for him, but sometimes he weighed her down, having to be responsible for him weighed her down. He might be King of Norway, but he would never know how to be a king, it was up to her to rule on his behalf, to fulfil his father's expectations for him. Having been brought up in the abrasiveness of the English court, with her father and brothers councillors, she knew how to rule with diplomacy. Though the individualism and ungovernable nature of the Norwegian people would certainly present a problem. How much easier it was for Queen Emma's son Harthacnut, ruling Denmark, a civilised country – moreover the country Canute had earmarked for Sweyn to rule. But while Canute had been away in Rome, Emma had tricked the kingship for Harthacnut: and Canute would have lost face if he had admitted that he had been outwitted by his wife. So here she was, Elfgifu, confronted alone with the problem of Norway – a country at this very moment at war with its former king. A civil war she had no stake in. Olaf couldn't win – but suppose he did, what then?

'Are you angry with me?' asked Sweyn.

'Angry with you? No, my dear, what makes you think that? Worried about the battle that's going on, that's all.'

'Have you seen the sea-eagles?' he said. 'Over there, soaring above the cliffs. They are so huge and free. I would love to fly.' The sea-eagles' wings were sunlit, arced outstretched, tipping this way and that now and then for balance; the sun at last free of the shutter that had crossed over it, the day once more blue and beautiful.

Elfgifu put her arms around her son, she embraced him, she hugged him tight. Her head on his shoulder. Comforted by the wiry strength of his thin body, though she knew the mental strength had to be hers.

'Your poor hands,' Elfgifu said to Thore Hund three days later in the great hall.

Thore stretched them out to the firelight, letting her see back and front. Broad strong hands, a couple of fingertips missing, a vivid slash across the palm of his left hand, a cut across the back of the right. 'I got off lightly,' he said, 'thanks to that reindeer-hide coat of mine. I bought a dozen of them last September off a Lapland magician, and I shared them out among my men. Amazing, they were. There was King Olaf, raining down blows on me with his gold-hilted sword that was forged by the best blacksmith in Nidaros - holding it two-handed and smashing it down on my shoulders. Should have cleft me in two but that coat of mine blunted his sword. Miraculous. So I was able to slide my sword up under his mailcoat into his belly and he was a gonner. Sad how life goes, it has to be said. Olaf and I - we were friends when we were boys, you know. What he wanted to come back to Norway for I don't know. Nobody here wanted him, he'd alienated too many people by forcing them by the sword to convert to Christianity. Believe or die, that's what he said. As if anyone could change the faith they'd grown up in like that. You need to persuade people of what is right. Old Olaf was doing fine in Russia, the king had offered him the kingdom of Vulgaria. Not that he wanted it. His heart was set on becoming a monk. That's what he'd always wanted. To be reclusive, to devote his life to saving the souls of heathens in a more peaceful way than he had done as a king. It was his men who persuaded him to come back here. Dag Ringsson – Dag's always been an impetuous fool, what on earth did Olaf listen to him for? I suppose his men all wanted to return from Russia to their families, to their farmsteads and boats, back where they felt they belonged.'

'Our own land always has a hold on us,' said Elfgifu, thinking wistfully of how long she had been exiled from

England, her own homeland; land of her family, land of her people. Canute always insisting on keeping her out of Queen Emma's malicious reach.

'It was too late,' sighed Thore. 'The time for return was past. Olaf must have known it. Most people just want a quiet life. No more bloodshed. Just being able to get on with life in a peaceable way. Farming, hunting, providing food for your people... Strange, isn't it, that one has to fight for that...'

'Sit down,' said Elfgifu. She could see that Thore Hund was wavering on his feet and guessed that he had been wounded more severely than he had revealed to her. She poured him mead thick and sweet with honey, she cut spit-roast boar for him. He folded it into his bread.

Sigurd the skald had followed them into the hall, and Elfgifu asked him to sing. The song of the Battle of Stiklestad it was, sung to the weary and wounded victors in the dusk of the great hall that was misted with wood smoke, the rafters black with it. The embers of the log fires glowed orange. Outside an early frost nipped at the grass. Sigurd's throat was dry and he coughed, and Elfgifu poured him mead into an ox-horn to soothe it. He drank the mead and then he sang of the valley to which Olaf's men had fallen back, where on one side were laid the bodies of the slain, and on the other side the wounded had cast themselves down, the wounded and those who were utterly exhausted by the length of the fray and the sheer weight of their weapons. They could not go on, which was a physical fact, not weakness at all. That utter exhaustion... The nurse-women had lit brushwood fires, they were making leek soup and offering it to the wounded so they could smell the depth of their wounds. They crouched over their patients, their hair bundled up in scarves, their sleeves rolled up. Dark aprons that didn't show the blood, with big pockets into which they might slip the occasional gold ring or heavy torc or silver-inlaid knife, which they took as payment for their services. Wood smoke curled up into the ebbing blue of the dusk, the evening star shone steady to the west. Olaf's men were Christians, they died assured of their place in Heaven.

Elfgifu said to Thore Hund, 'I thought you were Christian too. Yet you went to a Lapland magician.'

Thore laughed. 'I'm pragmatic,' he said. 'I believe in anything that works.'

Elfgifu was sitting on King Sweyn's left; to her left was the phalanx of their Danish advisors. Grease dripping from their chins, loud laughter erupting from them occasionally. Not integrating with the Norwegians at all. The Danes shorter, squarer, more richly dressed, better fed. Planning increases in taxation to be imposed on the Norwegians; planning that Danes living in Norway would have greater rights than the native people. Elfgifu was opposed to both proposals, but how could she go against what the counsellors whom King Canute had appointed advised?

Elfgifu retreated into her own thoughts. She was thinking: I live in a half land, a shadowland. That liminal space between belonging and isolation. I'm part of the government, I have duties, commitments, a role to play. And yet I am alone. Who is there that cares about me, cares for the person that I am? To my son Sweyn I am just a mother. Defined by my role again.

Have I faded from Canute's consciousness?

What am I, essentially? Is anyone ever more than the role they play?

I am an exile from my own land. I yearn to be back home. I am an outsider here. An alien. I don't care about these people. I can never belong. I can just do my duty.

I am a lover, I think. I love Canute, I love our sons. I love the wide world and the open air, the trees and the wind and sun. I love to step out of the great hall and feel the sun warm on my face. Then I feel alive. How good it is to feel alive.

42. Canute, England, 1030

Canute was coming home from his second visit to Rome. *Home*, he was thinking, obsessively. He thought of his feather bed in his own chamber, and his wife to welcome him and make him comfortable, to wipe his hot forehead with a linen cloth dipped in water fresh from the well, to cool and soothe away this wretched fever that had afflicted him since he left Rome, crossing the Mediterranean and rowing through the Straits of Gibraltar, then suffering the great storm that struck them, the huge waves in the Bay of Biscay, where he was washed overboard yet clung to the blade of an oar with desperate strength, strength that seemed to descend from the Lord above, he clung on, arms and legs wrapped round the oar, body pressed tight as a barnacle to its rock, so when the crew succeeded in manhandling the oar aboard, even when Canute was safe in the belly of the boat, they could not make him let the oar go; the din of the wind in the rigging and the singing waves, and his head crowded with prayers and with the dragons and sea-serpents and white ghosts of statues summoned up by his fever, so he felt for his sword at his side to stab or behead them, but no belt, no scabbard, his body ached and burned, he was sick and swathed in a sodden white nightgown though the day was bright, the bright sun making rainbows in the spray of the breakers, pretty colours, a diamond, diamond-butterflies in his head.

Home, and his head was nodding as he jogged along on his horse, feeling dizzy and insufficient in himself, wanting his wife, wanting to rest, no more travelling, to sleep, not this relentless ever onward, he couldn't go on, he was afraid he would slip from his saddle, he had slipped and a man running at his ankle had caught him in his arms like a babe, light like a baby from the fever, Canute the great king like a baby, and home was the last waystone on the road to Winchester, his eyes were closing and...

He was on his feet and here was his wife at the door, summoned and coming reluctantly from her meeting, so they said, and something was wrong, it was not her, it was the other, the other one who braided her blonde hair in bands of iron and laid down the law, the lawyer, the reader of books, stout short and fierce, and she had run right past him, she hadn't glanced at him, he glanced round at her back, she was beside the baggage mules, she was demanding the men unpack the bags from off the mules so she could see what gifts he had brought her from the Pope and Conrad the Emperor of the Holy Roman Empire, he slipped to the ground, he had dirt engrained in the palm of each hand, Palm Sunday, he held them up to inspect them, dirt deep in the pale skin of his king's hands, and she had unpacked a silken cloak, priceless and patterned with peacock's feathers, she was holding it high and Alwyn had seized a corner of it and held it higher, the cloak shimmered in the sunlight and she was exclaiming, oh, oh, her mouth a round O, hands greedy as a sea eagle's talons, and two men raised him up, hands under his armpits, his arms across their shoulders, his feet stumbling, dragging, not working, they were carrying him to his chamber where pitchfork devils danced at the junction between ceiling and wall, he was more frightened than he had ever been, and he wanted Elfie to sit beside him and soothe him, he was crying for her, if Elfie were here she would lie by his side and sing to him and everything would be right he was certain, he was frightened to let go of this world he couldn't make sense of and to sleep, he cried out in fear like a boy in his first battle, why was the other one here? Emma – 'I don't want Emma,' he cried but she hadn't come, she didn't attend to him, she was on her knees ferreting through his travel bags for the fingers of saints, the broken tooth of St Peter, kneeling, fingering through Persian carpet bags, rattling silver dirhams, dripping the silver coins through her plump fingers...

Oh. His cool chamber. The organic bulges of his wattle and daub walls. Tapestries hung on them, ones he'd commissioned to celebrate the battles he'd fought, stick figures slain and recumbent, ready to rise up and avenge their deaths in his dreams; a full moon and stars in a dark sky; and the horse that he loved and the silver stitched threads of his sword blade, the church of Ashingdon that he had founded and built, the singing of the monks at Ely – you couldn't have singing in a tapestry, that was wrong, but he heard it in his ears, the music trembled in the hollows of his ears, *nunc dimittis, non nobis Domine* – sweet to lie in his cool sheets...

'Canute. My liege lord.'

'Yes?' He turned his head on the pillow, stretched out his hand to touch her. But it was still the other one. He pulled his hand back. His nightgown was soaked with the sweat of his fever: 'Bring me a fresh shirt.' He amended it: 'Have Hakon bring me a fresh shirt.' Because this one would not help him. Once she had the son and daughter she wanted by him she would not let him touch her. I need you, he said to her once, I have such need of you, and she laughed in his face. She was too old for such things, she said, her time for child-bearing was past. Yet she was intimate with Archbishop Stigand, or so it had been told him. The power that she wielded in the Church was useful to him. The Church was the greatest landowner in the country, and she ensured that it paid its taxes. She was older than him, and slow in walking, a matter of dignity rather than disability, he thought. She walked very erect, with measured paces. Her crown, on feast days, settled among her greying braids. He had long ago given up his crown, the weight of it gave him a headache.

He had a headache now. A woman, a slave woman who spoke Cornish, came with lavender, she bundled it into a jar by his bed. 'Do I smell so foul?' he asked her, and she washed him in cool water with a linen cloth. He did not know this woman's name. She combed his hair with a buff-coloured comb. 'Is that walrus ivory?' he asked her, and she said yes, in her Cornish accent, it's walrus ivory from Greenland, and he said, 'I don't know if I will ever travel there now.'

'I would like to go there,' she said. 'I would like to sail on to Newfoundland. To be one of the first people in a new land. That would be good.'

He gave her a gold ring from off his finger, with his blessing. 'Thank you, sire,' she said solemnly, and she rubbed his skin with scented oils.

'You may sell my ring,' he said. 'Then you can travel there. Say a prayer for me when you are in those far distant parts.'

'I will,' she promised, and knotted the ring on the strap of her apron, so she could not lose it. 'Let me prop you with cushions,' she said. 'A messenger is come from the King of Sweden.'

'No need to exert yourself, my lord,' said Emma, and Canute and the woman were both startled, having forgotten her presence. 'I will deal with him.'

This weariness. The scented oils were making sleep drift over him in waves. He yawned. He could let her... let Emma...

That was how it began. He had not even been aware that Emma was in the same room as himself. He had felt that moment of intimacy with the young woman, had identified with her desire to travel and explore, and that was how he allowed it to begin. Emma taking over control of his kingdom from him. Of course it had happened on occasions before, just recently when he was in Rome, often when he was in Denmark; sometimes when he was fighting the Norwegians, sometimes spending time with his sons and Elfgifu; but this was the first time that it happened when he was present. He was ill, he was exhausted, he allowed Emma to grasp the reins of power.

Emma dealt with the messenger from the King of Sweden. King Onund sent news that Olaf, the erstwhile King of Norway, had crossed his territory with four hundred men, determined to recapture his throne. 'I have given him little support,' Onund had said. 'It seemed best I left him to go on his way unmolested. Your son will have no problem disposing of Olaf, in the unlikely event that he succeeds in crossing the Swedish forests and wild bogs with his ragtaggle army.' And at the end he said, 'Queen Elfgifu should be told of the threat that Olaf poses to her.'

And Emma said: 'I will deal with this matter. I will ensure that a messenger is sent to her.' But she made sure no messenger was sent. As it happened, it made no difference, as the battle of Sticklestad had already been fought and King Olaf was dead.

211

That was how it began, Emma taking up the reins of power, holding them firmly in her small plump hands. She liked the way her assumption of power made people bow down to her with great respect, she liked the way people sent her rich gifts. She had a windowless chamber built in which to store the gifts she was offered. She would take a candle into that dark chamber and see how its light glittered on the gold, she would polish the gifts with a soft woollen cloth. She always listened to the causes of people who gave her rich gifts. The poor were of no importance.

Einar who had fought alongside Canute in many battles sent him a stout ash walking-stick with a dragon head in gold: a dragon so smooth-backed it made a round curve to the hand, its wings just gentle bumps, its mouth agape with ivory teeth, its garnet eyes a purple glare. Emma ordered that the gift should be put in her treasury, but Richard who was charged with the task took it instead to Canute. 'Thank you,' he said feebly, and rose up from his bed with Richard's help, and, leaning on the stick, walked around his room, and out into the yard, where there were men and horses, and he felt himself almost like a man again. Free.

But Emma heard of this, and sent Richard into exile, and Canute never saw him again. 'Where is Richard?' he would demand, and Emma would say, 'I don't know who you mean.' Then Canute would wonder if he was going mad, with that madness that afflicts old people. Yet he was not old, he was merely unwell, he would soon get better. Give him time and he would recover.

His men brought Canute his horses, he went riding in the forest, he hunted for wild boar and deer. Emma was angry when she saw blood on his clothes, she summoned him to chapel and had him kneel for hours to repent of his sins. His head was muddled; he had lost the strength to resist her. He did not know if he was right or she was right. She seemed always so certain, and he... He thought of the woman in Rome whom he had briefly loved. He thought of Elfgifu and her sons and how happy they had been, the four of them together. *Our sons are grown up now*, he thought. *The whole world has changed.* He had Alcuin write to Elfgifu to ask her to come to him, but Emma kept close watch on him and substituted blank parchment for his letters. He lay on his bed and sent Elfgifu thought messages – *Come home, come home, sweetheart* – but he felt that the stone walls of the palace blocked the transmission of his thoughts, which had always reached her before. He wanted to live again in a timber house, as he had as a child, but Emma would not hear of it, she said that timber houses were for the poor and for peasants, not fit for a king. And sometimes his fever returned, and he spent days in bed again. And he'd dream of the timber house where he had lived as a boy, how it was made of logs that had been living trees, and that first year, because the trees had not long been felled, they came to life and put forth green shoots. Twigs twisting from between the logs; green shoots bringing hope and energy into the world. Renewal. A new season, a new spring.

When the king was ill, Archbishop Stigand went to pray over him. There were some of the king's council – particularly the Mercian and Northern nobles, whom Queen Emma did not favour – who said that Stigand's prayers kept Canute as a cypher, that they drained him of will. Some even suggested that Stigand was drugging their liege lord; but no evidence was ever found of this. And it surely could not be true, because Stigand was the queen's friend.

43. Elfgifu, Norway, 1030-1031

At the far end of the headland was a place where one could scramble sideways down the scree, clutching at clumps of grass for handholds; down to where a rock made a safe ledge in the cliff. There you were hidden from the houses behind you, and the cliff-face dropped almost vertically in front of you, so you felt as though you didn't belong to the land, but were a part of the immense sphere of sea and sky; a spherical blue world where the horizon was veiled in mist, so it seemed that if only the air were clear and you opened your eyes wide you would be able to see for ever, to the farthest limits of the Earth. It was a place where you felt in touch with the invisible and unknown lands across the sea. Close to them. Close to England, maybe. As if you could take a giant leap and step out on to its shore.

In early June Elfgifu was perched on this ledge, arms looped around her knees, knowing she could not be seen by anyone. She stared out over the waves, all her concentration on the misty horizon and the worlds beyond. She was free to send her thoughts flying, there was nothing to stop them, no let nor hindrance, the soft wind would carry her thoughts through all that emptiness: Canute, she was thinking, Canute my lover, it is two years since I last saw you. I last saw you a month before you set out for Rome, and I miss you, I need to be with you again, my flesh craves you, my mind too, I long for you utterly in a way I cannot express in words, I long for you with my whole body, my whole heart. What is the reason you don't come, why don't you come, I long so much for you to be here, with me, beloved... *take my hand.*

I was not wise to give my heart to a king. Is it some business of state that keeps you away? Or do you have another love now, has someone taken my place in your heart? Has Emma - no, you could never love her, it must be someone else. Am I, in truth, nothing to you now, have you forgotten me? I want to know, I can't bear this emptiness, this hollow hurt, this not knowing. I have to know for certain that I have lost your love. Have I lost it altogether, or do I still have a quarter, or a third, some small portion of your loving? A chamber of your heart. You have always been so generous with your loving.

I think you've turned away. Turned away from me. Buried your head in politics. In the business of being a king. The meetings, the talking. Have you succumbed to flattery and so become other? I heard the story of how you had your chair carried down to the shore and taunted the waves, how, with your courtiers looking on, you commanded the rising tide not to dare touch your feet. And when the tide paid no heed to your commands, but rolled ever inwards, rattling the shingle, crashing in white spray against your legs, you laughed aloud and said to your men, look, I have no power, I cannot command the sea, I have no true power, all the power on Earth belongs to the Lord above, and you must stop praising me...

They say you have never worn your crown since.
Ruler of four lands.
You have never been proud, my Canute.
I am listening to the wind and I cannot feel where you are.

In the old days I knew you were there. Before, I have always been able to sense you. We were so close that I felt whenever you were thinking of me. As if waves of air, an invisible, unfeelable breeze, were bringing your thoughts to me.

Often when she sat here and thought intensely of him she felt as if their minds connected, as if there were invisible threads in the air, finer than spiderwebs, that connected her thoughts to his. Then a week or a fortnight later a boat would bring a letter from him in which he avowed that he had been thinking of her at the same time; in which he hoped that she and Sweyn were well and the situation in Norway good; and he'd give her all the news from home, something about their mutual friends, and how the weather was etcetera, and she'd be reassured.

But these last six months or so that connection hadn't worked – all she'd received from him were those strange blank missives stamped with his seal – and she was afraid that something had happened to him, or to the relationship between them. Or maybe it was that her present thoughts were so negative (these Norwegians are utterly ungovernable, Sweyn is retreating more and more into his own head, I despair of making him interact with anyone, my Danish advisors are alienating the local people, they will not obey the law, I don't know what to do). Even if she were to send Canute thoughts of the weather that would be bad – a second cold wet summer had caused the grain to rot in the fields, which would leave the barns almost empty for the winter. Resulting in famine. Starvation. Babies that were loved and had been longed for were exposed on the rocks, or in bogs, that death more humane than a long-drawn-out one from gradual starvation.

The fish even, usually plentiful around the coast, the silver shoals of them had swum away northward. Or southward. Not here anyway.

And the people held her responsible. 'I am their leader, Canute,' she cried, 'and they say it is all my fault. I should be able to manage things better. They say this lean time will be known for ever as Alviva's time. They won't even call me by my name, Canute, they call me Alviva, they say my name is unpronounceable. Canute, I need to talk to you, I need reassurance. I have no confidence in the Danish advisors you appointed for me, they are so prejudiced against the Norwegians that they even insist that in disputes the word of one Dane is equivalent to that of ten Norwegians. That can't be right, Canute, can it? And yet I've signed it into law...'

She was talking loudly, almost shouting. The gulls soared over the cliffs, regardless of her, they didn't reply.

Just the empty space in front of her, the vast space empty of replies or advice. She sighed, and scrambled up the scree, more disconsolate than ever. She had a meeting with her Danes and she had no idea what she should say, no idea how she should act.

They were in the chamber ahead of her, sitting round the table. She took her seat on the carved and cushioned chair at the head. They did not stand, they did not welcome her. She guessed she was in disgrace for being late. 'Sometimes one needs time to think,' she said. They sat there mutely, except for Halfdan and Gudrod, who were talking together in undertones. 'Perhaps you would like to share your discussion with the rest of us,' Elfgifu said.

They paid her no attention. The whole room smelled of sweat, the greasiness of unwashed hair. One of the younger men, a natty dresser, had scented his hair with pine cones; the smell of them made Elfgifu want to sneeze. 'The Norwegians are murderous bastards,' he was saying, 'so habituated to killing that they won't pay the fines we impose on them for it. Fair enough to give compensation to the murdered man's family, they think, but they don't see what business it is of the state's. And, moreover, why the state should profit. Murder is a private affair, they think.'

217

Halfdan stood up. 'Perhaps we should first of all discuss how Norway is to be governed,' he said, 'in view of the accident to King Sweyn.'

'What accident?' said Elfgifu.

'Obviously the king should not have been climbing an ash tree,' said Gudrod, 'putting himself at risk of falling in such a manner.'

'Sweyn's fallen from an ash tree?' Elfgifu demanded. 'Is that what you're saying? Why did no-one call me? How is he? Where is he?'

The boy was on his bed in his chamber. Eyes closed; ashen-looking. Unconscious. One of the wise women was attempting to straighten his broken leg; another was bathing the wound on his head, another mixing a concoction in a pewter vessel. 'Oh, Sweyn, what have you done?' cried his mother. She longed to hold him in her arms, to succour him with all of her love, but could not get near because of the ministering women.

She paced up and down while the women did the best that they could for him. How terrible it was not to be able to help him herself. She grabbed the arm of one of the wise women as she passed. 'Will he recover?' she demanded.

'His fate is in the lap of the gods,' the wise woman responded

44. Elfgifu, Lapland, 1031

I should not be doing this, Elfgifu was thinking. But the wise women are useless. All their expertise, their herbs, their potions, they have done my son no good. I have no choice. I do not know what else I can do. How else to help Sweyn.

She was walking along a narrow earth path crisscrossed by tree roots that stretched like sleeping snakes in the dappled sun that fell through the silver line of birches that separated the path from the lake. So quiet it was. Far from town and village and farm. All breeze had stopped, birdsong had stopped, the water had stilled its ceaseless lapping.

I am afraid, Elfgifu was thinking. I am so afraid. But she had not known what else she could do. 'This magician,' she had said to the Norwegian Thore Hund.

'What magician?' he had said.

'The one who cast a spell on your reindeer hide coat,' she'd said, 'so that it kept you safe in battle. So that it resisted the blow of every axe or sword or spear.'

'Oh, that magician,' said Thore. 'The Lapp.'

'His magic must be very powerful.'

'Many of the Lapps can do powerful magic.'

'Will he know any spell to make my son Sweyn better?' She had tried praying to her Christian god, she had prayed till her knees were sore, but the answer to her prayers had so far always been *No*.

'She,' said Thore.

'What do you mean?'

'The magician. She is a woman. A witch. Gyda is her name.'

'Aha.' A woman will know better than a man how to make a child better, Elfgifu thought, a woman will understand a mother's love.

'She is a Sami. She lives in the north. She has an iron staff.'

'Where will I find her?'

Thore took her by boat north along the coast. The weather was clement, a gentle breeze blowing from the west. An easy sail. The weather was warm, the sun yellow, the sea blue. The men lazed on the rowing benches. Go quicker, Efgifu's heart sang, I need a cure for Sweyn's disability, I need to make him strong again. But her journey took as long as it needed.

Then Thore had abandoned her part way up a river, where rushing down from the mountains it dashed against rocks: white spray caught in sunlight turned to rainbows. Salmon leapt silver in the falls; otters were sleek against the banks. Thore had turned back with his men. 'This is a journey you need to take alone,' he had told her.

'Stay. I wish you to come with me.'

'No,' he said. 'The journey is part of the cure. During it you must formulate what you most desire. You need solitude for that. Then you can tell Gyda, and she will say if she can help you.'

And so here was Elfgifu on the narrow path by the lake on her own in the silence in the shallow bowl of the hills. The still water was strewn with lily pads, their white and yellow flowers floating to her left, and on her right lazed a field of golden buttercups and great grey rocks like yawning monsters. The field dwindled into a forest of dark pines, very tall, very old, they'd never been felled, they'd been there from the beginning of time; they led her away from the lake and she could sense their moist ancientness, the damp, the bogs, the mossy rocks and the ferns, the dark pools among them; and she was afraid. Now and again came a sharp *crack* as of a breaking twig, and she wondered what was there in the forest with her, a raven or a bear or a pack of stalking wolves; or an elk with young to defend; deer, or heavy musk-oxen lumbering along. Or a spirit – the spirits of this place – you could sense them lurking invisible, you could hear their whispers in the breeze among the pine needles...

She wanted to turn back, to run back to the others, she could pretend she had spoken to Gyda, what need was there to tell the truth? No one would know. A queen should not venture alone into a forest like this. Too vulnerable.

She was afraid. She wondered if this was Thore's cruel joke; a Norwegian joke on a ruler they didn't respect. A test of her. Maybe there was no witch here at all; maybe they had simply decided to abandon her here alone in this godforsaken place. Who would know? *Canute my love,* she thought, I am here. I am doing the best I can for our son, whether the magic is true or not. I am testing it. The bishop's prayers and laying on of hands have had no effect. Older spirits live here, spirits from the birth of the world, I can feel them. They frighten me. Oh Canute, listen to me. Listen. Tell me that what I am doing is right. She thought the words with all her heart and her soul but again she felt no response.

I am doing this for Sweyn, she thought grimly, the image sharp in her head of her son who was half man and half boy, recumbent on a bench in the great hall, or lying on a reindeer hide on the grass beneath a tree, wherever she directed men to carry him; and with her whole heart she wished him strong again and that he had never fallen from the ash tree. Let him grow strong as the ash, she thought, let him grow strong as an oak, let these great pines impart their strength to him. And she thought: maybe the witch will have tapped these trees for their strength and preserved it like resin in a jar; maybe she will let me have some of it and permit me to carry it back to him.

She had brought treasures with her to pay the witch, five gold rings, a silver cup that was once a chalice in an Irish monastery, that had a century ago been stolen and carried off to Norway by Viking raiders. I will give the witch all my gold rings, Efgifu thought, if she will only fill my chalice with the strength of a tree, so that I can take it back and give it to Sweyn, to make him strong again.

She adjusted the straps to the basket on her back, which held her treasures, and walked on, concentrating on her footing on the uneven path; concentrating on continuing her journey, her quest.

The smell of birch smoke. Elfgifu sniffed the air. Birch smoke: a fire. The witch's fire, it had to be, because no ordinary person would choose to live here in this wilderness. She quickened her pace.

The path became stepping stones across a bog, grey stones in a green bog; she hitched up her skirt and jumped from one stone to the next. The birch smoke smell grew stronger; she could see the mist of it drifting between the pines. The smell of decay now, of rotting flesh: sacrifices made in a clearing. Triangles of rags festooned a dead tree. A horse hide hung over a branch, the head still attached, flies all over it, maggots erupting from the eyes and muzzle. Elfgifu had brought nothing to sacrifice with her. She cringed from the paganism of it, the old, pre-Christian ways. She had been a Christian all her life. She'd been thinking of the witch as a healer, a beneficent spirit, and this – this was different. She was scared of what she was about to confront. She crossed herself, she repeated the Lord's Prayer to protect herself from any evil that might lurk here.

On the far side of the clearing stood a log hut raised up on stones; nine courses of logs to the walls; a steeply pitched roof on which grass grew. A goat stood on it, grazing. The open door hung crooked. A woman peered out, holding on to the doorpost; she stepped down the four steps to the ground. She was skinny and unkempt, her black hair tangled as the twigs of a bird's nest; her dress – if one could call it that – was a shift of hare skins roughly stitched together. Dirt was engrained in the wrinkles of her creased face. She smelt of sweat and of some kind of strong liquor.

She stared at Elfgifu with sharp blue eyes. 'The two men you have come about,' she said.

'I thought I might not understand you,' said Elfgifu, surprised at the woman's cultured Danish accent. 'But it's not two men. It's only one. My son. He fell from an ash tree. Thore Hund told me you might have a potion to make him recover.'

'You are friends with Thore Hund?'

'I am his queen.'

The woman stared, then shook her head. She pursed her lips. 'An ash tree is not good. To fall from an apple is better. The other man – he is a long way away. I cannot sense him. But you love him. Is it a love potion you need?'

'A love potion? No, no. Just my son. It's my son I've come about.'

'You will pay?'

Elfgifu offered her gifts. The woman took the five dragon-engraved gold rings and arranged them in a pattern on the earth; she rubbed them in the dirt, slipped them dirty on her skinny fingers, held them up to inspect them. 'The dragons are old,' she said. She frowned. 'I can do nothing for the other,' she said. 'Not unless you have something of his.'

'I don't know who you mean.'

'He who is also present in your thoughts.'

Elfgifu considered for a moment. Whom had she been thinking of? 'My son's father?' She did not know why of recent times Canute had been so much in her head. A kind of nagging worry, as if he were not well; but she had received no ill news of him.

'I have to prepare myself,' the woman answered. She poked the embers of the fire; she fetched dry birch logs and piled them on it; brought four small ivory boxes from her hut and mixed different coloured powders from each in an earthenware bowl, stirring them together with a silver spoon. She sniffed the mixture, sneezed, added a few more grains of the orange powder.

Elfgifu watched. She was weary from her long walk here, and thirsty; she longed for a drink of water but didn't dare ask for it, for the woman was so intent on what she was doing. She had fetched a cloak of feathers from her hut, she'd spread it on the beaten earth, she was kneeling, straightening each feather out. Elfgifu prickled with fear of the alien world she had come into, this woman so unlike any healer she had ever met before. Her legs felt weak, she squatted on a log at the clearing's edge, hands around her knees. Her throat was dry; she licked her lips. The fire was blazing now, gusting smoke toward her, and she coughed; was convulsed with coughing. She ached to suppress it but she couldn't. She felt faint.

The woman continued with her tasks. She fetched an iron staff from her hut, she put on the feather cloak, she banged the ground eight times with the iron staff, and cried out a name. She took a draught of some liquid from a horn beaker; it was strong, to judge by the way she swayed and her pupils dilated. The fire was blazing now; flames swam up toward the sky.

Elfgifu pulled down her skirt to protect her legs from the heat. She was mesmerised, watching the woman. What supernatural powers did she possess? Were they of our Good Lord or of the devil? she wondered.

The woman sniffed the powder in the bowl; she sneezed, sniffed again, and shook the rest of the powder on to the flames. A strange smell arose, such as Elfgifu had never smelt before: of toadstools and damp places, cut with the sharpness of juniper, blended with the saltiness of oceans and the spice of stars, the darkness of the night. Her head swam; she felt as if she'd fall, she shifted her hands to grasp the log to keep her balance. Her eyes stung and prickled.

The woman danced around the fire, her feather cloak swinging wide, all the time singing words in a language Elfgifu had never heard, yet which was familiar, as if it were the root of all language, as if it were the language from when all men were one, before they divided themselves into tribes and nations. An old, old language she could not understand, which was spoken not just by men, but by every fir tree, storm and deer, by salmon and the musk-ox and the raven. If I could make myself simple, at one with them, I would understand, Elfgifu thought; but all she could do was sit and let the waves of the words wash over her. The scents from the fire enveloped her, they transported her to another place and time, to her fury and desolation when her brothers were blinded, to the warmth of sleeping with Canute under the stars, to Sweyn starting to walk when he was a twelvemonth old: toddling and falling, pulling himself upright again.

Now you are fifteen, pull yourself upright again.

Into her head came a vision of Yggdrasil, the world ash: the great ash tree from which Sweyn had fallen, and a man was fashioning a branch from it and giving it to Canute, laying it on his bed, but she did not know why he lay in bed. The ash stick a stiff companion to him, not her, herself rejected... hurt often makes people drive away those who most want to love them.

Elfgifu fainted maybe; or maybe she slept. When she woke the fire was low, the woman in her hareskin shift was resting head in hands on the third step up to her hut. 'Gyda?' Elfgifu queried. The woman's name.

The woman raised her head wearily. 'Sometimes there's nothing I can do,' she said.

'Ah,' said Elfgifu.

'The double magic of the ash was too strong for me. Here, take back your dragon rings.'

'No, keep them. You tried your best.' Elfgifu had come to this woman with so much hope that her disappointment did not for the moment register.

'I will give you a powder to ease your son's pain. For your husband, I can do nothing.'

'There is nothing the matter with him. I have had no ill news of him.'

The woman gazed levelly at her. 'The spirits do not always tell the truth,' she sighed. She stood up wearily; she seemed to have aged by fifty years. She brought back from her house the silver chalice that Elfgifu had given her, half filled with a white powder. 'It's an extract of willow bark,' she said. 'Any competent herbalist will make it for you. I cannot help you more. You are strong, you must help yourself. You will know what to do.'

Elfgifu's hands were shaking; she cupped her fingers together to hold the chalice steady, so none of the powder would be spilt. She felt so weak that she did not know how she would complete the long walk back to Thore and her men. But gradually, as she walked, her knees found their strength again. At the bog edge she knelt and laid her hands palms up among the reeds, cupped water in them and drank. The water was muddy-tasting, like her thoughts. She stood up, straightened herself, swung her basket back up on her back; carried the white powder in

the chalice carefully, thought how she would kneel by
Sweyn's bedside and give him the powder mixed in water;
and his pain would be eased. He would get up from his
bed. They would walk outside into the dark night, beneath
the stars and the silver crescent of the moon.

'Drink it,' said Elfgifu. She knelt by Sweyn's bed, she had
the silver chalice in her hand. 'Taste it,' she said. How still
he lay there, eyes closed, lashes spidering across his
cheeks as they had when he was a baby. 'Such a lovely
child you were,' she whispered.

Heat radiated from his body. 'Open the door,' she
whispered, but there was no movement behind her and
when she turned her head she saw that she was alone
with her son. 'One minute,' she sighed, and got up and
propped the door open with a stone. A chill breeze sighed
in. The day was suffused with the yellow-grey of morning.
She folded the blankets back so the breeze might cool him.
His dog was outside and she called him in: 'Terror! Terror!'
She patted the bed and the dog jumped up and lay close
against the boy's side. 'Feel him,' said Elfgifu. 'Feel him,
Sweyn.' She lifted the boy's hand and placed it on the
dog's soft head. 'He's damp with the dew,' she said. 'He's
just come in from outside. He's probably been chasing
hares.' The dog, full of life, wagged his tail, slapping it
against the bed, and licked Sweyn's hand with his rough
tongue. 'He loves you,' said Elfgifu.

'I love you,' she said. In the room was the damp smell
of the dog's fur and the sweat stink of the boy, the foul
breath that came from his beautiful mouth, the stench of
his leg where the thigh bone when it broke had torn the
skin, and infection was setting in. She had done her utmost
to keep it clean. The bruise on his temple was swollen,
vivid blue-black.

'The reason I've been away a few days, Sweyn,' she said, 'is that I've been up north. On my travels I met someone who'd caught a white gyrfalcon. I brought it home for you. I know how much you loved the one you had.' And yet he had set it free. She stroked his arm. His left eyelid fluttered half open. 'When you're well – as soon as you're well – you can fly him.' Tears pricked her eyes. 'You have such a feeling for birds, Sweyn.' The magician's white powder is his only hope of surviving, she was thinking. 'You and the gyrfalcon can hunt together, Sweyn. Terror will go walking through the forest with you. You will hunt together.'

She had never asked the magician how to give Sweyn the powder: whether to give it all to him in a single dose, or to spread it out in several doses over a week. She didn't know whether to dilute it, or to give it him in a spoon. She dipped the tip of her finger in the powder and tasted it. Oh, it was bitter! She would mix it with honey, to sweeten it. Perhaps Sweyn would take it from a spoon. She fetched a wedge of honeycomb from the storeroom, crushed it in a bowl and added half the powder to it. The taste, when she tried it, was now mostly of wax. 'This will make you better,' she told Sweyn. 'The magician who sold it to me promised that it would.' She couldn't help remembering the magician's uncertainty, and wiped it from her mind, not wanting Sweyn to sense her doubt. 'This will make you better,' she repeated. She didn't know how aware he was. She rested the full spoon on his bottom lip so that his mouth opened, and she pushed the powder mix into his mouth. It will dissolve in his saliva, she thought.

His lips were dry and cracked, his cheeks flushed with fever. She sat beside him for a while.

How he has always loved the outdoor world, she thought, and she went out into the fields around and fetched armfuls of buttercups and plantain, blue campanula and red sorrel and those wiry daisies, and arranged them in earthenware bowls all around the room so the room was like a flowering meadow. 'Does that remind you of the places you love to be?' she asked. Cotton grass from the edge of a bog, tall field grasses gone to seed; a goblet of sea lavender; a thimbleful of pink sea thrift. Pine branches broken from the forest; that resinous smell. Cloudberry twigs, the berries not yet formed. His room was beautiful and full of the outdoor world, but he was no better.

He was racked with a bout of coughing, and in a panic she mixed the remaining powder with the honeycomb and pushed it in to his mouth. 'You have to get better, Sweyn my beloved. You have to get better. I can't bear it if…' She couldn't utter what she feared.

She sank down on to her knees, she knelt at his bedside. She bowed her head and prayed, her whole bowed body was a prayer that he would recover.

45. Emma, Shaftesbury, 12th November 1035

'My lady.'

Emma turned her head. It was her maidservant Balthild hesitant in the doorway to the chapel. A timorous slip of a girl whom rumour said was the daughter of Bishop Stigand. Certainly it was he who had recommended her to Emma's service, and as the girl was awkward and ill-looking, so no kind of rival, Emma had accepted her. And since so far Balthild had been compliant and capable, Emma had seen no reason to get rid of her.

'My lady.' Balthild's voice was more urgent now.

'*Praise him for his acts of power.*' Emma continued to chant the last psalm, disregarding her.

'My lady.' Balthild again.

'Oh, what is it, girl?' Emma snapped. The cold in the chapel had seeped into her bones, it made her tetchy. The smoke of the candles and incense had mingled into a sweet cloud toward ceiling height. The thick greenish glass in the single window weakened the wintry daylight seeping through.

'My lady, your husband, his royal majesty...'

'What of him? Spit it out.'

'They say he is very weak, madam.'

'Why should I concern myself about that? He has been weak for months.'

'His doctors recommended that I should fetch you, my lady.'

'What are they fussing about this time?'

'They requested that you attend his majesty with great expediency, my lady.'

'Oh, what now?' But nevertheless Emma consented to allow Balthild to lay her sable-lined cloak across her shoulders, hood her greying hair and fasten the brooch at her throat, then hurry her along the hawthorn-hedged avenue that led to the king's chambers: an avenue today heavy with white hoarfrost that bristled on the dark twigs, the still air trapping a deep chill and a mist so thick that Emma could see no end to the avenue she was in. But Balthild led her on, in at a side door that appeared out of the mist, and through a hall to a low-lit chamber in the vast carved bed of which Canute had lain for many days, sometimes tossing and turning with fever, sometimes quiet with exhaustion, in his weak voice rambling meaninglessly about past battles, and often about Elfie, his dear Elfie...

'What terrible hallucinations he is suffering from,' Emma was wont to say.

But this time when Emma approached him and stood at the foot of his bed he lay still. 'Is he...?' she asked of the dozen stern men attending him.

'He departed this world an hour since, madam,' one of them offered.

'Ah.' Others might have been expecting this day, but her heart was rent with disbelief, shock and loss, as if an eagle had dug its claws into the red muscle and was tearing it from her body. She rubbed her chest hard. She had never meant... it was nothing she had done... her games, the potions she had given him, they were just to keep him calm so she could rule as she wished, this death was no consequence of any action of hers, she needed Canute, he was essential to her, she would never willingly have hurt a hair of his head. A whisper: 'I would never have hurt you, beloved.' She knelt by his bed, she buried her face in the silken cover of his quilt, in the prickly wool of his blanket, and sobbed.

One of the men in the end put his arm around her and raised her up. 'Madam,' he said. 'My lady.'

Emma pulled away from him and rubbed her eyes. She steadied herself on the end of the bed, averting her eyes from the still face of her dead husband. He had left her; and without him she was powerless. She knew that. 'I will send a message to Denmark, to my son King Harthacnut,' she said hoarsely. 'He is the heir to the throne of England. I will order him to come immediately. He must obey me instantly. This great kingdom of ours cannot be without a ruler for any length of time.'

46. Elfgifu, Bradwell, 20th November 1035

Elfgifu folded her son Harald's letter, tucked it back inside her dress to keep it dry. As close to her heart as possible. It is my one human connection with this living world, she thought. The people I love most have died. But my son Harald wants me. He has summoned me to him. Mother, I need your help, he has written. He wants me to speak for him to my Mercian family, to help him gain their support so that he may be king. King of England, like his father. As is his right. The more so because I am English. The blood of King Alfred runs in my veins. My grandmother – she said she was kin to Alfred. Harald is Canute's and my second son. Now his brother is dead, he is Canute's true heir, without a doubt.

Harald was different to Sweyn. Mother and son had never been close, he had always held her at a distance. Treated her with suspicion. She wondered if that was her failing, that she had had so much love for her firstborn in their infancy that she did not have enough love to spare for him. She wanted to love him but he always slipped away from her. He loved to travel. He had led his first expedition, to Sri Lanka, in search of garnets, when he was fifteen.

The same messenger who had always brought her news from Canute had brought Harald's letter. This was a link, a certainty that the letter was authentic. Harald had written the letter himself, the writing was ill-formed, the letter was not written by a scribe. It was not a trick, not Queen Emma seeking to ensnare and destroy her.

After so many years, Elfgifu was going home to England. To where she belonged. Her heart was crying out to be home, her feet ached to walk on English soil. From the hull of the boat she sailed in she could smell the land now: wood smoke and mud and trees. Her boat was almost there.

A bank of low cloud rested on the horizon: a constancy. Not cloud. England. It had to be. 'Oh, take me there, quickly!' she cried to Edwin.

'We can't land here, we are too far south,' he said. 'People here may well be supporters of Queen Emma, and hostile to Harald the Far-Travelled. I'll land when we get as far north as Ely.'

'My husband loves Ely,' she said. 'We stand on the shore of the lake and listen to the sound of the chanting of the monks drift across the water.' How many years was it since they had done that? When their sons were little...

Loved, she should have said, Canute loved to listen to the chanting of the monks; didn't one use the past tense about people who had died? Which was nonsense, because they lived on in your head, they lived on in what they'd done, what they were accustomed to do. Canute was still a presence close at her side, though they'd been apart for years, and he was young and she was loving him, she was grasping his hand, she was bringing it to her lips, she was kissing it, he was pulling her to him, the hilt of his sword was catching her hip, it was bruising her, the bruise would last a month... It had been such a long journey, their journey together. A blessed journey. But his part of it was over. He had gone without her; he had left her behind. She stood up in the boat, holding tight to the mast. 'Take me closer to the shore,' she commanded.

She had been an exile from her homeland for so many years. It was a new ache, this longing to be there, a new ache among all the wounds of loss. Too much loss, more than she could bear. Sweyn, her son, the king of Norway, her liege lord. Norway lost too, to its rebellious people, its mad people who had made his murderous predecessor into their saint. Saint Olaf – what a cruel joke to declare their previous murderous king a saint. While her beloved

Sweyn, he was disregarded, her fair gentle boy with his blue-eyed smile, whom no one and nothing could help, not magic nor herbs nor prayers nor even the doctor trained in Padua when he came at last.

She had written to Canute. Come, come, she wrote, come to your son, your presence must heal him. Nothing else has worked. But Canute did not come, he could not come, for he was not well himself, and when Sweyn died she wrote to him, now may I come to you? Will you permit it? There is such an emptiness in my heart and I am desperate for the consolation of your arms.

Then had come the news: Canute was dead. Her true love, her laughter, the sanity she had believed would always stand beside her. Gone.

Everything lost in such a short space of time. Queen Emma had buried him in Winchester Cathedral. St Peter's Minster. His erstwhile warm body crated up in cold stone.

We live in a brutal world. I know that. But still I cannot make sense of it.

She shook her head.

'It's not your imagination,' said Margaret, at her side.

'What?'

'I thought I was hearing things at first too. Then I realised what it was.'

'I don't know what you mean.'

'It's amazing how sound travels across water, isn't it. The bell.'

'What bell?' Elfgifu put down her hood and listened hard.

How quiet the evening. The boat slow under sail on the calm of the estuary. The men resting from rowing, Edwin at the helm, hand on the steering oar, eyes fixed on the width of the river, the salt marsh ahead. The only way one could tell they were moving was by the slow procession past of the banks on each side. It was as dreamlike as if they were adrift in a ship of the dead. A ship of ghosts.

Only the bell was tolling. The bell was summoning her.

'That must be the chapel,' said Margaret.

'I don't see a chapel.'

'There.' She pointed again, and Elfgifu saw the pallor of a thatched roof rising in a vee beyond the dark humps of oaks. 'It's too high to be a house roof,' Margaret said. 'What else could it be but the roof of a chapel?'

Elfgifu did not know where they were. She did not know what day it was, or why a chapel bell should be ringing. But the monotonous repetition of that sound, the tinniness of it in the wide space of the estuary, spoke to her as nothing had for weeks. She was suddenly certain of what she must do, the knowledge broke through her numbness. She jumped up off the chest in which were stored her and Sweyn's few treasures, and she stumbled across men's outstretched legs to the stern: Edwin, she said, Edwin, put me ashore, the bell is calling me, stop the boat, I must go to the chapel.

'That would be madness, my lady.'

'I have to go.'

'Have patience, my lady. We will soon anchor for the night. In the morning we will reach Ely, where you will be safe.'

'Look, there's an old jetty, set me ashore there.' It was a ramshackle structure, weathered and battered by storms, the timber of it bleached by the sun, the barnacled piles that held it up all on a slant.

'We are too far south, my lady. People here are opposed to the Danes. Think of the battles of Ashingdon and Maldon, they were fought not far from here, and many brave men were killed. Everyone here will be supporters of the old order, and Queen Emma. We'll rest up in the marshes for the night, and sail north tomorrow. You'll be safe in Ely, you'll be among friends.'

'Edwin, you'll do as I command.'

'My lady, it's not safe.'

'I want to go to the chapel.'

'Tomorrow, my lady, when it will be empty.'

'No, now.' She wanted to do this simple thing, to achieve something concrete. She could not bear to be thwarted any more.

'It's not reasonable to risk the sailors' lives on a whim.'

'I will go on my own. Margaret will attend me.'

He shrugged, and swung the steering oar round so that they headed toward the jetty. This same slow pace, this dreamy drift over the quiet water. The subdued rattle down of the sail, the muffled oars' splash in the estuary as they drew near. One of the men held the boat steady against a post, and she heaved herself up, rolled sideways on to the lichened planks and jumped to her feet.

'We'll come back if we see you here again, mistress.' That was Edwin.

Margaret was moving to follow her, but her hesitation, the way her foot slipped on a rowing bench and she stumbled, made Elfgifu think, how terrible if the illogic of my own need were to put her life at risk, and she said, Don't come, I want to be on my own, it's important to me.

'Not on your own, mistress,' she pleaded, but, 'Yes,' Elfgifu commanded. She turned her back on them all and ran.

The sand of the beach was ridged with banks of empty cockle and mussel shells: her feet crunched over them. She crossed up to the trees, where a footpath led into the dark shadows. A circle of light at the end, beyond the trees.

She headed toward the light, where a chapel stood tall, built of stone in a clearing. High windows; the sound of chanting drifted from the open doorway.

Stone, in this area of mud and sand. It must have been reused from an old building, she thought; a Roman fort, maybe; it was said the Romans had brought stones over from France. Why bother when there was so much timber round about? Scraps of old brickwork were mixed in with the stones; the mortar was rough, containing shells. Beyond the chapel stretched ploughed fields, the ridges running east to west. The clouds glowed bright with the sun behind them. A road; a well-worn track with ditches either side to drain this flat land.

A peasant in the chapel doorway called out, 'Will you come in, mistress?'

Elfgifu hadn't realised she was hesitating. She drew herself up straight, put back her shoulders, and went in.

Inside was a stone altar at the eastern end, a wooden cross upon it. The nave was filled with benches crowded with peasants. A space on the right where she could squeeze in. She knelt on the earth floor to pray. The priest continued with the Creed. *I believe - oh, I believe...* Amen, she said at the end with all the others. They were poor people, people of the land in simple clothes. She was conscious of the silk dress she wore and drew her woollen cloak tighter around her though she was not cold. She slipped off her earrings and cupped them in her hand, slid her bracelets up out of sight under her sleeves. No point in making herself a prey to thieves.

The Magnificat, the Nunc Dimittis - the familiar Latin praise played out in that simple chapel was a reassurance that the world had in fact not changed. This was a constancy. God's in his heaven; we each have our place.

Sunlight glided up the aisle like a blessing. When Elfgifu looked back to the doorway she saw that the sun had broken through the clouds: it was a radiance against which the trees at the far end of the fields were silhouetted. The ploughed land was gilded. As were the members of the congregation behind her; the outlines of their cheeks and brows, their hoods and hair glowed as if they were angels.

She thought of Canute, she thought of Sweyn. This English sunlight was a blessing.

47. Harald, Northampton, 24th November 1035

This English sunlight, thought Harald the Far-Travelled. It's so weak at this time of year. So chill. The days so short. But it's good to be here. Back from Constantinople. The colours there, the warmth, the noise, the press of people in the streets. He'd brought his sick father pomegranates and dates, lemons, grapes and wine. Strange sweetmeats, jellied delights, pastries sticky with pistachios and honey. You will love these, he'd said to him, but the old man had barely lifted his head from the pillow, when he drank the wine had dribbled red from his mouth like blood. Staining the pillow. Old man – he could not have been more than forty, and yet he was so feeble. 'Tell my council, he had said to his friend Gabriel, 'tell them I want Harald to succeed me.' This was after he had heard the news of Sweyn's death.

Harald was not yet twenty. A slip of a boy. Blond, thin and tall, just as his father had been. He stood in the doorway of his mother's hall in Northampton, he stared out at the great oaks being stripped by the wind of the last of their golden leaves. *Catch them, catch them,* his mother used to shout to him when he was a child, running after the flying leaves herself, and Sweyn would run after them too, but he...

Sweyn had always been his mother's favourite, and now Sweyn was dead. Their father dead too, so all the family Harald had was his mother. Not true. He'd married young, taking after his father, he had a son named Elfwyn. Not a family name. He'd wanted to begin a dynasty that was new. That had him as its centre.

He didn't know if he wanted to be king. It was his duty, he supposed. To his father. Nobody would want his half-brother Harthacnut of Denmark to be king of England. An arrogant, officious brat given power before he was old enough to wield it. The two of them had never seen eye to eye. And dammit, there was no justification for Harthacnut Emmasson to be king of England as well as of Denmark. He was already proving himself badly stretched in fending off attacks on Denmark from Norway and Sweden.

48. Elfgifu, Winchester, late 1035

It was not wise to go to Winchester, it was stepping into danger, Elfgifu was aware. The core of Canute's troop of house-carls still guarded Queen Emma and the royal treasure; some were men who had been with him when he came to Denmark; Elfgifu knew them well. She feared that if they saw her they might betray her presence to Emma; and Emma, she was sure, would find a speedy way to dispose of her.

In the shadow of the great stone wall of the cathedral, she pulled the loose leper's clothes she wore closer round herself, veiled herself more tightly. In this disguise she would not be allowed to enter into the cathedral where Canute's body lay, but she could at least get close. She did not care about her safety for her own sake, but she was determined to help their son Harald be crowned king, and for that she needed to be alive. For herself, she felt she had nothing to live for. But she had to say goodbye.

The stone walls were inimical, they bade her *keep out*. She thought of Canute's dear body prisoned in there: his strong hands, the height of him, his face that could be fierce and yet for her was always gentle; his loving eyes. A sensation of distance filled her heart; a feeling of long-ago. She was angry with herself for not having come to see him in his final illness, but she had not known, she had thought there was a breach between them - and it would not have been permitted, he would not have wanted it, he had always kept his two lives separate. Standing there in the grey December drizzle that dark morning, she beat her fists against the stone wall of the cathedral till they bled.

And yet: that was not Canute in there. The man she loved could never be prisoned up in stone. He should have had a Viking funeral, his body in his beloved Sea-Dragon sent burning out on the grey infinity of the ocean and his spirit set free to rise to the stars, to Heaven or Valhalla or wherever he ultimately finally believed in.

Oh, Canute.

Canute. She said his name over and over, a mantra, a prayer. *Canute.* She thought her heart would shatter with the pain of loss. *Canute.*

Something touched her arm. She looked down: it was the steel point of a spear. She turned around.

It was Einar. 'Go, woman.'

'Oh, Einar,' she said. 'Are we come to this?'

He stepped forward and put aside her veil. 'Oh, mistress,' he said sorrowfully, 'I would recognise you anywhere.' He paused. 'You were not here,' he said. 'You did not know. He would not let me come to tell you. But he was ill. He had been ill a long time. He could no longer do the things he loved, and the time was right for him to go.'

'Oh, Einar. And our son, our son Sweyn – he who should have been king – he – he was dying. I had to care for him.' She stared gaunt, wide-eyed at him, held out her arms as if for help. He folded her in his solid embrace. How comfortable his arms were, how comforting his strength, the male smell of him. She leant, sobbing, into the beat of his heart.

When she had control of herself again she stepped back, she held his wrists, she looked up at his lined, sad face. 'It is your duty to tell Queen Emma I am here,' she said. Her voice came out small and scared.

'I cannot do it,' he said. He released himself, he pulled the leper's veil back across her face. 'Go, woman,' he said loudly. 'Be off with you. Get out of town right now. We don't want your kind here.' He picked up her leper's bell, he shook it and gave it to her. He picked up a stone, threatened her with it.

She went off wailing, her sandals slapping over the cobbles; off up the muddy sunken lane that led out of town.

It chilled her, the way merchants heading into market skirted aside from her and shunned her, afraid of the disease they thought she carried; and yet one, seeing her stumble, called out, 'Here,' and laid a meat pie on a stone for her to pick up as she passed by.

'God bless you, mister,' she cried out. The pie was still hot from the baking; its warmth seeped into her cold cupped hands.

Beyond the fields around the town, distant from any human dwelling, there grew a great forest of oak and beech and birch: huge ancient trees. It was here that

Elfgifu had asked the troop of Harald's men to wait for her; and they waited for her still, although the low winter sun was setting and the sky was suffused with red. It was chill among the trees, a thin mist settling among them like ghosts. The fire they had built was low, dull red embers. Gabriel, the leader of the men who had escorted her here, jumped up at sight of her and kicked the remaining logs apart, making small flames crackle and shoot up like orange darts, or spear points, vivid in the dark. 'Let's get away from here,' he said. 'The greater the distance we can put between the town and us, the safer we will be.' He had Elfgifu's mare – a gentle daughter of Delight – brought to her, and helped her mount; but she swung round and stared down at the tiny darting flames.

'Wait,' she said. 'Wait, there is something we must do.'

It was this: they must build a great fire that would send flames shooting higher than the tallest oaks in the forest, a fire that would soar and crackle and roar and bear Canute's spirit high, that would set him free from this land-locked earth, send him out on to the astral plane.

'Not here,' groaned Gabriel. 'Not here, within sight of Winchester. Such a great fire will attract attention, it will summon Emma's forces here. Canute's former house-carls, madam. We are only ten men, we do not have the strength to withstand them.'

'Nevertheless...' she said; and because she was their mistress they had to do as she commanded: drag great branches thither that had been brought down by last autumn's storms, and were now half-dry. The men stacked them high on the embers of the little fire; and first one twig caught and then another, and soon there was a great roaring log furnace. Tongues of flames licked up into the evening mist and sent smoke like ghosts into it, a surreal world of darkness and dancing spirits. 'Canute,' Elfgifu called. 'Canute!'

Attracted by the flames, people came close to see – merchants homeward-bound; a cohort of Emma's men, sent out because the queen had seen the flames from a high window in her distant palace, and was fearing insurrection as an aftermath of Canute's death. 'I will not have it. Go there and extinguish it utterly,' she had ordered her men. But when they reached the place they found Elfgifu, still in her leper's dress, like a thing possessed, invoking the name of Canute, calling on his spirit, and of a sudden under the bare trees of the winter forest there was a rush of wind, a chill whirlwind like a dervish that sucked up dead leaves into itself and span them into the tall shape of a man with sword raised to the skies. The heat of the flames sucked in the leaves and whirled them higher. Then it was as if his very spirit crossed over out of the heavy stone walls of the cathedral and floated heavenward and free upward with the leaves and smoke and flames, as if his spirit, or his soul, whatever you liked to call it, was set free, into the wilderness of space, the unexplored that he loved: and happiness filled Elfgifu as if she were a goblet topped to the brim. She had done the best she could for him.

Men gasped, onlooking, rooted to the cold earth at the roots of trees, they saluted him: 'Canute, farewell!'

The flames sank down and dimmed. Men departed. Embers glimmered. Elfgifu rubbed her eyes, that were still stinging from the smoke. She took hold of the reins of Delight's foal and swung herself up into the saddle. 'Let us go on now,' she said. 'Five miles, and we'll be at the convent, where we can find refuge for the night.'

49. Emma, Winchester, August 1036

Emma stood in the treasury in Winchester.

The walls of the tower room encircled her; they pressed close against her. A single ray of sunlight fell from the high, small window. The great door with its huge hinges and iron bars, its studded nails, was locked; no man could enter. The key hung at her waist, so big that she found the weight of it hard to bear. The stone dimness smelled damp; in the still air five candles burned with straight flames on the round oak table. Her most trusted men stood guard outside.

She unlocked one of the brass-bound chests; heaved up the heavy lid, leaned it back against the curved wall. Inside it lay some of her most prized treasures: the head of St Ouen, the tiny gold reliquary holding the tooth of St John the Baptist, a jewelled gospel, a little toe of St Antony. Leaving the lid open, she crossed to another chest: inside lay the crown and sceptre, the symbols of the kingship of England. She stroked the oak planks of the lid. She was determined never to relinquish them other than to a son of hers.

Why would her son Harthacnut not come and claim the throne of England? She wanted to keep her power here, but as a woman she didn't have the right, she had to shelter behind her son's actions. And he wouldn't do anything. He seemed paralysed. He was too busy in Denmark, his message came, he couldn't come to England just then. She longed for him to be here. She wanted to witness his coronation; his wearing the crown, holding the heavy sceptre, seated on his throne. Being anointed with oil. Ah, then her life would be fulfilled! Her son succeeding her husband on the throne of England. This nonsense he argued about needing to defend the kingdom of Denmark and make that secure – there's a danger of invasion from Norway, he kept saying - but there was more danger of losing England since that dreadful Elfgifu woman had come over here, and was engaged in bribing the great men of the realm to support her and her son Harald. She was holding all sorts of feasts and jollity in her hall in Northampton: how inappropriate that was so soon after the death of the king. But it was the English way of doing things, which amounted to bribery – Emma had never supported it, believing that right was all-important. Harald had no right to the throne, he was not Canute's true heir, as Elfgifu claimed; everyone knew he was her son by some petty shoemaker. Emma had been instrumental in spreading that rumour far and wide (though she still had her shoes made by the same shoemaker-fellow – soft scarlet leather, gold fringing at the ankles, shoes to yearn for.)

It was Emma's own son Harthacnut who was the rightful heir to the kingdom. There was no doubt about it. King over England and Denmark, the same as Cnut had been. For heaven's sake – she paced round and round the treasure chamber, her soft slippers soundless, her skirts whispering against her legs – for heaven's sake, even her sons by King Ethelred had more right to the English throne than had Harald the Far-Travelled.

Her sons by King Ethelred – she hadn't thought of them in years. Her relationship with them had been a matter of self-sacrifice at first, of course. The suffering of enduring sex with that terrible old man to begin with, in order to conceive, and then, oh, the suffering of renouncing her motherhood! The bowls full of tears she had wept for the loss of her first set of children! When she married Canute she had put aside her past and abandoned all thought of her children by Ethelred. She had begun her life again.

Anew. As if she were a mere girl and a virgin all over again. In her second marriage there had been no place for her children by her first husband. They didn't belong. She had to get rid of them. She disposed of them to her brother in Rouen. He was an archbishop; he'd see that they were brought up properly, she had no reason to care.

But the fact was that now Canute was dead those two boys definitely had a legitimate claim to the English throne. If Harthacnut was indeed turning down the opportunity to become king of England – which is what in effect he was doing by his desultory tardiness – her sons by Ethelred would assuredly dearly love to claim the position. After all they were the sons of the true Saxon king rather than the Danish invader; their claim was sound and likely to be approved of by the *witan*, the English council. They would certainly be more legitimate than That Woman's bastard offspring. And if one of them were king (she could not quite recall which of them was the older) then she, Emma, would retain her power as queen. Queen Mother. Queen Emma, for evermore.

She unlocked the door of the treasure vault, she turned the great key and the guards pulled the heavy door open. 'Lock it,' she commanded, and they did, and gave her back the key, which she hung from the ring at her waist. 'Send a scribe to me,' she ordered, climbing the steep stone stairs to her chamber.

The scribe was a young man whom she was not familiar with; he did not bow as deeply as she felt was owed to her dignity when he entered, and she reprimanded him, told him of the respect that was due to his queen. 'Your pardon, madam,' he babbled, embarrassed.

She scowled. 'Sit down,' she commanded. 'Write this.' She hesitated for a minute, unsure how to address her sons after not seeing them, nor even asking after them, for nineteen years. She cleared her throat and dictated: '*To my dearest sons Alfred and Edward.*' She hesitated a second; was it Edward or Edwin? It had been so long since she thought of him. Edward. First thoughts were usually most accurate. '*God be with you, and send his just blessings upon you. The time at last has come for you to abandon your exile in Normandy and return to England to take up your rightful position as princes of this great realm, with all the riches and honours that are due to you. You owe a duty of obedience in this to me, your devoted mother, who has been most cruelly prevented from seeing you in these past years by her late husband. You must now abandon your common lives, take ship from Normandy and sail into glory. I, Emma Queen of England, command this. Therefore return at once. Come, quickly, come.* – Read it back to me,' she ordered the monk, and he did. She nodded intently. 'Finish it: *From your ever-loving Mother, who has been yearning for many years that our enforced separation might end, and who awaits you in her palace of Winchester with rich gifts for you, and arms open to welcome you and enfold you at last to her bosom that throbs with longing to see you.* Fine. That should do it. Dust it with sand. Very well, you may go.'

The scribe left the letter open on the lectern, and when he had gone she stepped away from the window and crossed the room to read it through. She was shorter-sighted than she had been, and did not like to be seen reading, having to hold the paper close to her eyes. She could not bear to admit that she was ageing. She was older now than Ethelred had been when she married him; and she knew how very old he had seemed to her then. It was commendable that she had always acted with dignity, in a stately way befitting a queen: thus the slowness of age was less noticeable. She was certain that that concubine

Elfgifu, whom she had heard had always been inclined to run and dance and generally behave in a disorderly manner, must have aged more noticeably.

She considered again whether it was wise to write to her sons; whether it would be better simply to be patient and await Harthacnut's arrival. The danger, of course, was that Elfgifu's son Harald – no son of Canute, whatever physical similarities there certainly were between the two men – the danger was that Harald would be crowned king in the meanwhile, and it would be difficult to oust him in Harthacnut's favour; impossible without fighting, in fact, and she was proud that Canute, with her at his side, had been able to maintain peace in England for so many years. She was determined in as far as she was able to keep England at peace. Peace was necessary for prosperity.

'Madam.' It was Stigand beside her. Her and Canute's old friend and adviser.

'I didn't hear you come in.' She stretched out her hand to him; he kissed it. 'I'm glad you have come. I wish to discuss the succession.'

'Madam, your son Harthacnut...'

'He won't come, damn it! He won't leave wretched Denmark until he's got the Norwegians under control.'

'You must persuade him, madam. Otherwise the throne will fall to Harald. Elfgifu's son.'

'No, I won't allow it! I've written to my other sons to come and claim their inheritance.'

'Your other sons...'

'I forget how young you are. I had two sons by Ethelred. Before your time. Read my letter.' She waved her hand toward the lectern, watched Stigand stand and read it. She felt a fondness for him; had known him since she became queen the second time. Canute had appointed him chaplain of Ashingdon in 1020, when the king built the chapel in memory of the battle that had been fought there. He was the person in the kingdom she most trusted.

Stigand vacillated, fingering the gold cross on his chest as if he were looking for divine guidance as to what to say. 'Madam.' He paused. 'You are aware you may be putting your sons' lives in danger by summoning them back to England?'

'Nonsense. They have more right to the throne than that pretender Harald.'

'However, Harald has a great deal of support in the kingdom. Your sons – two princes who were exiled from this country as little children, and have never returned – however legitimate their claim, one cannot imagine that the people will be ready to look to them as saviours of our realm.'

'I'm not inviting them to take up Canute's throne, simply to fill the vacuum until Harthacnut is able to come over. To prevent Harald gaining dominion over Wessex as well as Northumbria and Mercia. Imagine if he ruled Wessex – I'd never be able to stay here in Winchester. It's where I belong, close to my husband's grave in the cathedral.'

'Is that sufficient reason to imperil your sons' lives, madam?'

'You are worrying unnecessarily. Elfgifu would never dare confront me directly.' Emma picked up the quill and dipped it in the ink. She signed the letter, sanded and sealed it; summoned a messenger to deliver it to her sons in Normandy.

50. Alfred and Edward, late 1036

Alfred stood in his brother's hall. The letter from their mother was open on the table between them, a knife laid across the parchment to keep it from rolling up. 'What are you concerned about, Edward?' Alfred was asking. 'It's quite straightforward. Now that King Canute is dead, our mother Queen Emma is at last able to invite us home to take up the positions we are entitled to by birth. Of course she favours us, we two are the surviving sons of King Ethelred of England. We are her firstborn, we have an absolute right to the kingdom. Naturally our mother respects that. That's quite clear from her letter. Why are you hesitating?'

'It's not that simple...' Edward began.

'Bullshit! It's absolutely cut and dried.'

'The last king was Canute. He had two sons by his first wife, Sweyn and Harald. You can forget Sweyn, the damn fool killed himself falling out of an ash tree. The people in the north of England want Harald as their king. Harald is in England already, claiming the kingdom. He is of no account – he's not even legitimate – he's the son of a shoemaker, or a priest, some such story, not of King Canute at all. But people are so credulous... they like the fact that he's got an English mother. Then there's Harthacnut, our half-brother – our mother had him with Canute, after the death of our father. He's her favourite to succeed Canute. But he's tied up by fighting in Denmark at the moment.'

'Well then, we must act quickly and grab the English throne before either Harald or Harthacnut can,' urged Alfred, his eyes bright with conviction. 'Not me. You. You're the rightful king of England. Ethelred's oldest surviving son.'

Edward turned away. Alfred grabbed his shoulder and spun him round. 'For God's sake!' he cried. 'Our mother has summoned us home. Our mother, man! Queen Emma of England. The most powerful woman in the whole world. She wants us with her! What a great event that is! It's the first time she's written to me in the whole of my life. I've got to do as she commands.'

Edward scratched his nose. 'Maybe she is not well-advised to invite us back. The situation is complicated. Harald...'

'He's Canute's concubine's son! A thing of no importance!'

'He is the heir to the man who ruled England in peace for many years. By Germanic law he is legitimate.'

'Not as legitimate as we are. As you are. Our parents' marriage was blessed by the Church. The throne of England is yours by right, Edward. The only reason you're not claiming it is that you are so prosperous, you don't need the money. You're a coward when it comes down to it, you want to play it safe. But I'm different. I believe in justice. I'm prepared to gamble everything on our mother's love. Why would she summon us if so doing put us in any danger?'

'Alfred, I'd like to believe you, truly I would. But our mother has misled people in the past, and I don't know what we would find once we had crossed the Channel.'

'You coward! Well, I shall go on my own.'

So Alfred stood on the beach at Wissant, the great sand dunes at his back, the open sea before him. A January day. Last night's storm had swept the sky so clear of cloud that he could see the cliffs of Dover: the yellowish haze of them across the turbulence of the grey-green water like a step up into the sky. His homeland. Land of his birth. Where he belonged. Where his mother lived, his mother who had at last avowed her great love for her sons. She was going to welcome him into her arms, she was going to share with him the great riches that belonged to her kingdom. All would be well in his life. All would be well, for ever and ever.

He stepped across the hard sand down to the water's edge, and waited. And here at last from the south sailed the fishing boat that would bear him to England. He intended to travel light, with no fuss, and perhaps twenty armed men; he would land quietly on shore and make his way to his beloved mother, who would put right all that was wrong in his world. He would kneel at her feet, couch his head in her lap. All would be well. He pulled off his boots, rolled up his breeches and paddled out, heaved himself up into the boat. The sea swelled and surged; he clutched at the sides, feeling queasy. But no matter; he could cope with this insecurity because all would be well in the end. He was certain of that.

Edward had been eight when he last saw his mother; old enough to be instinctively more wary of her, more aware of her self-centredness and manipulative nature. He had never felt loved by her. Had never seen any evidence of her loving his younger brother either. She had wanted nothing to do with them. Had rejected them when she remarried, put them aside. He would have liked to believe that she had had a change of heart and had come to appreciate them and to want the best possible for them, but he wasn't a great believer in myths. Their returning to England would be in her own interest: their having power in the kingdom would secure her own position. A woman couldn't rule, that wasn't allowed, but through her sons she could have dominion. Think how influential King Ethelred's mother had been, when she was a widow.

He would not venture unsupported into England, a strange land he did not know. He needed forces. He had fifteen boats of his own, and his uncle the duke of

252

Normandy, always angry at the way his mother had treated him, loaned him fifteen more. His father-in-law loaned him a further ten. Altogether that made up a fleet of forty vessels. A formidable fleet assembled in the bay; a fleet that any enemy would take seriously.

My land, Alfred thought, stumbling ashore, his legs uncertain. He scooped up seawater to wash the sick from his beard, grabbed a handful of sand and held it high. 'My homeland,' he shouted to the men on his boat. 'At last I'm back where I belong, in the land where I was born!'

It was a quiet stretch of coast. A windmill spun, its sails circled in the sea breeze. Alfred climbed the steps into the half-dark inside, into the dusty smell of grain being ground. The burly miller had hefted a sack up high, was intent on dribbling grain between the turning quern stones and did not immediately notice him. Quern stones from Norway, Alfred would have been prepared to bet – he had recently imported two sets for his Normandy estates.

The miller did not see him. Alfred coughed loudly, cried, 'Good morning, good sir.' But the miller did not understand his Norman French, and Alfred had forgotten how to speak his native tongue. 'Queen Emma,' Alfred tried.

'Not here,' the miller replied. 'I'll take you to Earl Godwine.'

'King Harald, he's who I support,' said Earl Godwine, a well-fed fellow at the head of a long table in a timber hall; he would not listen to Alfred's protests that he wanted to be reunited with his mother. 'What proper man would want that? I suspect you're a spy,' he said, 'sneaking into England in an underhand manner like that. If you are indeed a prince, why did you not come with an escort befitting your rank? Why are you not appropriately dressed?'

Alfred smiled weakly, not making sense of Godwine's anger. He saw the great man rise, his fist swing out, knuckles cracking against the young man's lips. Alfred's knees buckled from the blow. What was happening? Why the truncheon blow to his head, why the black fog it enveloped him in? Why the iron taste in his mouth, why the manacles prisoning his wrists and ankles? 'I'm the son of King Ethelred,' the young man cried, but the name meant nothing to the Earl, time had moved on and new dynasties of kings had fought and ruled. Ethelred was a has-been, dead and gone twenty years since. He belonged in history, he'd been the vicious murderer of the father of Elfgifu who had been wife to King Canute, and whose son Harald would shortly be crowned king and secure peace in England.

'I'll send you to Harald, to do with as he sees fit,' Godwine said.

A long journey Alfred had of it, trussed up on horseback and bitter cold that January coming into February through forests bare of leaves, where wolves howled in packs: a nightmare he could not explain and could not understand. They have taken me for a Viking raider, was the only interpretation he could put on events; and he tried to comfort himself with the thought that whomever he was being taken to would respect his situation and treat him with honour. At last his captors set him free and he could walk, or rather stumble, his ankles being so sore; and when he sought to do his business behind a tree he made a run for it, but they chased him with dogs – his heart pounded, the dogs slathered at his ankles, they nipped at his heels. The men called off the dogs and caught him, and the most terrible pain was inflicted on his face, and then

Alfred could not see at all: the whole world turned black, he felt blood coursing down his cheeks. He dashed his sleeve across his face.

The world consisted of nothing but pain and sounds. At one point he heard a woman's voice, clear and full of pity. 'Mother?' he said, but she wasn't. 'They've done it to you too,' she said. 'I can't bear it. They blinded my brothers. And now you. When will men ever learn?' She gently washed his mutilated face. Rough men took him away from her. More journeying trussed up on horseback, then he was laid on a hard bed which he'd have said was in a monastery, because of the bells that rang from time to time, over, and over and over. A fever: he had a fever, he was no longer cold, he was burning in fiery flames.

'There was no evil in it. Ethelred's men did as much to your brothers,' Earl Godwine blustered, defending his men for blinding Alfred.

'Nevertheless, we must learn to forgive,' sighed Elfgifu. 'It is not a fate I would have wished on any man. If we cannot learn, what purpose is there to living? I've no wish to behave as Ethelred did. I have made Alfred as comfortable as I could and had him borne to the monastery at Ely. It is a lovely place, and the monks there are caring. Moreover Queen Emma has bestowed great gifts upon it, and so the monks will do their best for her child. They are gifted in healing.'

The cold wind blew clean air across the lake. The monks chanted their joyful anthems. But Prince Alfred could not fight off his infection, and he died a few days later.

Meanwhile Prince Alfred's older brother Edward landed his forty ships near Southampton, fought against and defeated a large English force, and then, shocked at his mother not sending troops to his aid, decided that he needed a much larger army if no one was going to rise up spontaneously in support of his legitimate cause, and so sailed back to France. Better to preserve one's life than lose it fighting for what was rightly his, he felt. Time would pass; events move on. He would bide his time and await a better opportunity.

In due course, in an as yet unforeseeable future, he would indeed become king of England. King Edward the Confessor. Sainted monarch.

51. Elfgifu, Northampton, 1038

The Northampton hall was empty. The tables were littered with the debris of the feast: gnawed bones and apple cores, fragments of bread, the shells of nuts. The scent of spilled ale and wine and mead permeated the still air. A couple of benches were overturned.

A red squirrel paused in the open doorway; failed to see Elfgifu because she was keeping so quiet, scampered inside and jumped up on the table. It picked up a hazel nut, cracked the shell and sat to eat the kernel. 'You can't have all the leftovers,' whispered Elfgifu, and, holding her apron open, swept into it the scraps of bread and carried them outside, where she scattered them in the yard for the birds to eat. Down they flew straightway: thrushes and goldfinches and blue tits, starlings and robins and black crows, they all pecked at the crumbs.

The yard was muddy and uneven, trampled by the hooves of the horses of King Harald and his court. No matter, Elfgifu thought, I'll get the men to rake the surface smooth again. It was a good night, last night, she thought, like in the days before my father died. Merry-making, an abundance of food and wine, the music of the lyre and the skalds singing songs about former times of heroism and valour. She was glad she had been able to help her son renew the ancient traditions. As if England had never changed; as if it were once again the good old days of her childhood. Those sociable days, days of generosity, gift-giving, celebration and feasts. Days of honour, when people were loyal to each other.

She stepped back, shaking her head. Sadness had of a sudden closed like a claw to grip her heart. Why, she wondered, what reason have I to be sad, when I should be utterly happy to see my son and his friends doing so well? But their happiness in her hall had reminded her of her own childhood, her parents and her brothers, how carefree they were, they too believing the good times would never end. When she looked at her son Harald, when she listened to him, he reminded her intensely of Canute when he was young, when they were just married. The likeness between father and son almost broke her heart. The memories of how happy they'd been.

She wished so much that she had her brothers still to talk to, to gossip with about their childhood, the old times. Those lovely long summers in Northumbria. The fun they had in the palace with the princes, all the palace children together. And then after his marriage to Emma King Ethelred had seemed to go mad, had had her father murdered and her brothers blinded. How determined her brother Wulfheah had been to still manage the family estates, not to devolve all the responsibility on to her. She suddenly remembered the stone eye that he had carved at the summit of the hill, and she itched to see it, to run her hands across the rough stone, and to feel again the passion that he'd felt in carving it. Such a fierce longing for the past. *You and me together again, Wulfheah.*

No one was around and so she went to the stables and found Delight's foal, and, talking gently to her all the time, whispering in her ear, she harnessed her and saddled her up, led her across the muddy yard to the mounting block, and then rode through the forest on the tracks that she used to know so well. They were less trampled and so drier than the lanes, and by late morning the hill on which Wulfheah used to sit in the sunshine and chip away at his great stone was rising before her. His monastery lay over on her right. She heard its bells ring out, she heard the monks begin their plainsong chant.

She dismounted and climbed the hill, leading her mare. You must have felt the strain of climbing this hill just the same as I do now, Wulfheah, she thought, the way it makes your legs ache. She was climbing against the low sun to begin with, and she saw the silhouette of Wulfheah's stone as a dark pimple in the sun's eye. The eye is the key to the soul, she thought, climbing on: thinking of her eyeless brother chipping away at the stone over days and days: his devotion to his task. His need to make a mark on the world.

When she reached the stone she found that it had changed. It was pitted by the weather; but more than that, over the years other carvers must have climbed this hill with chisels and mallets and added to it. Serpents now twisted across the stone, their long bodies crisscrossing in a geometric interlace; and at every intersection perched a bird or an animal: a pheasant, or a crow, or hawk; or a hare or squirrel, a stoat or otter. Elfgifu traced their shapes out with her finger, thinking how much these carvers with their observation of animals had softened the fierceness of her brother's stone eye. There was writing too: not curved as in the leather-bound volumes of the gospels and psalms that she knew, but the sharp angular writing of Viking runes, easier to carve into stone than the curves of the Latin alphabet. She ran her fingers along the shadowed lines of them. Maybe they were the names of the carvers who had come here and continued Wulfheah's work. Or maybe the runes conveyed a message she could not understand. Some kind of magic? she wondered. Transforming pain and hatred into love of the natural world... She was glad that the carvers had softened the eye that her brother had carved with so much intensity by adding to it the intricate pattern of the interlace, and that the animals had been carved with an accurate observation that spoke of love and study.

This is how the world should change, Elfgifu thought. Over the years it must soften. You must not perpetuate hatred. Nothing stays the same. The peacemakers must win.

It was said that it was the role of women to be peace-weavers.

Whom has she hated most in her life?

Queen Emma, she thought. She used to hate her for being Canute's other wife. For robbing her of the time that she and Canute should have spent together. For stealing the happiness that was her due. For being a more successful administrator than herself. Well, Emma had the easier task, the English were more amenable than the Norwegians. Perhaps because they were for the most part more affluent, living in a kinder climate.

But now the world had changed. After his father's death Elfgifu's own son Harald had been elected and in due course crowned king of all England, and Queen Emma had been driven out of Winchester, stripped of her treasures and put to flight: not to be with her nephew in Normandy, as might have been expected, nor with her son Harthacnut in Denmark – but instead she was staying in

Flanders with her niece's stepson Baldwin and his wife Adela. People of little account.

Flanders was but a step to England, of course. Maybe she was waiting there. Unable to accept the turn of events. That Harald was king. Harald the Far-Travelled, Elfgifusson. *I cannot abide how things have turned out*, Emma would be thinking. *I must change them.*

It had come to pass that Elfgifu was the queen mother now. The worthy one, the dignified one, walking tall. She had a secure position in English society. She was respected. Everything seemed settled and certain. Moreover, she had her little grandson Elfwyn to play with and educate. Harald's heir. He was such a sweet and gentle child; more like his uncle Sweyn than his own father. Elfgifu planned to do her best to ensure that he would be a wise and peaceful king in the future. 'Come, my little one,' she said. 'Sit down with me. Let us do our lessons.'

52. Elfgifu, Northampton, dawn 11th March 1040

At dawn on that March day, when faint light crept around the edges of the shutters in Elfgifu's bedchamber, there came a loud knocking on the door of her chamber, where she lay in the great high bed she had shared with Canute when he had been free to come to her. Her little grandson Elfwyn lay beside her now, snuffling in his sleep because of the disturbance. 'What is it?' she hissed, only half awake; that familiar claw of fear around her heart. 'Come in.'

It was a messenger, the lamp in his hand illuminating his grim and sweating face, his sodden hood thrown back to show his dripping hair. 'Madam...'

Foreboding gripped her. These last two years she had learnt to be happy in a quiet way, but now: 'What is it?'

she repeated, sitting bolt upright. 'What can the matter be, that you come in such a state?'

'King Harald, madam. Harald the Far-Travelled. Your son.'

She pushed her blankets to one side, slipped out of bed and shook her nightgown down to skim her bare feet. 'For God's sake, man, what news of him? Tell me.'

'An illness, madam, very sudden. He turned black...'

'What?'

'A sudden illness, madam. He... he complained of the taste of the wine...'

'He still drank it?'

'Yes, madam.'

'How is he now?'

'Madam...'

'Spit it out, man. What have you come to say?'

'I dare not tell you, madam.'

'Tell me,' she hissed, 'quietly. Do not wake the child.'

'King Harald is dead, madam.'

'No. That's not possible.'

'It was very quick, madam. Even when I left to come to you, they were carrying his body in procession to be buried at Westminster Abbey.'

'This can't be true. He is only twenty-four.' Sweyn had been younger. To lose her two sons, and her husband, in such a short time, that wasn't possible. Her family extinguished... She pressed her hand to her chest to still the sudden bounding of her heart. Her and Canute's fine strong boys... at least he was spared this grief. 'Was he poisoned? Queen Emma, it's said she's well-versed in herbs and their effects...'

'No one knows the cause of it, madam. Only that he is dead.'

She sank to the floor, head in her hands. *My dear Harald dead. The Good Lord rest his soul.*

My son. My hope. My love. My future. I cannot bear it. Bitter bile came up in her mouth.

My God. Lord God, save us. How my world will change. How all our worlds have changed.

In the last few years she had gone from being the beloved of the greatest king in Christendom, with two sons who were heirs to the throne of England, to being nothing. She was nothing now. A nonentity. Owning nothing, belonging to nobody. How lonely she felt already. Her only loyalty was to her grandson. Dear sweet Elfwyn. Him she needed to protect. Suppose Emma decided to put out his clear blue eyes, as vengeance for the blinding of Alfred. Elfgifu must take him with her, and flee. She had to be strong for him. 'Elfwyn,' she said, shaking him. 'Wake up, my boy. Today we are going on an adventure.'

53. Emma, Winchester, 1042

Life is so much a game of chance, Emma thought. She was back in the library at Winchester, standing among those shelves of tall dark books that walled her in with their leather bindings set with jewels. She loved the richness and the smell of them, the gleam when you opened them of the gold leaf on their pages, the bright colours of the illustrations, the beauty of their words and the careful transcription of them, the many hours the scribes had taken to copy them, their authority and the learning they represented, their certainty, their fixity, their arrogance: their conviction that they told the truth. She had once said to Stigand, How do we know that what is written in books is the truth? He had said: Be careful what you say. To even think that what is written might be untrue is blasphemy.

'I am thinking of commanding to be written, "The Life of Emma, Queen of England",' she told him.

He didn't answer.

'That would surely be fitting matter for a book?'

He had merely shrugged his shoulders, intent as he was on preparing a sermon to welcome Edward, Emma's son by King Ethelred, as co-ruler with Harthacnut, her son by Canute, of the kingdom of England; it was what Harthacnut had declared he wanted, he didn't want sole responsibility for governing England.

What is written in books becomes the truth, Emma believed.

Encomium Emmae Reginae, her book would be called, she decided. *A Document in Praise of Queen Emma*. She instructed a Flemish monk from St Omer, whom she had met when she was in exile while Harald the Far-Travelled was king, to write her book. His script was easily legible, and he was young and foreign enough not to have the self-assurance or knowledge to contradict her version of events. *The story of my life*. She sat with the young monk for hours in a sun-filled chamber of her palace, having the servants close the shutters at sunset; watching the black ink the young monk's quill trailed along the lines he had drawn on the parchment, and the movement of the muscles in the back of his slender right hand that he rested in a fist on the parchment.

The story of her life: and yet she banned from it all mention of her marriage to King Ethelred whom she hated, left the reader to assume that Edward, Harthacnut's half-brother, was her child by Canute rather than Ethelred. She belittled Elfgifu by claiming that she was merely Canute's concubine and had been unable to bear his children, and that the late King Harald's father had been a mere shoemaker, never mentioned that her own mother Gunnor's relationship with the Duke of Normandy was the same respectable one of Germanic marriage that Elfgifu had had with Canute. If you write your own history, Emma was certain, you can make sure that your own version of it is the definitive version. And it will still be able to be read, and believed, in libraries a thousand years hence.

She dreamed of a great red brick library that might one day hold the whole of the world's knowledge. A woman centuries into the future, when all women would know how to read, as was their right, would step up the white steps into the library, and stand before a desk and say, I want to read the *Encomium Emmae Reginae,* and a monk would fetch it from a treasure chest and with white gloves lay it open on an oaken table; and the woman would turn the pages and read it and honour Emma's status and her wisdom. Her wisdom would be honoured through ten centuries, through a whole millennium; or till the end of time, whichever was the sooner.

What a wise woman was this, every reader of her book would say. What a wise woman. She would be revered like a saint.

54. Emma, Winchester, 1044

Two years later, Emma stood in the small garden of her house in Winchester. She held a small knife with a jewelled handle, and was using it for cutting sprays of orange rose hips, deep crimson haws and green sprigs of rosemary. Holding them in her gloved hands to avoid being scratched, she carried them through her garden gate and across to the Old Minster, the church of St Swithun, where she planned to lay them on the tomb of her late husband

King Canute. Dead these nine years now. You would never have thought this was how events would have turned out.

A priest, hooded and simply dressed, bowed with age, scurrying across the misty churchyard, turned aside to greet her. It was Stigand, with whom she had for the greater part of her life been good friends. 'Rosemary for remembrance,' he remarked, and then his worried face relaxed into a smile and he said, 'Do you remember Normandy, the year of the famine, when you'd sought refuge there – how you and Elfsige of Peterborough went round buying up holy relics at knockdown prices? What riches you brought home for the Church!'

'Have you heard of King Edward's latest excess?' Since her thankless oldest son's accession to the throne her voice had developed a whining tone in which she conducted most of her conversations. 'He has stolen the head of St Ouen from the treasury and had it taken to Malmesbury Abbey.'

'It's criminal,' agreed Stigand.

'But not as bad as what he has done to you, dear friend.' She took his hand. 'Depriving you of your bishopric and taking all your possessions. As if that could make you into a common man.'

'While I may still enjoy the grace of your presence, your majesty, I shall never feel bereft.'

'Edward has robbed me of everything. All my gold and silver, all my land. A little he has given me back, I'll admit, but only enough to permit me to barely exist. He has made me into a pauper. My own son! My firstborn! How could he do it to me! You can tell the vengeful blood of King Ethelred runs in his veins. All thanks to that wretched ingrate Harthacnut inviting him back from Normandy. What did he want to share rule over England with his half brother for? Who would have believed it when he had all the power in the world? The pair of them have been so cruel to me, their mother, to whom they owe their very existence! Oh, so cruel, Stigand! Do you know, Harthacnut accused me of banishing him to Denmark when he was a child because I hated him! When instead I'd been making him a king. Building a great future for him. Outwitting Elfgifu, that peasant's daughter, for his sake…'

'Madam, the good Lord has seen fit to punish him.'

'He wasn't the only one, others went into convulsions at that marriage feast. What a revolting sight it was. Absolutely disgusting. People collapsing and writhing about on the floor in agony and screaming. To be honest, it was almost a relief when Harthacnut was still at last and gave up his spirit to our Lord in Heaven.'

'Something in the wine, it seemed to be, I understand. You didn't drink any, madam?'

'No, indeed. I had a presentiment. A warning from the Virgin Mary. But now of course Edward's been left with sole power over me. Hasn't he made the most of it, in the two years since Harthacnut died. Depriving me of every honour, as if I were a peasant. You'd think he must hate me! Because I had him fostered by my brother, when that was what was proper for a royal prince. He thinks himself so pious and so saintly. 'The confessor' is the nickname the people give him. Edward the Confessor. Pah!'

'Madam, do not concern yourself over him. You are always beloved.'

'I have done well for myself, haven't I, Stigand? I may be living like a poor recluse, but I am still the king's mother. I have for many years been the wife of the greatest king of England in this millennium. Canute who was king over six kingdoms. The Emperor of the North. I tend his sacred tomb and do him honour as befits his grieving widow.'

'You have triumphed over Canute's first wife, madam. Your sons have replaced hers as king. You are honoured in the land for your Christian learning. What more could you wish to achieve?'

Emma moved the bunch of rose hips, rosemary and haws into her left hand and took his right hand in hers. 'We are the victors, Stigand,' she said. 'We are the ones who have always done right. We have earned success.'

55. Elfgifu and her grandson, France, 1040 onwards

'Come,' said Elfie. She took her grandson's small hand in hers and led him away from the chapel and through the trees to the beach at the edge of the estuary, out on to the rickety jetty where she had landed when she returned to England after Canute's death, where Edwin had promised to meet her with a boat. How grief-stricken she had been then; and how sad she was now to be once again leaving her native land.

The jetty was empty, a dark frame of broken timbers in a wilderness of tidal marshes. Gulls wheeled and cried; desolate. A bitter wind blew from the east. 'We will have to wait,' she told Elfwyn; and the two sat cross-legged on the bare wood and she wrapped her fur-lined cloak around the two of them. More around the boy than around her. Her life was in the past, she felt: his lay all before him. She had to keep him safe. He was heir to Canute and Harald, nephew to Sweyn; he would grow to be a good man, she was certain of it. She kissed the top of his blond head and he pushed her away. He was eight years old. You are all I have left to love, she thought.

She didn't know where to take him. Not England, nor Denmark. Not the Holy Roman Empire, because although his half-sister Gunnhild had died, Edward was still closely allied to her widower, the Emperor. And Edward, like his mother, was filled with hate. They would seek out and kill the boy if they could, just because he was Harald's son.

She thought of the countries she knew at the rim of the world; the eastern lands from where jewellery and silks were traded; Ireland and Mann in the west that were ruled by warlike Vikings whose language she could speak but whom she would hesitate to trust. 'I don't know where to go, where we'll be safe,' she said out loud, and Elfwyn began to sob. She knelt up, she hugged him close to her. 'All will be well, my dear little one,' she said. 'Do not fear.'

But still she did not know what to do.

Still no boat came. They stared together into the emptiness of the grey mist.

Elfwyn lay on his belly on the boards of the jetty and watched the fish nosing among the submerged grasses. 'I'm hungry,' he said, and Elfie gave him some of the dry bread that she had; a chunk of cheese.

Elfwyn's eyes were sharper than Elfgifu's, and the next day he spotted a fishing boat far out in the estuary. He jumped up and down and shouted, and the fisherman changed course toward them. 'Give me your fur cloak, madam.' He fingered it, stroking Elfie's breasts as if by chance. 'Give me your fur cloak, and I'll take you to France. Or I could just throw you overboard and steal it off you.'

'I would kill you if you did,' said little Elfwyn, and the fisherman laughed at the boy.

France was not where Elfgifu wanted to be, because of Emma's family in Normandy. 'We will become pilgrims,' she told Elfwyn. 'We will go on a pilgrimage to the shrine of St James in Santiago de Compostela. We will have new names. I will be Margaret, you will be Leo. Can you remember that?' Elfwyn nodded.

They walked south, seeking the charity of monasteries and convents, sleeping side by side on thin beds in cold dormitories, and up at dawn for Lauds before setting out once more. 'My name is Leo,' said Elfwyn, over and over again. 'This is my grandmother Margaret.' They walked south towards the sun.

By early autumn they were walking through a forest down a steep hill into the town of Conques, in Aquitaine. Elfgifu sat upon stones and bathed her feet in the cool river. The sun shone through the dappled shade of trees to bless her, it sparkled on the water. Elfwyn, barefoot, was racing sticks against each other, pretending they were boats. A girl appeared and joined him in his game. 'I'm Theresa,' she said. She looked to be the same age as Elfwyn, had dark hair she wore in long plaits.

Her mother came over to talk to Elfgifu. It turned out she was Irish, had been captured by the Vikings, enslaved and sold in Normandy. A musician's wife. She'd lost touch with him long ago. She had been resold and then brought south, where she was freed by her master, a tanner, who had since died. She had taken on his business. Theresa was their daughter. 'Why have you come here?' she asked.

'On pilgrimage,' Elfgifu answered.

They had the Danish language in common.

The single church bell clanged and small birds twittered. The mother shared the bread and peaches she carried in her shawl. Discovering that Elfie knew how to write and add and subtract, she invited her to stay and help her in her business.

'Very well,' said Elfie, whose feet ached from walking. She gazed up at the high-forested hills and thought how similar they were to the strong timber walls that encircled Danish forts, and she thought, here we will be safe. Nobody will search for us here. And so they stayed. In due course they gave their true names, which were written down when on adulthood Elfwyn persuaded the local authorities to rebuild the church and grant him the office of prior of the monastery of Sainte Foy.

Meanwhile Elfgifu dreamed of one day resuming her pilgrimage to Spain. To the coast where she would walk to the shore and stand upon rocks, white-haired and frail and leaning upon a stick. She would watch the setting sun lay its road across the western sea: that flickering glitter on the undulation of waves that would in time summon her to step out across the water, straight toward the horizon, to the greatest light there is.

There she would once more have the companionship of those whom all her life she had loved.

Printed in Great Britain
by Amazon